EDEN BUTLER

Infinite Us

Copyright © 2017 Eden Butler

Edited by Sharon B. Browning
Copy Edit by Kiezha Smith Ferrell
Cover Design by Murphy Rae, Indie Solutions
Print Format by Alexandria Bishop and Tee Tate

ALSO BY EDEN BUTLER

SERIES

Chasing Serenity, (The Serenity Series Book 1)

Behind the Pitch, (A Serenity Series Novella)

Finding Serenity, (The Serenity Series Book 2)

Claiming Serenity, (The Serenity Series Book 3)

Catching Serenity, (The Serenity Series Book 4)

Thin Love, (Thin Love Book 1)

My Beloved, (A Thin Love Novella)

Thick Love, (Thin Love Book 2)

Thick & Thin, (Thin Love Book 3)

My Always, (A Thin Love Novella)

Swimming in Shadows, (A Shadows Series Novella)

Shadows and Lies. (The Shadows Series Book #1)

STANDALONE NOVELS

Crimson Cove

Platform Four—A Legacy Falls Romance

I've Seen You Naked and Didn't Laugh: A Geeky Love Story

For everyone who learned to love blindly.
May the world follow your lead.
#StayWoke

"We are only human, and the gods have fashioned us for love.
That is our great glory, and our great tragedy."

— George R.R. Martin, A Game of Thrones

EPIGRAPH

Once there was an ordinary girl who held an extraordinary hope. She did not wish for things that went beyond the apothecary labor her father's work provided their small village. But the girl still believed in the brilliant wonder that came with being loved. Love, after all, is a mighty force, born into every beating heart formed by the Almighty's careful touch. The elders promised so, and the girl knew that what the elders promised came to pass. It was that force, the same divine brilliance, that brought her into being: the Craftsman that formed cells into limbs, bone, and muscle, and the braided bundle of hair atop her head, had also fashioned to life kings and rulers, diplomats and paupers.

All, she decided, deserved to be loved greatly—fiercely—and to see that fine love grow and strengthened. And so this ordinary girl found her great love. She held it tight, made of it all she could, cherished and protected it like the precious thing it was—eternal, beloved and solely hers for the keeping.

But for the girl, like men and women before her, love was not an easily tamed beast. Sometimes it came to her, wrapped her in its clutches because it was greedy, because she did not mind being coveted. But then her husband or lover would defy the Almighty, incur His wrath, and love would fall between her fingers like brittle petals from a wilted sunflower.

But the memory remained and went through her, twined with her dying sighs, into the ether.

Sometimes, love came when her body was changed, when her shoulders had widened and her chest flattened. It came when *she* was *he*. It came when he was seeking no more than a meal and found instead a love that fed his soul, nourished it the same as his empty belly. And still, like all the lives before, all the forms inside of which that great love breathed, all the people he would ever be, that love died, sometimes slowly, sometimes not easily given up.

Other times, love came to him in the hungry touch of a girl that could never be his, the sweet forbidden touch that had his vagabond heart breaking when it ended, when death came and disintegrated all the hope that had built and settled inside his chest.

But the memory remained, passing into one life, onto the next, through bone and blood and cells that made up one life and then another.

Still, that love lived inside veins, inside the blood that moved through bodies, through all those bodies. For a brilliant time, perhaps for dozens like them, that love lived. For then. For now. For always.

And the memory endured.

Nash

Midnight. There was darkness, and the thump of a rhythm that wasn't welcome, when the aching started. Brooklyn was loud that night, full of chaos, adding to my sleepless misery. But noise wasn't the only thing keeping me up. My head felt thick with numbers and algorithms that coated my vision like some Pollock piece blurred with a toddler's finger painting. My body? Stupid with tension—the kind of tight coil that twists your spine and keeps your shoulders from any damn thing but bunching pain.

The numbers, the darkness, the kindergartener's chaos, all fought for space inside my head, dimmed by the noise I heard above me. That infernal thumping, a drumbeat from some clueless asshole's speakers in the upstairs apartment, tamped out the jazz pouring from my headphones. Coltrane was wicked, the smooth slip of his sax like the voice of God: the heady mix of condemnation and praise, pain that both harmed and healed in every note. But even the long, sweet whisper of the sax couldn't overcome the thumping of the trespassing drums from barging in, or keep out the noise of the crazy bitch singing out of tune one floor up. Had to be a woman. No dude's voice could be that high-pitched or whining.

For the fourth damn night.

Insomnia had first become my side-piece in college. Every night for four years, the noise of frat brothers stepping in line to DMX and his gravely-voiced barks in "Get It On the Floor" in the quad, the Alpha Phi Alphas and Omega Psi Phis vying for bragging rights of who was the flyest with every step-dance they made, and the general disturbance of new-held adolescent debauchery kept sleep from me. Those Omegas always won.

I'd trained my mind then, let the insomnia linger until there was an uneasy relationship between us—me tolerating the elusive hum of sleep and that affliction keeping me from it. I'd wrangle four hours of sleep, plenty for a computer science major, enough to ace my classes. Enough that I didn't look like an old man when I left for MIT. By then, insomnia had become the ride-or-die chick that refused to leave me. Got tied down to that bitch. Now I wanted a divorce.

That racket from the apartment above was not helping.

The noisy upstairs female started a louder chant, something that reminded me of the weird mess my twin Natalie watched every Halloween with her friends when we were kids back in Atlanta. Some movie with three white chicks from Salem, singing about spells and sucking the lives out of children. The one with the redheaded woman that my assistant Daisy says likes to burn Kim Kardashian on Twitter. That shit was funny, a hell of a lot funnier than the movies she was in that made my mom laugh so loud when I was six. It was a Broadway phase she kept from my pops. Nothing like the witch mess from that old movie—that nonsense was crap. And that's what my new neighbor sounded like.

Four nights. Four nights of this bullshit. Four nights too many.

Coltrane fell silent when I pulled the headphones off and moved across my apartment, not giving a damn that my T-shirt was wrinkled when I picked it off the floor and tugged it over my head, not caring whether or not that loud woman would get pissed if I interrupted what had to be some nightly juju ritual.

My skin pebbled in the cool air from the vents at the elevator ceiling, but I didn't shake or cross my arms to get rid of the sensation. It fed me as I slipped into the elevator, ignored the quick flash of my reflection showing the bags under my eyes, the streak of muscle that twitched when I stretched my shoulders. Maybe it wasn't the best idea to confront this chick, but I was tired and annoyed, and before I stopped to think about what I was doing, the elevator dinged and I stood right in front of 6-D's door. There was a sliver of light at the bottom of the door; the only shadow I could make out slipped around that light, probably dancing to whatever voodoo junk pulsed from those speakers.

Coltrane was music. Spirit music. Deep, heart-aching music that seeped into your soul, filled in all the fragments that life left empty. This garbage? Hell, no. This wasn't music at all.

Two bangs of my fist on the door was all it took. I stood there, arms braced against the doorframe, loops of black tattoos— things I wanted to remember, things I could never forget— running over my forearms, moving as I twisted my fists on the wooden frame. I didn't care what I looked like, a tall, inked black man breathing fire at her door. Not worried that this woman might see something of a threat in me, wide-shouldered, thin, wrinkled shirt, jeans slipping low on hipbones. Instead, I focused on that mean ache of messed-up calm and lack of sleep crowding in my skull. The longer it took this female to open the door, the more amped up I got. Waiting, I envisioned that I'd yell, I'd unload on her, then get the hell away before she could react, stalk back to my own apartment with my anger leeching out behind me. Then maybe Coltrane would work and I could get at least a few hours' sleep.

The drumbeats stopped. I heard footsteps, the turn of a lock. I was breathing anger through my nose, eyes glaring, like a bull ready to charge.

Everything changed in the second the door opened. With the smallest creak of a hinge, the softest slip of light, a perfect shadow was silhouetted in front of me, followed by what felt like a whip of wind moving through the park, the memory of plastic beads and forgotten parking tickets on Bourbon Street the second Fat Tuesday ended, the spray of waves that had crashed against the quay. It slapped across my subconscious, a whoosh, a break of something that could have been a kiss but was likely a punch in the gut, though no one touched me. Before I finished one blink, there she stood, a foot from me, staring at me like she knew me, like she'd been waiting on me to knock on her door.

"*Oh.* Oh no, honey."

It was her. The girl I had seen through my window, and again a couple of times on the elevator. The girl—no, the woman—new to the building, who had not only caught my eye but caused me to stare, even though I'm usually not so stupid as that. Once, coming home, I had noticed her walking a block in front of me, and had followed her like a stalker, not even realizing how creepy I must have seemed. Every time I saw her, her presence had lured me like a crazy moth to a flame, but I had been too wrapped up in my work and my own damned mind games to even consider that she was real, and approachable, and living nearby.

And now she stood in the open doorway, only inches away.

Her touch brought me from my gawking stupor. At least, it made me move. She touched me, and it felt like a bolt of electricity. Fingers warm against my skin, gripping, pulling me forward like she expected me to follow, as if resisting her was not an option.

Her grip tightened as I followed her inside, and a voice started screaming in my head to back up, to get away from this chick before I did something stupid or got blamed

11

for it. But then I looked at her again, and the voice retreated to a whimper.

This woman wasn't like anyone I'd ever seen in my life. She was tall, heightened by dark tights and the loose, bright top, with swirls of green and yellow which might have been flowers, that cupped her small waist and drifted nearly to her thighs. But she was no delicate flower; she reminded me of a bunch of balloons, the kind that jackass clowns twist into animal shapes to impress stupid six-year-olds. There was so much color and noise in this woman—the whiteness of her skin, the loud shade of her lipstick, the jingle of the stack of bracelets on her wrist, and the thick bundle of long, chestnut colored hair that hung in a riot of waves and curls past her waist.

But it wasn't the chaos of colors she wore that kept me from bolting. It was the stare she gave, the pause before she spoke, as though she knew exactly who I was and why I'd pounded on her door.

I had forgotten *why* I had pounded on her door.

I couldn't explain the sensation if I had a billion words to describe it. It was something weird but familiar, something I didn't recognize in her expression, in the slow, sweet smile that moved across her face as she watched me. As if she knew me. Like I was supposed to be right there, standing in front of her, waiting for something to happen.

Hell. I *was* sleep deprived.

When she stopped watching me, when that little smirk

vanished from her features, she squinted, looking over my head as though she was considering something, like she needed to figure out what kind of flaw I had.

"It's bad." She waved her long fingers over my head, swooping one hand up and down my body, breaking the moment and confusing the hell outta me. "It's just the wrong color." Another wave, and I finally wrestled my thoughts under control enough to step away from this crazy woman even as she tugged me further into her apartment.

I finally found my voice and my reason. "That shit is too loud," I said, mustering all the good damn sense I could, as I looked around her cluttered apartment.

"What?" she asked, her brown eyes wide, innocent.

My gaze settled on an old ass record player in the corner, spinning, with the needle up. "Your record...that turntable?"

She frowned, but more confused than unfriendly. She had one of those faces that some females do, like tears and worry and rudeness wouldn't—couldn't—keep her from being beautiful. And she was. Beautiful. For a tall, skinny, white girl, she was damn beautiful.

"The turntable, the speakers, you got to cut that noise down. I can't sleep as it is, but that fucking ..."

"*Oh*, you shouldn't curse like that."

Again she reached for me, fussing at me, bossy as hell as she led me to what I guessed was supposed to be a sofa but looked like a stack of fluffy mattresses with the loudest looking blankets and pillows thrown around them. The entire place reminded me a circus caravan—colors that were deep and rich, tapestries and blankets draped over all the furniture, covering the lampshades like some drifter's wet dream, and flowers, both dried and blooming in vases along the window sill and across the mantel. The thick scent of something that smelled a little like weed clouded in the air, something sticky and sweet, but too flowery to be anything worth smoking.

She stared me down, gaze hard, critical, and I brought my attention back her, trying to dismiss the fact that I'd gotten nosy eyeballing her place but not wanting to give in entirely. "Um…mind your business about my mouth…"

"Sit." When I folded my arms, keeping another curse between my teeth for God knows why, the woman moved her brows up, those coffee-colored eyes matching me pound for pound. I meant to tell her to fuck off. I thought about just rolling out without so much as a word to her, but that look on her face, the one that was both severe and tempting all at the same time, kept me stuck to where I stood. Damn, it would be a mistake to underestimate this woman, doe eyes or not.

After the glare went on for damn ever, she nodded at the sofa, staring at me like she'd lost her own shit a long time ago and hadn't bothered with finding it. After few seconds and several long, furious blinks, I gave up, too damn tired to fight with some crazy woman I didn't know.

Somehow, she got me to sit, damn the good sense God gave me. No one bosses me, but this woman found a way to get me inside her place and on her sofa with half-a-dozen words, all of them bossy as hell.

"Now, I want you to relax and breathe deeply. I'm going to focus your aura…"

"Look, lady…"

"Just relax. I need to assess where the problem is." Another glare and she relaxed her own expression, her nose flaring as she inhaled deeply. "Now, close your eyes." Even as she commanded it, she did it herself. I closed my eyes, but damn if I wasn't still completely aware of her.

The image of her, the long cascading hair, the softly chiming bangles, the blouse shimmering around her body, they were all lingering behind my eyelids. She smelled like jasmine, a weird scent that I only recognized because Luke, my college roommate, thought he was *Erykah Badu*'s soulmate and was gearing up for the job by shopping at some funky head shop that sold all kinds of crazy essential oils. Jasmine was Luke's scent of choice, and of all the nasty oils he brought into our room, the jasmine smelled the least like ass. On her, it smelled… well, better than any damned oil, essential or not.

"There's a misalignment in your auric field, I'm afraid." Her voice went still, deep, and through the half-light when I squinted to peek at her, I caught the expression on

15

her face—all studious; the deep line between her eyebrows that hadn't been there a minute before giving her a focused, worried look. She, at least, thought there something serious that needed fixing, and that something serious seemed to be me.

Her face was round, a sort of heart shape that made her look like a kid. But then I got a good look at her eyes when she looked at me and caught something in them that I hadn't before—stories and legends. That's what my Gramps used to say of folk whose past was clouded right in their eyes. Stories that became legends; a life so unbelievable or sad, so lived, that it showed in the stare someone had, how they held it, kept it as though every story would live in their eyes, but they'd never speak it out loud. "You had to look," Gramps would say. "You had to look hard."

I didn't even know this woman's name, but inside of three minutes I knew there was something belly deep she kept to herself.

"I just finished cleansing my own aura." It came out like an afterthought, something she said to fill up the space between us as she moved her hands around my body, motioning like she meant to rub my skin, my limbs, but without touching me. Not once. She moved weirdly, hands and fingers stretching all over me; head, shoulders, chest, down to my knees and feet, then back up again, to my shoulders and neck, around my aura, whatever the hell that was, until she finally rested her fingers against my traps, exhaling hard as she worked her nails up and along my neck, her thumbs rubbing in circles just under the back of my head. "It's probably why yours was so easy to notice."

"That right?" I tried for skeptical, but my voice sounded far away. I forgot about the stupid music she'd blared through her apartment over the past four days. I forgot about the sleep that wouldn't come to me. I forgot about all the worries and work that had kept me up… all gone as I gazed at her face. I'd never seen skin that smooth or freckles up close like that, lips that ripe. If I moved a little, brought her close, I could touch my mouth to hers, in a fraction of movement.

Damn. Where'd the hell had that come from? I wasn't into white girls. Never had been. I wasn't against messing around or hooking up with them, maybe dating for a little bit, but I'd never really been into them. I'd always been into Latina girls, and sisters, definitely, but white chicks? Not really. Despite my current tatted image, I'd spent high school locked up in the library or the computer lab, away from everyone but my teachers and tutors. College for me was Howard, a historically black college, before I transferred to MIT. Not a lot of opportunities for white women to enter my orbit. Not a lot of women, period. There was no reason for me to want to watch her the way I did or think about how she'd taste, what it'd feel like to have that smooth skin against my tongue.

"Oh…" Surprise worked across her features, the harder she massaged the muscle of my neck. "*Oh…*"

"Oh?" I saw her expression focus, become determined, deep, and when she licked her bottom lip I almost lost it. Just like that, I forgot about what type of girls I'd always been into.

"It's…" She blinked twice, her gaze moving around my head, as though she saw something I couldn't. "It's changing colors."

"Weird." That was lame, but I couldn't think of anything else. I kept the frown on my face, as if that wouldn't give away what was in my head, but I got the feeling this chick didn't buy it. At least, she didn't act like it, not the way her cheeks flushed brighter the longer she rubbed my neck.

She paused, and I watched her, wondering what was making her smile like that, wondering why the hell I returned it with one of my own. She noticed.

"You've got a great smile." She moved my face in her hands, and I spotted the dimples that pressed divots in her cheek. "I like it."

Then, just like that, she went all focused and bossy as hell again. "Close your eyes." That demand came out soft, the smallest hint of something deep between each syllable, like she wanted to say please, but wouldn't ever. "The tension is here." There was a small graze of nail against skin when she touched my neck, and I breathed deep, liking the way she smelled, how that soft, firm touch warmed my tight traps. "There's so much tension…you don't…You don't sleep well, do you?"

When I opened my eyes, ready to answer her, she brushed her fingers against my lids, making them stay closed. "No." I didn't bother sweeping her hand away. She worked some kind of juju on me, and for the fucking life of me, I couldn't stop her. Didn't want to. "That's why I came here. Your music…"

"It's the Cistercian Monks of Stift Heiligenkreuz. Well, their chants, anyway. They relax me. You should try listening…"

I opened my eyes despite myself. "That wouldn't relax me. That's why I came banging on your door."

"What would?" She didn't stop me when I looked at her, but her hands relaxed on my shoulders, just for a moment. "What music would relax you?"

"Coltrane."

She frowned then, back straightening as she rubbed against my muscle firmer, deeper, something I thought she did to avoid looking me. I couldn't read her expression. "You don't like jazz?"

"What? No, I do." She corrected that frown, her features returning to the sweet softness again. "My *świenty dziadek.*" I frowned, and she waved a hand in apology. "Sorry. I meant my great-grandfather. Our people were Polish. Some things stuck. Anyway, he loved Coltrane." She smiled, remembering. "He'd sit in his office, smoking a cigar, sipping on a glass of bourbon, listening to Coltrane's *Spiritual.* Maybe Louis Armstrong if he was feeling 'a little New Orleans,' he'd say." She seemed to be lost in the memories, her face both sweet and sad. "He'd do that for hours."

"Why does that make you sad?" That made her glance at me, as if she was surprised that either she had been that open, or that I had been that observant.

"He died. Last month." She moved her chin, her expression evening out as she refocused and stretched and moved her fingers around me, away from my skin. "He was over a hundred years old and I...I loved him a lot." She shrugged, exhaling like she needed it. "Coltrane makes me a little sad now."

"Coltrane is supposed to make you sad." She pushed on my shoulders, and I sagged back against the pillows, dismissing how weird it was that I was letting this woman touch me, trusting her to touch me, and not putting up my guard. "That's what good music does."

She moved her hands away, head tilting as though she hadn't heard me quite right. "Good music makes you sad?"

"Nah. Good music makes you *feel*."

It always had for me. Jazz, blues, especially, maybe really good rap like Rakim, P.E. or Common, old school beats that went deeper than the bragging rights most artists spit out these days, back when lyrics had something real to say. Music should be elemental. It should be bone deep. All those thoughts ran through my head, but I wasn't about to start preaching to some pretty woman I didn't know, the same woman who somehow managed get me on my back with her scent and fingers all over me, working some weird new wave bullshit over me while remembering her granddaddy and his afternoons with Coltrane. Hell, I'd only come up here to get her to cut off that dumbass chant music. I'd done that. I needed to jet.

So why the hell couldn't I move?

"Maybe." The word came out weak, like she didn't buy the line I'd fed her. "Maybe it should sometimes. But I can't listen to Armstrong or Coltrane or smell those Padrón cigars or catch a sip of Pappy's without it reminding me of him and how he's not here anymore."

I shouldn't care. Not about this woman. She'd kept me up for four nights straight. Looking at her, seeing how she carried herself, how bouji her place was—despite the Technicolor boho mess—how she looked as though she'd never known a hardship in her life, I knew we had nothing in common. We were completely different people. But I still wondered what she'd been through, why she felt the way she did. I shouldn't have cared about this woman. God help me, though, I did.

"He was a good man?" It was out of my mouth before I could think about how stupid it might sound.

Without skipping a beat, her face lit up with the most beautiful smile. "The best."

There was no doubt in her reaction. She believed no one had a better grandfather, and I could understand the feeling. I let the moment chill, and when her face started to settle again, I cast around for something to say. "Remind me to tell you about *my* granddaddy one day." My sister Nat and I only got to live with him for four years after our mother died, but those years had made an impact. My mother's father had been a good man. He'd been the best, too.

It was an invitation I didn't mean to make, telling her I'd give her that story, but again, something had spoken for me, some weird, stupid thing that had me itching to let this woman know I'd be back around. She didn't miss it, and it seemed like my suggestion had pleased her, even as she tried to distract herself with the tassel on one of her bright red blankets. "Does that mean you'll come back?" Before I could answer, she shrugged, fronting like it didn't matter, but there was a wisp of teasing in her voice. "That mean my chanting music or my aura cleansing didn't completely scare you away from ever speaking to me again?"

She went back to fiddling with my aura, all business, or at least pretending that she was. Long, thin fingers moved over my arms, again not touching but coming close enough that I could feel the heat of her body on my skin. She moved closer, and again I saw something a little hungry come into her eyes, a look that housed a thousand legends. Something thick bubbled in my stomach, the closer she came, and when she glanced at me, reaching forward as though she would touch my face, I realized I hadn't answered her question. "Maybe."

She smelled so good and the heat between us grew, ran into something that felt like muscle memory, familiarity that made no damn sense to me. Something old and primal seemed to move her, and she came closer, leaning on an elbow to bring herself near enough for me to catch a whiff of her breath— spearmint from her toothpaste, gum maybe, enough of a distraction that I didn't think of those lips for almost half a second. We moved together like magnets, the force unbreakable, undeniable, and out of our control. But at the last moment, the scent of her breath and proximity of her body jarred me from whatever small spell we'd been under, enough that blinking to clear my head did the job, brought me out of whatever fog I'd stepped in the second I had sat down on the sofa.

It was as if the air had cleared, and a kind of understanding came to me. After all, pretty women aren't all that uncommon in New York. There are models and actresses, folk coming in from all parts of the world, adding to the melting pot. Pretty women are everywhere, and I was sitting right in front of one of them, but she wasn't what I wanted, not right now, anyway, not with everything else bearing down on me. Yes, she was beautiful. She was sweet, weird and bossy as fuck, but she wasn't for me.

Maybe it was me moving back, maybe it was just the spell breaking for her, too, but she went still and stiff, as though realizing where she was and what she was doing. Then suddenly she jerked her hands back, staring at them as if they belonged to someone else.

"I don't…" Her gaze didn't leave her hands, as though she half-expected lightning to shoot from her fingertips. There was a hard line between her eyebrows, and when she closed her eyes, scooting back to put distance between us, I thought maybe I'd done something wrong, had said something that put her back up.

"You all right?"

"What?" she said, distracted, waving her hand, looking like she wanted to shake something that ached her from her limbs.

She moved her gaze over my face like she'd only just realized there was someone else with her in her apartment. The confusion was plain, though that expression, the low dip of her mouth, did nothing to take away the sweetness of her features. Still, she seemed unsettled, continuing to stretch her hand, extend her fingers as though her joints ached. And when the seconds lengthened and she went on without speaking, without doing a damn thing but looking worried and confused, I figured it was time to make an exit.

"You want me to go?" Before she could answer I left the sofa, moving slow, cautious, only a little worried that she was a dramatic chick that would act a fool if things didn't go her way.

A few more blinks as she watched me move toward the door, and she finally got to her feet, holding her arms over her stomach like she needed to keep herself together.

"I'm sorry…it's…Your aura is so…" She sighed, head shaking. "There's something about you, and I can't figure it out."

"Maybe it's my bitchin' about that." Again I nodded toward

the record. The turn table went on spinning, and as I pointed it out, the woman moved toward it, flipping down the power button so that spinning stopped.

"It's not that. And I'm sorry." She faced me, curling her arms together again. Her body was stiff, and I got the feeling that holding herself like that was something she did to keep her hands off me. Wasn't real sure why that bothered me, but it did. She took a step closer, body still rigid, but her eyes held that hungry, eager look again; I wondered what she thought of me, and why the look on her face seemed so familiar.

"I'm a little thrown off, to be honest," she said.

"By me?" I tilted my head to watch her close, not getting what I'd done to throw her off.

She watched as I took a step, that hungry, confused expression not moving from her face. There wasn't any fear or worry in that look, but her stance didn't change, and she kept on holding herself together, knuckles white as she balled her hands into fists, like she was worried what she'd do if I got too close.

Took all I had to not smirk like an asshole at that thought.

"By your aura…your…presence." She waved a hand, again motioning at something around me, not at me exactly. "There's something I can't put my finger on."

I didn't buy any of this aura mess. I knew I had a

body, a good one for how hard I worked it. I knew that somewhere inside there might be a spirit or soul; wasn't real sure the difference, but I suspected there was more than zeroes and ones to this world. I still believed I was part of it. But auras and cleansings and all the hippie crap she seemed to believe in? Nah. That was a pill she offered that I didn't have the stomach for.

But that didn't mean I couldn't shake the feeling of there being more to her. More to the feelings I caught in the half-hour I'd been around this crazy white chick.

My mentor Roan had always taught me to listen to my gut, and right then, my gut told me not to jet. Not just yet.

"You...you wanna finish?" I grabbed at anything that would keep me in that apartment. The juju shit was weird, but seemed to be strangely... good. "You know, finish with the..." quick wave around my body, at the invisible whatever-it-was that I guessed was supposed to be my aura, "the ju...ah...the aura cleansing?"

The whites of her knuckles had returned to their original pink color, and I relaxed a little, moving slowly back to the sofa, arms spread wide on the back: an invitation to work me over again. Her frown disappeared, and she dropped her arms to her side, relaxing as she moved toward me.

She knelt in front of me, still cautious, movements slow as she dragged her fingers to the back of her head to braid her long, chestnut hair. She worked quickly, efficiently, flicking long strands behind, in between, around another as she worked, not watching me as she spoke. "Not sure how good it'll be now."

"Not sayin' I believe all this," I waved a hand, grinning when she rolled her eyes, "but I'd hate for you to blast that chanting nonsense all night because you couldn't finish the job." She smiled when I shrugged, and I guessed she didn't buy my nonchalant act. "You seem like a chick that likes to finish a job."

She purposefully ignored my crappy attempt at flirting and moved her hands to her lap, sitting straight. "I like solving problems." She was dead serious.

"You think I got a problem?"

"Hello, you can't sleep. Even without my 'chanting nonsense' music playing." Her laugh was quick, a little loud, and I liked the way it sounded, even if it was poking fun just a bit. Reminded me of the noises blue jays made when I went to the park on my lunch break. The woman recovered from her humor, head shaking.

"You got a point?"

She moved slowly, but all those colors and sounds came with her as she crawled closer, a few loose strands of hair falling out of the braid as she sat next to me on the sofa. "You offered. And yeah, maybe I do need to finish the job."

"I'm Nash, by the way. Nash Nation." It came out in a whoosh of air, like something I'd kept to myself but wanted out in the open. Had no idea why I'd said that.

"Oh…okay." She started to say something, and I

interrupted her, answering what I knew would be the same smartass question I'd heard my whole life. "No, I'm not from Nashville. Never been. Don't much care for country music. Nash was my granddaddy's best friend in the war. I got landed with his name because he'd saved my granddaddy and their entire unit on the beach in Normandy." The small pillow at my feet was blue and red with small sparkling rhinestones edging the seam. I picked it up, to have something to do with my hands as she watched. The silence stretched. "You got a name?"

"A few, actually."

She didn't bother looking sorry for the smartass comment, and I didn't bother calling her on it. She knew who she was. "Okay then, wanna give me one?"

She shrugged, a casual gesture I tried to pretend I didn't find hot. That smile, though, even a monk would be affected by that smile. "Willow."

"Like the tree?"

"Like the movie."

For a split second—hell, for longer than a split second—with that teasing look coming from that bold, Technicolor woman, I thought maybe that smile and her flirting might just make me forget about the kind of women I'd dated. All of them.

Nash

No juju worked on me. That's what I told myself for the hour Willow tried clearing my aura, and I'd been right. Sleep continued to be evasive. The still-griping side piece insomnia was too damn clingy that night, but this time it was mainly because the smell of jasmine clouded my sinuses and stayed on my skin despite the overly long shower I'd taken when I finally made it back to my place.

I hadn't touched Willow in all that time. Not once. Not even casually. Still, my nose, my skin, all smelled like the smoking hot hippie chick who'd convinced me she could help me get some sleep.

I didn't see her much after that. She stayed out my sight, an on-purpose thing that kept me calm. It went on for a week, with me making no plans to see her. But Willow wasn't the type of woman you could hang out with—for any reason—and then just forget about. She made my already crazy-ass thoughts more chaotic, and I'd only spent an hour with her. When I'd left her apartment that night, I told myself I didn't need the distraction. That she wasn't my type, no matter how good she smelled or how warm her non-touch felt. That I had just been imagining that freaky connection we seemed to have, because I had been so damned tired. Yeah, I admit it, I used the sleep deprivation excuse every time I thought of her.

But we lived in the same building. There would be accidental meetings—passing each other in the lobby or at the mailboxes next to the manager's office. There were also times when we met at the elevator, the awkwardness a little thicker than in just some other random encounter. Still, Willow wasn't a woman that could be ignored completely, regardless of door banging and drum thumping and aura cleansing. I saw that clear enough when no less than three different fellas tried getting with her just in the time it took for her to get the mail out of her drop box.

She turned down each one, even Milo Wilson, the seventy-five-year-old janitor who cleaned the building in exchange for the five hundred square foot ground entry apartment next to the manager's office. Yeah, even he knew a good thing when he saw one.

"You know..." her voice came from the back of the elevator when I slipped inside, idly thumbing through my phone so I would seem busy, only pretending to notice Willow over my shoulder as Mrs. Walters got out on the second floor.

"What?"

She moved to my side, ever-present smile on her face as she looked up at me. "I wanted you to know that I can hear *you* clear as a bell from my apartment."

"Payback for those damn monks," I mumbled, still seeming absorbed elsewhere. She didn't like me ignoring her; she made plain enough when she grabbed my phone, taking Instagram from my fingertips and forcing me to look at her. "Willow…"

"I'm just saying I can hear you. At night." She slipped my phone in my jacket pocket as if she knew me. Like we were friends and not just neighbors who'd only met once. I had no idea why I didn't tell her to mind her own business. Jasmine didn't smell that damn good. "When you have your…you knows."

"My what?"

I'm 6'2, pretty built. Weights at the gym and the occasional CrossFit session sometimes are the only things that keep me from losing my head when the work gets too hairy or my business partner Duncan rides me too hard. I swear that man is worse than the naggiest wife in the world. But for as big and square as I am, Willow didn't retreat from my glare or get the message that I wanted her to stay out of my business.

"The noises you make…because you don't sleep. I hear it all."

I pulled my phone back out of my pocket, holding it in my left hand to keep it out of Willow's reach. "You don't hear anything."

"I do so." She sounded like a kid then, and acted like one, making a grab for my phone, which I held up, still out of her reach.

I didn't even look at her, or do anything but watch the floor numbers rise while she gawked at me. That killed her. I knew it did. Willow didn't seem like the kind of woman who was used to being ignored. Or liked it.

A few heavy sighs, that constant stare at the side of my face, and I had to fight the smirk that made my top lip twitch. Then she actually snorted.

"I can hear you pacing, Nash. Back and forth, up and down, all night."

"How you know it's me pacing?" One brief glance down at her, and I let the smirk pull up my lip. "There's other back and forth, up and down things I could be doing."

"That's not…" Her cheeks went pink, and my smirk became a full-fledged smile. "Oh…you aren't…"

"I've been known to do a few back and forth, up and down things…"

"That's not. Well…I mean, I don't think…"

I laughed. Couldn't be helped. Those round, sweet cheeks were completely red after that, and I heard her low curse as the elevator doors opened and I headed for my door.

"You need your rest, Nash. I know you do," she called after me. In the reflection of the wall of windows to my right, I spotted her leaning out of the elevator, that mop of curly hair falling into her face.

"Night, Willow."

"I can help you, you know…"

The last sound I heard was her yelp as the elevator alert

sounded for keeping the doors open too long. Then, there was quiet. At least for a little while.

Two hours later, one game of *Left for Dead* and three of *Call of Duty* still hadn't made me tired. Duncan had sent two messages while I was in the shower, then another one as I threw together two chicken Caesar wraps. I didn't respond to any of them. The man never slept and was always on the clock, reason enough for the two divorces he had before he'd hit forty.

I probably should have called him. I thought about it, thought about updating him on the new projections my assistant Daisy had sent from the contractors beta-testing our software. My plan was to revolutionize data security by perfecting the social engineering tech that kept banks and financial institutions from being hacked. The software had been free-sourced for decades, but mine piggybacked on the hacker's ISP, reverse-attacking them with a nasty virus I'd invented. Duncan had plans to go wide with our company, and it made him nervous that I didn't worry about it as much as he did. But then, worrying was his job. Mine was the product, period.

But later, as I lay in my bed trying to relax, Coltrane's sax soaking into my ears, not even my annoyance with Duncan could keep my thoughts from straying to Willow. Hell, I even ended up thinking that a tunnel-visioned asshole like him would have been smitten by Willow and her hippie vibe, if he ever had a reason to meet her. Everyone was smitten by her, and damn, I had to admit it bothered me, which pissed me off even more.

Four hours later, I was still awake, completely bored out of my mind. From my bedside table, the Ambien bottle seemed to stare at me, the blue and pink font a taunt, promising peace and serenity. All you had to do was pop that small blue pill into your mouth. One small pill would squash the insomnia. But only for one night. The insomnia would come back the next night and the next, I knew that. To get rid of it, I'd have to take those little blue pills every night, probably for the rest of my life. That cost was way too high, especially factoring in the side effects: the wild pounding of my heart and the fever that came out of nowhere; the listlessness; the empty, bottomless feeling that left me with zero desire to feel anything at all. The last time I had tried that mess, it took me a week to claw my way back. No, Ambien had to be a one-time-only, last resort. I wasn't that far gone, not yet.

For a second, thoughts of tapping on Willow's door popped into my head, but I ignored them as quickly as they came. She couldn't help, no matter how much she believed she could.

Instead I got out of my bed, picking up the tennis ball from the side table in the living room, bouncing it to the ground as I walked to the stereo. If Willow could play her monk chants at ungodly decibels, then she'd have to be okay with a little Coltrane coming from my surround sound. Headphones were fine usually, but sometimes you needed the music to fill the world.

Two long, drawn-out notes rattled my speakers, and I swear I felt that go deep, to my gut, as I kept my focus on the wall and returning the tennis ball to its surface again and again. That sax went on and on, leveling the faint crackle and pop that came from the speakers—there was a hint of breath in that white noise, something you wouldn't notice if you only listened a couple of times. But I was a Coltrane disciple. I knew each breath as they came, the cleft of the crackle and the pause just before the long tones, moving between B, A, and G, and a million other combinations came from that horn. I knew the direction of each chord and the steady beat of the bass as it thumped and rattled right alongside that slow, smooth sax. The song moved forward, the next started up and I zoned out, not even realizing how each *thunck* of the tennis ball against the wall was timed perfectly with the beat of the music. That is, until the rumble of a knock rattled my front door.

"Shit." It was the only thing I could think to say. A glance at my microwave over the open kitchen's wide, marble island, told me how late it had gotten. Another hard knock and I dropped the ball, muting the stereo before I opened the front door.

"You're kidding, right?" Willow had braided her hair again, not seeming to care that the double braids gave her a redneck, country girl vibe. "You cannot be serious with all this noise?"

"Noise?" My tone was harsh, and just to annoy her, I stood in the door way, crossing my arms before I leaned against the frame. "Coltrane is poetry, not noise."

"I meant the bouncing ball." She made to push me aside, but I didn't budge. "Nash, let me in."

"Why?"

She watched me then, frown pushing away the calm, simple smile she'd worn seconds before. "Because I can help get you to sleep."

"Oh? How you plan on doing that?" My gaze was purposeful, as penetrating as the slow, wide smile I gave her. The look was intentionally hard, slipping to her mouth, then down her body just long and slow enough to be insulting. It got me the reaction I wanted.

"Is it impossible for you to not act like a horny teenager?"

"I'm not horny." My laugh came quick, got louder when Willow barged passed my door. "I'm just teasing you a little."

"You're shamelessly flirting."

"Would I do that, Will?"

I could tell by the way she cocked her head, and how she smiled at me, that she liked that, the little nickname. It had come out of nowhere, but felt right, and I'd been rewarded with a smile I'd not seen before. It looked good on her. "Absolutely."

I stayed in the doorway while Willow took inventory of my

apartment, not judging, but probably recognizing how sparsely it was decorated, with a bunch of posters on my wall but little else. Tupac and Dizzy Gillespie, Einstein, and quotes from both Langston Hughes and Neil Gaiman designed by small-time artists. But Willow wasn't checking out my art or posters; she was assessing.

One nod of her head, an agreement she made to herself, then she faced me, pulling off the loud yellow sweater she wore, stripped down to the sleeveless white tee underneath.

"Okay. The couch will do."

"Do for what?"

She pointed to it without answering, throwing a stare so serious I almost thought she was sincerely pissed that I'd flirted. Almost. "Lay down." And when I didn't move, Willow adopted the best drill sergeant tone and pointed at the brown leather of my couch. "Now."

"It's not gonna work."

"It'll work."

"Stubborn fucking woman…" I flinched when she smacked me, pretending that little slap hurt worse than it did. "Stop beating on me."

"Stop being an asshole."

The scent of jasmine was everywhere; it hung like a cloud in my apartment as Willow's hair slid against my face. She touched me softly, fingertips over my temples, hair tickling my face as she stroked and rubbed my forehead.

I tried to keep it light. "I don't let anybody talk to me like that, you know. Not even my twin sister."

She stopped moving and I opened my eyes, staring up at her as she gave me a silly, fake-shocked expression with her mouth hanging open. I could sense the smartass comment before she made it. "Oh Lord, there's two of you?"

"Yeah, but we're not both bad."

"So it's just you."

"That's it; I don't have to put up with this nonsense." I sat up, had nearly made it off her lap when she tugged me back down. I tried to make it light, but I was really starting to get annoyed.

"Stop it. You need at least four hours of sleep. You said it yourself when I asked what you were working on the other night." She glanced at my open laptop and the incomplete code and blinking cursor I'd left waiting for me. "You said you have a meeting this week. The big one?"

"I'll manage."

"I doubt that." She made more sense than I let on. Still wasn't sure what about this woman kept me weak, sprung and stupid on a female I didn't even know. But still, I was immobilized, struck dumb and motionless by her commanding voice and the bossy way she made me participate in shit I just couldn't believe in.

Like the temple rub. The aura cleanse hadn't worked. Now Willow was trying massage and meditation. But no way I was gonna let her try "sonic meditation." Beautiful girl or not, she was not going to touch my stereo—Hippie-monk-chanting mess would come through those speakers.

"I should have never opened the door."

"Please. You couldn't resist."

She paused in the temple massage when I laughed, shaking my head as though I didn't appreciate the small jab. "I'm a baller. I can resist anything."

"No, Nash. You're a computer geek with insomnia."

I cracked open an eye, frowning with my nostrils flaring, wondering if she'd been checking up on me. But she just smirked and jerked her chin at the wall, right where my framed MIT diploma in computer science hung, telling her all she thought she needed to know about me and my baller status. "You are not invulnerable to my temptations."

I couldn't deny that. She came right in, and I didn't stop her. She bossed me around like I was her willing bitch, and I hadn't really complained. Still, I wasn't going to cop to that. "So you say."

"Hush." She held my head still, laying the pads of her thumbs over my eyelids. "Be still and concentrate…"

"Not gonna work…"

"And visualize a dark room." Her voice was low, but calm. It had taken on a deeper pitch, something that reminded me of an old-school club with cigarette smoke hanging like a halo in the air above a small stage. You give Willow something black and tight to wear, and I bet all the cash in my *Make It Rain* savings account that she'd pull off the part of sexy-as-fuck jazz singer, easy.

"There is no light. No noise. There is only the vastness of space, starless, soundless." As she spoke it, my mind went gray. There was a lull, the small, silent hum of nothingness you always hear when you slip between asleep and awake. 'Tween place, as my old Creole gramps used to call it.

Willow got me there quickly. It was less difficult than I thought it would be. For all my protests, this crazy white chick had my mind doing the 'Tween hum. The smell of her, that soft touch, her calm voice, so easily pulled me right to the edge of oblivion. "You are alone in that darkness, and your body is weightless. You are floating. Breathe. Keep breathing in and out. In through your nose, out through your mouth. One, two, three…"

"Not…not working." Fighting was useless. I knew it, but was too much of a hardass to admit that aloud. Especially not to Willow.

"*Shh.* Keep floating. You are light and free. There is nothing around you. Only space and the infinite expanse…you are floating…free…"

Willow's voice faded until it didn't sound like her at all. I gave up resisting and followed her lead, letting the image of the darkness consume me. There was nothing for me to see, no real images that came together from form and shape to make something real. It was a place I'd never been—in this silence, in the space where there was nothing. Something about Willow had put me there, and the harder I concentrated, the fainter her voice became. I floated then, imaging things that could not be real, things that seemed so usual, so familiar.

"Listen to my voice…"

I did. I listened so closely, so intently, that after several minutes, I could not hear Willow at all.

I heard nothing—not her sultry tone, not my own breathing, not even the traffic from the street below. Everything faded to silence.

Then there were other sounds; sounds that I couldn't make out at first. Sounds that had me shaking, had Willow's grip shifting from my forehead, traveling to hold my fingers tight.

"Nash?" she asked, and I knew it was because she was worried. But her worry was the last thing on my mind.

There, in the center of my living room, a woman I didn't know held my hand and rubbed my temples until her voice became a distant echo as I slipped away into sleep.

Behind that sleep and the fainting feel of her touch, I left Brooklyn.

Then, the dream took me.

New Orleans

For starters, no one had been able to drink hooch for going on seven years. Mama said that's where all the bad came from—bossy government people telling folk they couldn't have a drop to drink. Those meddling politicians called it "Prohibition." My Uncle Aron and his smart-mouth self liked to call it "Proha-bullshit." Anyway, the whole mess made people angry, and angry people did angry things. That's why Mama said to stay clear of Ripper Dell and those bad-seed boys. Never mind that Ripper got paid by every fool who ran a hustle on Rampart Street, my mama included. He had money, and men with money got whatever they wanted, even fifteen-year-old girls like me. But, I did what Mama said because if I didn't, she'd whip my behind until it was redder than the wattle of Mimi Bastien's rooster.

I wanted to be out at Bastie's swamp farm today, not running hooch between the corners where the white policemen kept their eyes tight on anyone that hadn't paid them their fair share of 'hush now' money. Mama said between

Ripper Dell and those fat policemen, we'd be lucky to eat come the rest of the month. It was another excuse she gave to that cat-eyed old priest during confession. "I got to feed my babies. Hooch makes that happen, Father."

Last Thursday, I'd sat in the pew next to the confessional as Mama spilled away the sins she'd racked up for a week, since the last time brought me and my stupid brother Sylv to St. Augustine's to get our souls right and sort out our sassy mouths. At least, that's what she called it.

She and her good friend Lulu Davenport made the hooch from an old recipe some cropsharer woman had given Bastie when they still lived back in Atlanta. That white cropsharer lady had gotten the recipe from her daddy, a poor hillbilly who died in the middle of a gunfight somewhere up in the Appalachian Mountains. Bastie fed the woman, gave her a place to stay in Atlanta because she'd married Bastie's cousin, and family was family, after all, at least to Bastie's folk. That lady'd been a redneck's daughter and married to a black man, which was two strikes against her, so no white people in Atlanta would lift a finger for her. So to thank Bastie, she gave my Mimi the only thing in her power to give—the recipe to make good, strong hooch.

Bastie wouldn't help my mama with making it, not with the policemen greedy to do bad to folk who they thought wouldn't hand out that 'hush now' money, but she gave Mama the recipe, and now Mama and Lulu paid Ripper Dell to keep them safe and paid the white policemen to look the other way.

No one was supposed to drink hooch. So said the law. But that didn't stop a damn person from doing it. Not in New Orleans. Sure not on Rampart Street.

"Sookie! Get your skinny backside over to Miss Matthews. She's waiting."

Mama was in a bad way today. It was only the end of March and already hotter than the devil's tongue, and the humidity around the city, was like taking a big ole breath, holding inside your lungs right before you jump into the cold, deep water. It felt like something was coming, and it was something nobody wanted showing up.

"Sookie, right damn now!" Her voice was loud, mean as all get-out, and I moved through the back kitchen of my mama's small bakery, pushing the Johnson kids out my way as Esther and Robbie, who cleaned the building for food, fussed at the boys throwing rocks inside the little shop.

Mama's bakery was just inside the Quarter, away from the fine businesses where the rich white ladies shopped. There weren't customers coming in to nibble on Mama's cookies and breads during the day, but she had a bargain with the hairdressers in the Quarter, keeping them and those rich lady types in sweets they pretended they didn't eat while they got their hair set and their fingernails painted and trimmed.

"I'm moving right now, Mama."

But brownies and cookies and rich little cakes weren't the only things my mama cooked up in that tiny kitchen just big enough for her, and, if they were really busy, just the right side of Lulu's thin body.

"You stay to the tree line and keep out of Ripper's sight."

"Yes, ma'am. I will."

She'd pulled one of Lulu's old scarves from the drawer in the back of the broom closet and tied two bottles of her 'special' hooch together. These bottles were of a stronger vintage, meant to give someone ailing a little relief, not get nobody drunk for fun. She put the bottles at the bottom of the basket and fitted a thin piece of pine on top, filling up the rest of the basket with some bread and corn biscuits and lots of pralines wrapped in wax paper before handing it to me. "Disguise," she called it a while back, when the policemen started messing with me and my brother Sylv just to see what we carried past the Square and through the crowds of farmers and performers and ladies whose business mama wouldn't talk about. Mama was good at tricking those white men, and I was glad for it. It was too hot to go running away from them if they got too nosy over what I carried in that basket.

Congo Square was more crowded than it had been all summer. The street performers danced and sang louder and longer than they had the day before, and I guessed that was because of the busload of Yankees in from up north somewhere that I heard Lulu telling Mama about while they poured the ready hooch into clean bottles this morning.

"Yankees from Boston," Lulu had said, drawing out the last work like it pained her. Lulu had met a man from New Jersey once— broke her heart clean in two—and I reckoned Jersey was just too damn close to Boston for Lulu's liking.

The crowd was heavy with curious white folks—all manner of rich people, the women in their fine, fitted, dropped-waist dresses and sweet little T-strapped patent leather shoes, the men in straw hats they waved in front their faces, complaining like a preacher in the middle of

Mardi Gras about the heat and humidity and smell of the city.

But I didn't give them much more than a passing glance. Mrs. Matthews had the cancer, and it was only the tonic Mama worked from the hooch that seemed to give the old woman enough sleep that she didn't keep her daughter and grandkids up at all hours. The white Yankees would probably still be nosing around by the time I got back, and so I hurried through the crowd, ignoring the sharp eyes that belonged to Ripper's crowd. They were just as curious as the Yankees, and I liked my behind the color it was right then. Didn't need my mama changing that color because I'd caught those bad seed boys' eyes.

"Sookie. Hold up." Sylv was slow as maple syrup in an ice storm and I figured, as I moved away from the Square toward Tremé that my brother was only catching up to me because Mama had fussed him good. "Damn, girl, you hear me say hold up?"

"Don't need a tagalong, Sylv."

He caught up to me, even though I moved along quicker, spotting Mrs. Matthew's granddaughter, Bobby, heading up the walk just outside her granny's small cottage. The girl had gotten taller in the few months since I saw her last, nothing like how she'd looked a year before when I still watched her overnight while her granny and mama were off to Baton Rouge to see a specialist.

"Mama would beat me bloody if I didn't walk with you." My brother smelled like sweat, liked he'd been out too late last night and up too early this morning.

"You shouldn't have been nosing around Lily Chamber's house so late last night. That's why Mama needs to whip you."

"Hush, you don't know what you talking about."

"I seen you coming home at two this morning."

My brother ignored me, pulling out a half-smoked, hand-rolled cigarette from his front pocket. He shrugged, like the frown I gave him didn't shame him even a little. "Don't you go sayin' nothing to Mama bout me smokin' or nothin'."

"She gonna smell it."

"Will not."

"Will...hey, Bobby, sugar. How's your granny?"

The girl's small smile fell a little at my question, and I felt a little bad for asking. Bobby liked Sylv, I knew that. But my brother was a boy, and most boys are too stupid to notice much about how girls act when they're around them, especially little thirteen-year-old girls like Bobby.

She didn't speak much, just kept her attention on the smoke floating out Sylv's mouth, then the loud, racking, coughing fit he had because he was a damn fool who didn't know nothing about smoking.

"Mama says to give your granny two tablespoons every couple of hours, but no more than that, you hear?"

"Yeah. I hear you." Bobby took the basket when I handed it over, but kept glancing at Sylv, as though she half-expected him to do more than lean on the street sign waiting for me to walk back to Rampart with him.

"We'll light a candle for her tomorrow night at Mass." I meant it, too. My Bastie wasn't as old as Mrs. Matthews, but I reckoned she would be one day. It would be nice if someone other than me lit a candle for her when she got old and sick.

Sylv watched me tuck the money Bobby gave me inside the collar of my dress and I pushed him to the side, head shaking when he looked a little too hard, probably from trying to see how many bills had been in that small stack.

"That ain't your money."

"Yours either. Let me see."

My brother reached toward me, and I stuck him good with my elbow, making that tall fool wince. "You leave the money be and stop acting a fool, and I won't tell Mama about the cigarettes…"

He blew out another puff of smoke, flicking ashes right at my feet, trying to make like he didn't give a fig if Mama knew he smoked. "Or that you left Lily Chamber's house later than is fittin' last night." Sylv watched me close, top lip curling like he was disgusted, and I knew I had him. "Ha! You so sad."

"Yeah, well, so are you."

"Not like you." He made like he might take another drag of that cigarette, but I beat him to it, yanking it from his mouth before he could stop me, tossing it down and grinding it under my heel. "Why you bothering me?"

"Your boyfriend is hiding again."

That had me stopping, watching my brother as he wiped a handkerchief over his sweaty head. Dempsey. What had he done now? "How you know?"

"He slept in the tree house last night. Uncle Aron told me this morning."

I didn't have to ask Sylv much more about what Uncle Aron said. Dempsey always ended up in the tree house in the back of Mimi Bastien's swamp house when things at his place were bad. Some nights he snuck away from Manchac where his daddy's land touched up against my granny's place and bummed a ride to the city because he need to see a friendly face. Least that's what the fool always said. We all did our part to watch over Dempsey because his own people wouldn't. Sometimes he hid for days and days inside Mama's tiny shop. Sometimes Uncle Aron got him a room at the brothel over on Bourbon because the woman running the place was sweet on Aron. They liked his light eyes, they said, how they looked almost green.

"Bad this time?"

Sylv shook his head, nodding toward the end of the street like he wanted to get out of the sun. "Aron said it looked like a split lip and a nice shiner on his eye."

"Damn his daddy."

My brother agreed, nodding once like he had every other time Dempsey ran away from the fine house his mama and daddy lived in with him and his hateful brother Malcolm. His mama especially hated that Dempsey liked sleeping in the tree house or on a cot in Bastie's pantry instead of their fancy place with the big columns and wraparound porches.

"You throwing something around in your head. I can see the gears working extra hard."

It was just like Sylv to have thoughts that he ought not let out his mouth, but my brother, pain in the backside that he was, had a heart. It wasn't completely wrecked just yet by the city and what it was having no daddy to speak of and a mama who worked so hard sometimes we went days without seeing her. Right down to his marrow, my big brother cared a whole lot about his folk, and loud coonass boy or not, Dempsey was our folk.

"That man, Dempsey's daddy?" Sylv said. I stared right back at him, not bothering to answer the fool because he knew I knew who Dempsey's daddy was. Everybody on the Manchac did. Mr. Simoneaux could scare the devil and have him running off with his tail wound around his pitchfork. But Sylv would have his say, no matter that he probably wasn't saying nothing I didn't already know. "Everybody knows there ain't a drop of good in him."

"That ain't a secret."

"So, little sister, what I'm saying to you is that you might wanna be careful."

He didn't like the look I gave him or the way I shook my head like he made no damn sense to me at all. But Sylv wouldn't let things lie. Not there. Not, I guessed, when it came to Dempsey Simoneaux and his hell-bound daddy.

"Listen to me a little bit." He took my arm, tugging me near a big magnolia tree with fat, sweet-scented blossoms peppered on every other limb. There were small gnats flying above our heads, and I swatted at them, mainly to encourage my brother to get on with his lecture. "This mess with you and that white boy, wasn't nothing to it when we was all little."

"Don't start with that stuff again."

Sylv's grip on my arm got tight, and I stood up straighter, giving him a mean frown as a warning. He stared a little bit before he dropped my arm, shoulders lowering because he knew he couldn't boss me. "I'm not sayin' you need to steer clear of him, Sookie, God knows that boy needs somebody to keep him alive."

"But?" The frown stuck, and I added a slow arm cross to keep the *warning between us.*

"Lord, girl, you smarter than this." Sylv rubbed his damp face again, tamping off the sweat that had collected against the back of his neck. "Dempsey's good people, we all know that, but his daddy and that no-account brother of his ain't. It's one thing with him nosing around the tree house or tagging after us when Aron needs a hand delivering the hooch, but Sookie, you ain't little anymore and neither is he."

My face heated then and I looked away from my brother, not wanting to see the look in his eyes; not sure if he'd pick on me or warn me for all the times I looked a little too long at Dempsey Simoneaux. "You ain't got to tell me my business, Sylv. I know just how old I am."

"Yep, you do, and so does Dempsey."

He came to my side, turning my shoulders so that I faced the Square. In the middle of that thick crowd, Ripper leaned against a brown brick building, hat tilted up as he watched all that was happening thick in the Square. But he shifted his head down, listening, when one of his bad-seed boys nodded toward me, and that hat went further back as Ripper moved the nub of a cigar to the corner of his mouth.

The look on Ripper's face made my skin crawl, made me itching to be back at Bastie's farm just so I could swim in the lake and be rid of the feeling of that man's eyes on me, looking hard. Looking like he wanted to see more of me. That look made my stomach twist.

"Dempsey ain't the only one, little sister. Ole Ripper sees it and he's looking damn hard, and he's a useless bully. You think Dempsey's daddy and brother don't see it too? You think every man in the city don't?"

"I stay away, Sylv." I turned back from the Square, from the eyes that stuck to me like a fly trapped on sticky paper. "I keep to Mama's kitchen and only go out with you or Aron or Dempsey, and even when I don't, I stick to the tree lines."

"That's not good enough. Not when every dirty man in the city—white, black, or whatever else—looks hard at you." My brother nodded, like he'd had his say and I needed to mind it. "You stick too close to Dempsey, and he's gonna get ideas."

I opened my mouth, about ready to tell Sylv to shut it up, but then, I knew I couldn't. It would be a lie denying what Sylv said, and he'd know it the second I opened my mouth. I knew what he meant. Dempsey had already gotten ideas. We both had. He'd held my hand just last week when Aron and Slyv walked in front of us back to Bastie's farm after the parish priests held a picnic down by the lake. I'd liked the way Dempsey ran his thumb over my knuckles, how my palm smelled like the sugar cane he'd cut down for me as we walked back.

"Nothing…" I swallowed, wanting the words to stay down in my throat. But Sylv's eyes went hard, a little worried, and I couldn't keep a thing to myself. "Nothing happens with us. Nothing bad."

He nodded, scrubbing his chin with his thumbnail as he led me away from the Square, away from the crowd. We weren't in a hurry to get back, not when the day was running hot. Not when Mama was sure to have us back in the heat for more deliveries.

"I like Dempsey. He's a nice fella, and he ain't nothing like his kin. That's a good thing, but sis, you got to be smart."

"He needs us, Sylv. If we weren't around, who'd clean him up when his daddy gets means and drunk and beats on him? Who'd hide him when the beatings are bad?"

"You ever think maybe it's us that gets Papa Simoneaux mean? You ever think that crazy white man beats on Dempsey because he don't stay with his own people?"

It might have been that. God knows I'd heard that hateful man screaming at Dempsey about being with the likes of us before. I'd heard the nasty things he'd called us and the things Dempsey's mama sometimes said about my Bastie and my mama. Hateful, all of them, but especially when they'd catch us swimming near the dock that splintered our two properties. Especially when Dempsey would run off to keep from getting beat on—and he always ran to us.

Sylv knocked my arm, pushing me a little, a tiny movement followed with a smile as we walked through the crowd. I knew then that his fussing was over. For now.

"You kiss him yet?" He didn't want to know, I could tell with how he rolled his eyes and made smooching sounds with his puckered lips. "Dempsey and Sookie sitting in a tree…"

"Oh, shut up." I messed his hair, popping him on the back of the head. "You tease me, and maybe I will go tell Mama about you and Lily." My brother's frown was hard and his eyes went all funny, like he was scared if Mama knew what he'd been up to there'd be a whipping in his future. But he tried to play it off, act like my threat didn't bother him none.

"Tell her." I didn't buy the way he shrugged or how he brushed *me off with a toss of his hand.*

"Okay. I'm going." And as I took off, jogging through the crowd with my fussing brother running behind me, I tried to stay tickled. I tried to not worry so much over Dempsey being hurt again. I tried something fierce to keep from reminding myself that the best thing for him, for all of us, would be to let him be.

If only I could muster the strength to do that.

Willow

Nash called me a witch. He didn't know I heard him, but I had. It came in a mumble as he drifted off, something low and quiet as I rubbed his temples, and I knew why. He floated, went where you're supposed to when you meditate. He could call me a witch all he wanted. I wasn't, by the way. I liked to think of myself as a healer, someone who touched and held and wanted nothing more than to help.

But Nash struck me as the type of man who needed to put a name to things he didn't understand. Usually, the wrong name. He was a man of science, of things concrete, that could be broken down and explained away. Numbers were his thing. They moved in and out of his head, sang to his soul because they made sense to him.

Two days after I helped him get some rest, he was still having vivid dreams. I knew he was. I heard him calling out in the middle of the night. But the sleeping itself hadn't remained, at least nothing restful. I heard him for the past three nights, moaning and whining, though he'd never own up to it.

It was Nash that took up most of my thoughts that day. It was Sunday, and the farmer's market had been packed. I'd been doing pretty well selling my cupcakes to folks ambling by, their bags full of organic vegetables and berries and plums. Everyone was in high spirits, at least until the skies opened up. Things thinned out pretty quick then; it came down in buckets, and each one, it seemed, was right on the top of my head. Cabs passed me by and so I ran, darting under awnings as much as I could, and then, God help me, I spotted that poor cat.

He limped toward my building, all skitterish and slinky, like he was doing his best to not be spotted because bad things happened to him when he was. I hadn't fussed much about the weather—it was only water, after all—but then the rip of thunder cracked as bright white lightning lit up the sky, and the thought of a poor little critter caught out in this storm had me worried. Skinny guy was alone in the world, and hurt, from the looks of him, and now soaking wet.

The rain came on like a broken wave; sideways, horizontal, it seemed to splatter and fall in every direction against my face, soaking into the small white boxes of what Nash called "prissy-looking cupcakes" when he caught me in the elevator the other night on my way to deliver said prissy cupcakes to a client. The prissiness of them sure hadn't stopped him from trying to sneak a swipe of icing.

The rain came so thick, so violently, I had to squint as I looked down the sidewalk, trying to catch sight of that poor, scrawny, limping cat. My thick Columbia hoodie was soaked through by the time I spotted him ghosting around the corner, and I jogged after him to the back of our building. There was water collecting quickly into puddles, so much that my feet and toes were soaked by the time

I made it midway down the alley. I dropped one of the sodden white bakery boxes when I tripped on a submerged crack in the pavement, cringing when two yellow-iced cupcakes floated down the temporary stream, leaving behind a cakey trail as they bobbed and twisted away. I dropped two more empty white boxes before I spotted the cat, who had scrambled up a tall pin oak tree which sat in the smallest speck of green space beyond the property gate. The poor thing had probably been looking for shelter from the rain, but seemed to be having second thoughts, given his sodden look, ears down, tail snapping. Determined to help him, I set down the rest of my boxes and tried to move a nearby dumpster with my hip toward the crooked limbs, intending to climb up and rescue the damned cat.

"What the hell are you doing?"

I jerked, twisting around with a small yelp, brushing my matted, tangled hair off my face. Of course it was Nash. "What are you doing out here?"

We had to shout. The rain spattered and crashed against the row of metal trashcans and three dumpsters that lined the back of the alleyway.

"I asked first. Damn, Willow, you're a fucking mess." Behind me the cat meowed, a loud, pathetic sound that tore at something inside my chest. Nash went on gawking at me like I was crazy, or clueless, but that sad meow sounded just like "help" to me, and I had to do something. But when I glanced up at the poor creature, then at the distance between the limb where he sat and the dumpster, I knew that it was too high. Too high for me, anyway. I looked around, looked back up at the cat, considered trying to coax it down, looked for any other way up, but there was nothing, all while Nash watched me, both of us drenched to the skin.

I am capable of a lot of things. My mama definitely didn't raise a dainty damsel watching out for a prince, but even I knew my limitations. As much as it pained me, I exhaled, turning back to Nash as his wet face scrunched up in a hard glare.

"Can you help him?" I came closer, pulling on his wet jacket, imploring. There was something in his eyes—hesitation, irritation, like he hated how drawn to me he was, yet still worried, wanting to pull me inside, to protect me from the mess I'd gotten myself into. But I didn't care how he looked or what he thought. He could look at me like that all he wanted, as long as he helped the poor cat. "Please, Nash, look at him. He's just a baby."

Okay. That might have been an overstatement. Even I knew the *baby* in question was the ugliest cat that ever walked the earth and was no baby, either. He was small, but scrappy, with a thick rat's nest of a tail that broke into a weird angle in the middle. And one of his ears looked to be eaten clean off with mites or some other disgusting mess alley cats got into. And he was filthy. And pissed off. Still, at that moment, more than anything, I wanted to help that cat.

My mother had taught me not to rely on my looks for

anything, but come on, sometimes being a woman gives you the upper hand. I adjusted my expression, working up a look that was worried and sad, because I *was* worried and sad, at least about the lost day and the sad little hurt kitty. But yeah, I laid it on a little thick, because I knew it could work.

And it did work. Oh, he looked me up and down, looked for a way out, but when he finally admitted to himself that my shorter arms and smaller-than-his legs wouldn't help me climb up that dumpster to rescue the ugly meowing little cat, he sort of gave up the ghost and resigned himself to helping out.

And I didn't plan it, but suddenly, without any warning, I sneezed, a racking, loud sound that made the cat jerk in alarm. "You okay?" Nash asked, and I knew I had him hooked.

"I'm fine," I promised, but I wasn't going to make it sound as sure as I felt. "Please. I'd get up there, but I'm too short to reach. You're a good three inches taller than me."

I did the sad eyes again just as yet another sneeze hit, and Nash moved over to the dumpster, climbing up it in a side to side motion while gripping the busted-up back gate in one hand.

"I swear to God, if this cat fucking scratches me..."

But the poor cat didn't do anything but stare right at Nash with a thick, raised tuft of hair standing on end straight down his back. From this angle I realized the cat's hair wasn't gray like I initially thought. The poor baby was white, completely white by the look of him, but he was so filthy, with greasy streaks of grease or mud or something smeared all over his coat, that he had looked gray from a distance.

"Easy," Nash said to him, leaning close with a hand outstretched. He teetered close to the edge of the dumpster, bobbing a little on his feet, and I actually got scared, imagining a scenario of Nash falling and breaking bones and how it would be entirely my fault.

"Be careful, Nash!" I blurted out, which was stupid, because it caused him to jerk, which in turn caused the cat to growl, a low, warning hiss that got louder and more threatening the closer Nash got. "Nash? Make sure you don't…"

"Will you hush, woman? You're gonna spook him!"

Turns out, the scrawny cat didn't want rescuing. Nash caught him by the scruff of his neck and the stupid animal hissed twice and scratched at him. When Nash let go, the "baby" leap-frogged from the limb without any assistance and dropped back into the alley, where he hissed once again at both of us for good measure before darting away.

"Unbelievable," Nash said under his breath, navigating away from the tree and gate, and then stepping gingerly on the dumpster before he jumped onto the pavement. "Happy?"

"I…" I started to say, but a sudden sneezing fit came over me, and Nash pulled me away from the nasty dumpster, guiding me back toward the alley. "Damn cat," I muttered, suddenly sad and soaking and in danger of breaking down into a crying jag. Nash must have heard the hitch in my voice because he tried to pull up my thin jacket over my head, but made a piss-poor job of it. We headed back toward the front of the building, but when we got to the boxes I had dropped, I stopped, bending to try and scoop up some of the cupcake mush.

"No matter how good they might have been, you're not gonna save them, either."

"They *were* good. These were my first attempt at Irish car bombs." I sneezed again, and Nash wiped the mash of cake from my hand.

"Come on, before you get pneumonia." I listened, following him down the alley without a backward glance at the cupcakes or the echo of the renegade cat. "That happens, and I'll be pissed about you not baking for me."

Willow

"When do you think Mickey will be back?"

"It's bingo night, remember? He doesn't ever call it early on bingo night unless he wins, and he never wins."

I liked Nash's place almost as much as my own, and that was saying something because I had totally fallen in love with my apartment. I still couldn't believe my luck when one of my Mom's old university buddies needed someone to take up the place when he decided to retire to New Hampshire. Rent control in Brooklyn? Hell, yes. I was never going to leave, unless forced to. I suspected Nash wouldn't either, and with how clean and comfortable he had made his place, I couldn't blame him.

I had no idea who some of the people on his posters on the walls were, except Gaiman, of course. Everyone knows Gaiman, and I guess I knew Einstein and Dizzy, too. I didn't mind that many of the other faces were unknown to me. It was like walking into some post-modern techie world that itched to be explored.

There were framed posters of musicians, writers, and scientists: beautiful men whose faces told stories, said things with one look. They contrasted against the utilitarian feel of the rest of his place—the clean, mint scent that wafted from his kitchen and the books organized on black metal shelves by color and size. There was very little in the way of personal items, only a few pictures of Nash and a girl who looked so much like him that she had to be his twin. They couldn't be more than eight in the picture, but there was a smile on his face, honest and open, his hazel-glinted eyes sparkling when he smiled at her. No photos of parents or friends. I couldn't help but wonder why only his sister warranted a frame on the center console of his entertainment center, but I didn't feel like I could ask. Not yet.

The last time I'd been here there'd been little time for exploration. Nash had been sleep-deprived and worn out. My focus had been on centering him and getting him to sleep.

Now though, I was stuck here, at least until the Super came back from bingo. "I can't believe I locked myself out." Another stupid sneeze. At this rate I'd pass out from lack of blood to my heart. Did you know when you sneeze, all your working parts just sort of stop? No heartbeat, no nothing. Sneezing is hazardous to your health.

"Here," Nash said, handing me something that smelled like the whiskey my great grandfather used to drink, but it steamed like hot tea and felt good against my cold fingers.

"What is this?"

"Hot toddy. Old family recipe." He pulled the towel from my shoulders and started to dry the ends of my hair, all familiar and sweet. Definitely not like him at all. I liked it—

Nash Nation, tough-looking, techie guy, taking care of me like he wanted to.

"Mmmm." The small, satisfied noise slipped out, without my permission, but I didn't try to cover the slip. It felt nice to have Nash fussing around me, in this quiet, almost but not quite intimate way. It felt...familiar, and I wasn't sure why that was.

"Drink," he said when I stared off into space, humming like an old woman when he worked that towel through my wet hair.

I listened to his demand, making a deeper, more satisfied noise when the toddy warmed me from the inside, a sensation that left me a little punch drunk.

"It's good, right?" he asked, and I could hear the humor in his voice. I must have seemed ridiculous to him, needy and pathetic, but I couldn't help myself.

"Willow?"

There was too much sensation, and my head felt fuzzy; a fog surrounded me, and now Nash combed his fingers through my hair, sweet and soft, too tender and yet welcome. What was in that drink anyway? I stifled a yawn, but Nash caught me up, tugged me onto the sofa with him, and I let him, liked how it felt to be moved around because I felt weak and helpless. I had never let a man do that to me before, but in that moment the warmth that surrounded me made me careless, left me stupid to warnings that might normally come into my head when I was alone with a man I didn't really know.

"Is Mickey back yet?" I said absently through another yawn,

but Nash shushed me, pulled me to the cushions with his arms easy around me. The room became silent in that space between fever and rest, right in the center of dreams and alertness. I nestled there, comfortable, free, and wondered where I'd landed; I wondered how long I'd stay there. It felt safe. It felt familiar, and so, I let the dream take me.

Washington D.C.

There were two spots on my new floral-print dress. I wasn't sure if it was ketchup from the burger I'd scarfed down on my way to the library or maybe droplets of blood from the straight pin I'd used to separate my thick lashes after I'd spent nearly an hour on my face this morning. It had pricked my finger when I'd gotten careless and those tiny blots of blood remained on the fabric.

Red against pink. Stupid really, but it reminded me of Jackie Kennedy's bloodied pink suit the day President Kennedy had been assassinated. God, had that only been four years ago? The thought came from nowhere, and I returned my attention to the small droplets. The spots were obvious, and I tried to keep Isaac from noticing. He sat next to me, huddled over the paper on the table in front of us, the long paragraph written in a neat, precise penmanship that reminded me of typewriter font. He leaned on one large arm as he wrote slowly, knocking his elbow against the worn copy of Countee Cullen's "Any Human to Another" I'd borrowed from him and returned when we met tonight.

"You think I should mention the work I did at my church? We had to rebuild after that first fire, and I got the pastor thinking

about a library. I built the bookshelves and even stacked the books when we got them in. Think maybe that will make me seem like more of a…what'd you call it? 'Viable candidate' or whatever it was you said."

"I think it couldn't hurt."

He smiled when I nodded, and not for the first time, my gaze stuck a little on his full mouth and the dimple pushing in his right cheek. "You really think so, Miss Riley?"

"I do." I touched my palm over my heart, an exaggerated oath, and instantly wished I hadn't. It brought Isaac's gaze to that red stain. "And I wish you'd stop calling me Miss Riley."

He looked down at my face, the light gold in his dark amber eyes seeming to sparkle a little, but then that could just be my imagination. I'd gone a little stupid over this man and was always inventing fantastical things that his eyes did or how his voice, so deep and sultry, spun its own sort of magic anytime I heard him hum or sing something under his breath.

"Some habits are hard to break." The easy smile my silent compliment brought onto his mouth slipped a bit, but Isaac kept watching me, eyes alert, as though he wanted me to understand some deeper meaning.

"You know that's not something that's expected here…"

The smile left him then, and he glared a little at my gentle admonition. "Here?"

"In. D.C. This isn't…you're not in Georgia anymore, Isaac." I moved my chin toward him, hoping I wasn't crossing any lines. He knew who he was and from where he'd come. The habit was a hard one, it seemed, since I'd been asking him to call me "just" Riley for over two months.

66

"Hmmm." It was an odd little noise, something strange and quiet that seemed to come from his throat without his permission. It was all the agreement I thought I might get.

"I just mean, around here, that's not how…"

"It's not?" He sat back then, leaning an arm behind him on the empty chair at his side, seeming to want to put some space between us. It had taken all my skills to get him to sit next to me, even at the same table. Isaac was big on how things would look, no matter that I was helping him with his admissions application to Lincoln University. No matter that it was nearly ten at night, and aside from his friend Lenny, we were the only ones left in the library. He'd still been skittish.

"No." I turned in my seat, facing him. "Of course not."

Isaac wasn't like other men I knew, aside from my Dad and brother Ryan. Most boys my age thought it was perfectly reasonable to talk down to me, as though a little simplification was required because I had breasts. Isaac wasn't like that. He didn't try to simplify anything for me, especially what he thought. He treated me like an equal. "Well, why don't you tell me all about it?"

But Lord above, he was fiercely stubborn.

"Are we going to have the same debate again?"

"Maybe we are, Miss Riley. Maybe it's a good plan, seeing as how you don't seem to get that you and me, we're different." I opened my mouth, the regular argument tickling the tip of my tongue, but Isaac cut me off with a shake of his head and the flick of his hand. "And before you start in on the same mess about your daddy being a civil rights lawyer and how you and your whole family have gone to marches and

sponsored black students and how that somehow makes things all level like, I'll remind you again that while that's mighty generous and much appreciated, it still don't mean that the whole world, even here in D.C., sees things the way you do."

"I realize that. I'm not simple, you know." I hated the petulant sound of my voice, how Isaac's assertions were likely correct even if I didn't want them to be.

"I know you're not. You're a sight more…" There was a lull in his voice, something that brought my attention to the way he held his breath, how he seemed to think on what he said, picking his words carefully. "Well. You got smarts, Miss Riley. I know that sure enough."

"And so do you, Mr. Isaac." He liked that; I saw it in the way the smile came back onto his face and how gentle that expression was.

Isaac was beautiful. There was no other way to describe him. He was tall, taller than even my father, who stood well beyond six feet. Isaac, though, was broader, with the shoulders of an athlete and hands that were large, fingers slender, and big knuckles that made three of his fingers slightly crooked. I suspected this was why he always popped his knuckles and stretched out his fingers after he'd worked for more than an hour on his application essay. Thinking of it reminded me of the first few times we'd met, how just a half-hour of writing long hand had made a heavy line dent between his eyes. The injury had pained him, but he was too proud to mention it.

"How's your hand? You've been writing a while."

"I'll survive." To demonstrate, he picked up the pencil, twirling it between his fingers like it was nothing. "Fit as a fiddle."

I didn't buy it. Dad had spent a good part of his childhood down South too, and the stories he told of how black and impoverished white kids were treated gave me nightmares. There were frequent beatings in front of the entire class, many meted out to left-handed students who were being forced to write with their right hands. I was pretty sure Dad had been one of those kids, and I suspected Isaac had dealt with a similar issue.

"My…my dad still has problems because of the awful school teachers in the South when he was a kid." Isaac stopped twirling the pencil and sat up straighter, like he was gearing up for another round of me acting like I had any idea what his life had been like. "Not saying I understand anything about your past, but Dad still does these exercises to stretch the ligaments and bones in his hands. I thought they might help you." He kept watching me closely, a doubtful expression on his face that I wasn't quite sure how to read. I shrugged, pulling the pages of note paper together as though it didn't matter to me at all if he wanted to go on hurting without at least trying to release some of the pain.

"I mean, if you want to try it, I could show you, maybe tell you about the massages my mom does to help when his arthritis is really painful."

The attention he gave me then was a little unsettling, and I didn't know what to make of it. There was a smile, though it was a little forced, and a fire lit in his eyes, the means of which I couldn't quite make out. As habit, I slouched a little and rested my elbow on my bag while Isaac kept on watching me. Suddenly the bag slipped from the table, and I nodded a thanks to Isaac when he grabbed it for me, our fingers touching for a second before he handed it over.

Every move I made was a weak attempt to distract myself from how closely he watched me, how I must have seemed like the oddest person in the world to him. He'd only been away from Georgia and all the realities of that life for a year. I'd overheard Lenny pleading for Isaac with Mr. Welis, the cleaning crew manager. He'd fussed at Isaac being late, something Isaac swore had happened because he'd gotten the bus schedule wrong. Lenny promised their boss that Isaac was still adjusting, still trying to figure out where he fit in here in D.C. or if he fit in at all. Mr. Welis was a nice man and hadn't been too irritated by Isaac's tardiness. He'd even been the one to ask if I could help Isaac with his application, despite how loudly Isaac had complained. It had taken a solid month for Isaac to return the "good afternoon" or "have a nice night" greetings I sent his way. It had taken another month for him to give me direct answers when I asked questions; trying to start up our first real conversation had provoked a response under his breath containing an insult I was sure he didn't mean for me to hear.

"Damn woman could talk the devil right out of hell."

"Well, that's true, I guess, but I wouldn't want him following after me." That little unexpected comeback had actually made Isaac smile and gave me my first full glimpse at the way his face would light up and how his odd eyes sparkled when he wasn't sullen and ignoring the world around him.

"You think that would help me?" he asked me now, wiggling his hands to remind me of the offer I'd made. "That is, you don't think it would be a waste of time?"

"Not at all." I twisted around in my chair, abandoning the task of packing away my things to face him. Our knees almost touched, and I pushed down the hem of my skirt more closely to my knees before I held out my hands. "Extend your fingers, as far as they can go, just like this." I stretched my fingers

until the ligaments felt tight, then balled them into little fists that whitened the tips of my knuckles.

Isaac made an effort, covering a wince with a half-smile when he tried mimicking my stretching movement. Then that half-attempted smile disappeared and two of Isaac's fingers locked up, making him curse low under his breath.

"You okay?" I didn't wait for him to answer. I didn't do much thinking at all. I only reacted as my parents had taught me. You see someone in pain, anyone at all, and you do your best to help them.

Isaac froze, body utterly still when I grabbed his hand. His fingers did not relax, neither did any other part of him, as I held his hand between my fingers, rubbing out the joints and knuckles, focusing on the movement of my fingers as I kneaded his brown skin with the pads of my thumbs. He didn't try pulling away from me, but he also didn't seem too eager to relax under my touch, something that caught my attention when I turned over his hand, working the massage on his palm. A long, deep exhale came from him then, gently moving the hair along my forehead. It was only then that I looked up from my work, coming to myself with a small shock at what I was doing.

"Miss Riley…" he finally said, gaze moving over my face like he was trying to map my features, to gauge the slightest hint of warning or caution that might have surfaced. But there was nothing there, I knew that, nothing but surprise at how forward I'd been, at how many assumptions I'd made without his permission.

I eased his hand down, laying it on the table before I swallowed and pulled away from him, unable to keep the shaking from my fingers or the tension from my belly. It was an awkward, strange moment, one that I'd never had with Isaac since I'd barged my way into his life with stupid smiles and dumb questions about the weather and what he used to clean the floors.

"Isaac…I'm so sorry. That was forward of me, and I don't usually…"

"I…I think maybe I liked it." His expression was a little amused, the corner of his mouth twitched and he lifted the massaged hand up, stretching the fingers and knuckles as though my brief touch had done some good at least. "Fact, I'm sure I did."

"Oh…"

The air in that small room went a little still, like nothing else moved around us, not the flickering of the lights overhead or Lenny's low humming a floor below where he was mopping the marble tiles around the reference section. The sound was soft, could be plainly heard from the open balcony below.

In that moment, I could only look at Isaac, a million thoughts and wishes floating through my mind, pumping the blood thick in my ears. Hopes too, those came rushing to the surface, silly, stupid things I knew would never happen, like Isaac telling me who we were didn't matter or, better still, like him taking my face between those big palms before he moved close, close enough to level his mouth over mine.

"I know…I mean, it was rude…"

"It feels better." He stretched his fingers again, ignoring my apology as he leaned forward, sending a jolt of surprise through my body when he got close enough that I could see just how thick and long his lashes were and that he had the faintest scar along his left cheek. He reminded me of a feather floating from the sky on a still, cloudless day where no wind rustles the trees and the air is thick

with heat. Isaac moved in that same minutely slow manner, fractions of inches that made up the single stroke of his thumb over my cheek and the slow, smooth sweep of him touching my face like I was something unusual—an alien he thought he'd never see up close.

I wanted to melt into that touch. I wanted him to stretch those fingers again, rest his palm against my face, to experience the smallest hint of what his touch would do to me—if it would cool or heat me, devour me with sensation.

"Isaac…" It was the smallest whisper of word, something that felt like a promise I wanted to make, but he blinked at the sound and his face shifted to an amazed, shocked wonder, as though he'd only just realized what he was doing. When he pulled his hand away, I wanted to stop him, bring back that touch without him arguing. But Isaac was stubborn, and there were those hard-lost habits he held onto like beliefs he'd never give up.

"I appreciate you helping me ease the pain and with my application essay, Miss Riley." He stood up, backing away from the table, and my chest ached, Isaac's dismissal a real thud of pain inside my heart.

"Isaac, wait a second, please."

He'd nearly made it to the stairwell, tucking the rolled up Cullen paperback into his back pocket. He didn't turn, not right off, and let me get a little more than ten feet from him before he faced me.

"You got a fella, don't you Miss Riley?"

That stopped me cold and I did my best to ignore the flush I felt warming my face. "How…"

"Folk talk around here. Folk who see you smiling at me, the same folk that tell me I need to steer clear of you, especially since you got that Trent fella picking you up most Saturday nights, taking you to places I could never go." He took a step closer, but it felt likes miles from me, those passive accusations that were nothing more than the truth thickening the space between us. "Lincoln ain't that big of a campus, Miss Riley. Janitors like me and the fellas who trim the hedges at your dorm, their cousins and women who clean out the bathrooms, they all talk. They all tell me about you because they know we here, all alone, so you can help me get into Lincoln."

"I…I don't care what people say."

He moved his jaw, working his teeth together so that the muscles along the side of his face flexed. "Sometimes, you got to. Sometimes what people say are the things that get the wrong people moving toward something stronger than words." Isaac tapped his finger to his temple before he frowned, making me feel, for the first time, like I was the one who needed lessons. "It's like I always say, we don't live in the same world. We won't ever." When I only stared at him, unable to keep my eyes from glassing over, Isaac lowered his shoulders, giving up something—a small, nearly insignificant thing he wouldn't be sorry to see go—that softened his features and took the snap from his tone when he spoke. "I don't say these things to be mean…"

"I know you don't." Those weren't just words spoken to ease the guilt he might have felt with his small rejection. But that didn't mean my chest had stopped aching, or that I'd rush to explain myself. Trent wasn't my "fella". Not like he pretended he was, and I knew people would gossip about me and Isaac up on the fifth floor organizing his letters of recommendation, trying to make his essay

seemed eloquent and appealing to the admissions board. We'd done that away from the gossip I knew circled around campus, just the two of us, cloistered from anyone who'd interrupt.

It would likely be best to walk away, free him from his worry that those gossiping people would go on fussing at him for the company he kept. But something inside my brain niggled fierce and persistent; it was the constant refrain that this man needed me, and louder still, that I needed him. Something beyond a whim, something familiar, something deep beyond reason.

"Well, then, Miss Riley, I suppose I'll see you next week, if you still want to meet with me."

He nodded when I smiled, taking two steps back to watch me before he moved down the stairs, and I watched him a good thirty seconds longer, until I couldn't hear his boots on the marble steps anymore, until I knew it was safe enough to sit back down at that table and let those poorly disguised tears fall.

Nash

The dreams felt real. Too damn real.

"Mr. Nash?" my assistant asked. "Mr. Phillips is on his way up."

"Fine."

They'd seeped into my head, interrupted my sleep, and now had taken root in my daily life, working their best to keep me from the things I needed finished. Like, you know, my damn job.

I loved what I did. I loved what we were trying to do with Nations, our company. I loved the planning, the programming, the stretch of time it took to finalize the source code and rework the software. I loved the late nights, the impossible deadlines, and the way total strangers looked at me and saw dollar signs. It made me feel good, better than any female ever had. Hell, better than almost anything.

Desire, drive, and ambition got me up every morning, hopping the bus to the city to work on making Nations a reality. It held me up through late nights at my office as I tweaked and molded my code into something unique. It had me putting up with Duncan and his slick tactics that I knew would someday pay off in stupid amounts of cash.

But the dreams that felt like memories? They were chipping away at my drive. They were turning my ambition, my desire, into stupid, simple things.

Two taps on the door and Duncan was barging into my office. "There he is!"

It was going to be one of those mornings where Duncan said a bunch of nonsense he must have thought I'd believe. Most of it would be flattery. It was how he rolled. He did this, I guessed, to show me he still was in; he didn't want me rolling out on him, especially since he hadn't convinced me to sign that little non-compete contract sitting on his desk.

"Man, have I got some good stuff lined up for us." He sat on the corner of my desk, folding his fingers together as he watched me. It was a tactic he used—give off that 'I'm your buddy' expression, even though I always called him on his bullshit.

I'd stopped paying attention to him the second he'd knocked on my office door. "No idea, man."

"Vegas." Even the way he said the word sounded filthy, like he thought throwing money at me—getting me laid, getting me drunk—would ease me into his contract. No denying it would put me in a good mood. It would damn well keep my mind off those crazy ass dreams, but I doubted it would get me to change my mind.

Duncan's smile was tight, a little forced, and I had to refocus on my monitor and the loop of code blinking back at me. This guy's excitement was fake, just like everything else about him. Like his veneers, and how wide and toothy his smile was because of them, or the perfect fit of his suit, the gold and diamond tie pin he wore, part of a set, all with diamonds, all too much for our small office.

He had a square jaw, something that reminded me of a Marine recruitment poster, but his eyes were too narrow and his mouth too thin, both of which gave him the air of a weasel: sneaky, stalking with a simple smile that never lit his eyes.

Duncan had snooped around an MIT alumni meeting, something he'd begged off an invite from a guy he claimed was a friend but who hadn't bothered to talk to him the whole night. Duncan had ditched him right away, I bet, and listened in on conversations, trying to pick up a tidbit of info, anything that would finagle his way into an introduction. He must have liked the way I'd called him out right away. Must have liked my moxie, thought it meant I cared.

"You're coming off as a poser," I'd told him as I'd handed over my glass to the bartender.

"Excuse me?" He'd held onto a half-drunk glass of Scotch that looked to be more water than whiskey. "Do I know you?"

"No," I'd said. "You don't, but I'm gonna do you a favor and let you know you're spooking the programmers. They don't like the eavesdropping, and it's pretty damned obvious that's what you're doing. You're not nearly as smooth as you think you are."

A warning. A small one, and I'd landed the shark, even

though I hadn't been trolling. He stayed and talked to me for an hour that night then found me on Facebook, taken me to lunch the next week. Squirmed his way into my life, and I was still trying to figure out how I'd let that happen. I didn't really like Duncan, but at least he did have a little imagination. He wanted Nations to succeed as much as I did. And to be honest, he was willing to handle the things I was not.

"No time for Vegas, man." A quick nod at the monitor and I started typing again. "I got work to do."

"See, that's what I thought, but then I came in here this morning, and you were just staring off into space."

He kept that smile tight and wide when I looked at him, my eyes narrowing. "You checking up on me, man?"

"No," he laughed, throwing a shoulder up in a shrug as though he thought I was simple. Then came a bigger laugh bunched up with an insult. "*I* pay *your* assistant to do that."

"I pay my assistant, Duncan. Don't get it twisted." He lifted his hands, a surrender he sure as hell didn't mean, and then laughed again, fast, hurried, failing at his lame-ass attempt to squash the tension he'd caused. "What do you want?"

"I'm just a little worried." He was circling; Duncan always did that. The predator, sniffing around, checking to see if I was full enough, juicy enough, to warrant an attack. But Duncan was a poser, a player of the game I was trying to learn. He was better at it than me, we both knew it, but he still fronted like he was only concerned for me, not the buckets of cash my program would make him one day. The laugh was gone, and so was the smile, and Duncan pulled his eyebrows together, forcing mock concern I knew wasn't real. "It's been a couple of weeks now, and you're still working on the same code. And you missed the meeting on Wednesday morning…"

"I can't oversleep?"

He waved, ignoring my question, speaking over me. "And then I pass by here this morning, and you're staring off into space, completely zoned out."

"Maybe I was thinking."

The head nod was slow, his eyes cool, as if he wanted to swish around his words in his mouth, like a shot of bourbon that would burn. The buzz was worth it, and Duncan knew it. He had me. I *had* been zoned out, messed up with Willow and the damn crazy dreams that wouldn't back off.

"Daisy tried buzzing you three times." There was a lot of accusation in his tone, and I stood, meeting his stare with a head tilt that let Duncan know I wasn't going to back down like a punk. Still, he watched me as if my bluster didn't matter, moving his teeth together like he wasn't sure if he should let the words on his tongue fly. "Weird, isn't it? Her calling, you here, and still you didn't answer."

"Maybe I was thinking *hard*."

He didn't buy it, not when I sat back down, tired already of the interrogation. In fact, he actually thought getting angry would raise my hackles maybe, because he let his temper flare, knocking a fist against my desk. "Man, what's going on with you? You…you thinking of fucking me over? Signing up with someone else, because if you are…"

Here we go. This mess again. What an asshole. "Give me a break. No, I'm not going anywhere but even if I was, what of it? We got no contract." Duncan stepped away from my desk, scrubbing his chin as he moved around my office. He looked like a tiger itching to pounce but I wouldn't let it get that far. When I spoke, I made sure it was with less attitude, that my voice was lowered, calm. "Everything's right down the middle until we land an investor."

"I'm not going to let you fuck me over, Nash."

I slumped in my chair, beyond tired of the argument and Duncan's nervous ass. "Duncan, I have no intention of fucking you over. Look, it's like I told you from jump, all this here," I waved around the office, pointing at the Apple iBook that I'd bought on credit, "is 50/50." The iBook came with me, so did the long coffee table made up of recycled palette wood and the sofa that Natalie had picked up at a thrift store and reupholstered herself. Even the file cabinets that looked slick and new were dinged up in the back, display models from Office Depot that the manager let me have for fifty bucks. I wasn't like Duncan. I didn't come to New York sucking on a silver spoon, or expecting I was owed one.

Everything I had, I got on my own. It was mine, and it came from years of scrimping, years of writing code that made somebody else money.

"You brought in the contractors and your connections, I bring my skill set. And Daisy. We don't owe each other a damn thing until there are investors and a board. Then we'll talk contracts and commitment. You agreed to that, man." He watched me, nodding so slowly it might have been a twitch, but I kept at him, hoping like hell this time he'd pull his head out of his ass and see reason. "And if I sleep in, and spend a few minutes zoning out, so the hell what? That only means I need a break."

Duncan popped his knuckles, a nervous, annoying habit he did when he was on edge, maybe to buy some time to try to come up with a valid comeback. There was no damn reason for me to recount stuff he already knew, but I'd discovered over the past six months that this supposedly top-shelf finder needed his hand held sometimes. He'd worry about the future without any real reason. Nothing was set and until it was, we could both walk away without a backward glance. It pissed me off that he forgot that. I mean, yeah, his job wasn't as concrete as ones and zeros, but it still was as solid as it ever would be.

"I need to hit this," I told him pulling my laptop closer toward me. "Just give me a little space and I promise I'll get my head right."

"All right, Nash. I hear you, just…" He bit his lip when I

exhaled, scrubbing my hands over my face. "It anything comes up and you need a break again, just say the word. We'll take that trip to Vegas to unwind."

"I got you. Thanks."

But of course it wasn't Duncan and the work that had me distracted. It was the dream. Sookie again. A face, a name, that felt so familiar. A life I couldn't shake, and it had kept me distracted. I'd doze off, and there she'd be. Beyond that distraction was Willow and the soft slope of her mouth, those damn lips. She'd fallen asleep on my sofa after that cat rescue fiasco, and the memory of her lying next to me, hair scattered like leaves all over my leather sofa, had kept me stunned stupid.

There was a problem now, and it had long chestnut hair and full, sweet lips. I knew that because last night while I avoided Sookie and that damn dream, sipping a beer on the roof deck, staring at nothing, at everything, Willow slipped into the seat next me like she'd known I'd be there. Like I'd invited her.

"There's no wind," she'd said, her voice so low and soft that I jumped when she spoke. My senses were out of whack, my instinct dulled because I'd gotten little sleep.

"No, I guess there isn't."

We'd sat there for nearly ten minutes, just watching the purple sky, staring up at the white dots of lights nearly visible above the smog in complete silence. I'd even passed over my beer, and Willow drank from it, like it had been the most natural thing in the world to sit next to me, drinking my beer. It *had* felt natural. But when that realization hit me, all of a sudden I got flooded in worry and confusion.

"I'm…I still can't sleep." That admission had left my mouth without much thought. That happened so damn much when Willow was around. Like being with her came with the permission to unload things I'd never tell anyone else. Except maybe Natalie.

She'd stopped mid-sip when I'd said that, holding the bottle just in front of her mouth with two fingers as she'd glanced at me, eyes a little wide, curious. But then she finished her sip and handed the bottle back, and I noticed that her eyes were puffy and red-rimmed.

"Sorry, but I can't help you." That'd surprised me. I hadn't expected her to dismiss me like that, when normally she was the one pulling me in kicking and screaming. In fact, putting together her red eyes with how subdued she was, and with how pale she seemed, made me wonder if maybe Willow had caught my insomnia. She damn well didn't look like she'd been sleeping much.

"What's going on with you?" I'd asked, gently. Or so I thought.

When she wouldn't look at me directly, instead seeming to concentrate on the sky sliding from purple to dusk, I'd leaned forward, setting down the bottle between us so I could catch her gaze.

"I'm tired," she finally said when she'd glanced away from the sky to look at me. "I'd be no good at trying to cleanse you again because I haven't been sleeping much either."

"You got a mondo cupcake gig or something?"

"Yes." She moved back, lying down on the wooden lawn chair identical to the one I sat in. Her hair had fanned out in a brown, frizzy bundle and slipped through the slats opened in the back of the chair. "Or something. But even when I'm not working, even when I'm bone tired, I still can't sleep. Normally baking relaxes me. I've always made cookies or brownies or something when I'm distracted, mad or worried. Now I'm…it's no good. I'm too…distracted." She stared back out at the horizon.

In the moonlight, even as pale as she had been—maybe because she was so pale—Willow looked like she glowed, like some wild child angel with her own aura buzzing around her pretty face and curvy body. Out of the stillness, a breeze finally rose up, meandering around us, and I caught the scent of jasmine coming from her skin and hair. Without thinking, I leaned closer, on my side, to get a better look at her, not understanding why I had the sudden urge to reach down and kiss her.

But my motion made the chair scratch against the roof deck and the noise brought Willow's attention back to me, which totally threw me off, like I had been caught doing something I wasn't supposed to. Not like she noticed, but still.

"You look tired, Nash. I'm…I'm so sorry." Willow reached for my face, like it was usual, natural, something she'd always done. She drew her fingertips along my bottom lip, a slow, steady trace, nearly touching my bottom lip, and I hadn't wanted her to stop.

"It's nothing I'm not used to," I'd said, voice hitting barely a whisper. "Been like this a while."

There had been something in Willow's expression I couldn't read: a little sadness, a little confusion, enough of something to make her look withdrawn and tight. Still, she continued to move her fingers in a trace along my lip, and even though I'd never allowed such a thing before, it felt familiar, and intimate. Without stopping to think about it, I'd decided to crush the cautious whine in the back of my head and do more than let the moment pass.

"You should be sleeping. I can try…" She broke off, failing to stifle a yawn, and moved her fingers from my face, but I grabbed her wrist, holding her palm flat against my mouth, I kissed her hand.

She was surprised, even more than I was.

"Nash?"

Her voice was soft, and sweet, and without stopping to try to make sense of it, I'd pulled her up, tugging on her hand until she lifted from the chair.

"Come here," I'd said, keeping my fingers against her wrist.

It was stupid to do. It was something I'd never been impulsive about—taking a woman I wanted, leading, demanding—

but right then it's what I'd done. I hadn't asked Willow to come closer, but even with that small demand, she'd come to me, warm and wild and without hesitation.

I hadn't had to ask anything after that. She'd moved like the slow breeze, barely any direction, but constant, sure, and before I realized what happened, Willow was on my lap, and I'd moved my hands to her face, my fingers in her hair, and she'd opened her mouth, an invitation that was sweet and certain. I took it, kissing her as if I'd always done it, like my mouth, my tongue, knew the contours of her lips and the taste of her breath.

It had occurred to me then that the kiss felt right. The scent of her breath, the warmth that fanned over my face, how it warmed me from the inside, all felt so damn familiar, not like it was me kissing Willow, but something deeper. Something I couldn't place, like a memory tucked far away in my head, hidden and waiting.

It had felt too good, too right. It had scared the hell out of me.

And right before the kiss had led somewhere else, had gotten us moving quicker, deeper, Mickey had banged open the rooftop door, letting us know he was going to replace the bulbs on the outdoor lamps, and we pulled apart, not reluctantly but kinda like kids who had almost been caught in the act of misbehaving. She'd blushed and laughed under her breath; I'd cleared my throat and held the door for her as she left, without looking back, but with a little sway in her walk that I'd known was just for me.

And damn, but hadn't that seemed like the right way for the evening to end? Don't ask me why, but it felt pretty fucking perfect. Even the way her perfume lingered.

And for once I slept well. Well, better than I had in a while. But when I did wake, it almost seemed like that night had been its own kind of dream, as if it, too, belonged to another place and time, and all the old cares and worries crowded in again.

For years I'd stayed focused, driven, and disciplined, always looking ahead. I didn't hang out and get shitty in college because I knew as a scholarship kid there was no room for fucking up. At MIT I worked to prove myself, determined to do more, be more, because it was expected. Now I worked to build the best program, the most efficient means to deliver a quality product to clients, with a board of potential investors who also believed in what I was trying to do.

There was no space in my life for distractions. There was no room for anyone who'd have me deviating from the game plan. I had zero time for Willow, no matter how sweet she sounded when I kissed her. No matter how much I'd liked the way she gripped my collar, like she needed to hold on to me before we fell from that moment.

So when I started out this morning and found a small white box on the floor in front of my landing, with the note *Thank you for the nap and the rescue and...all the other very good stuff. Let me return the favor,*

I didn't really know how to respond, or even what to think.

Up on that rooftop deck with Willow, everything had seemed so simple, so right. But this morning, reality hit me like a ton of bricks. I realized I had no clue what Willow really wanted from me. I only knew that if the dream wasn't distracting me, then Willow was, and I didn't have time for any of it. I had sleep to avoid and work to do. There was no time for dreams that made no sense, or for women, no matter how beautiful, who would do nothing but distract me from the life I wanted. Even if they made killer cupcakes.

Damn, I couldn't even concentrate. There were too many thoughts—of New Orleans and a kid in the '20s, of Willow and the sweet, sinful taste of her tongue, of Duncan and his needy, pestering drama that always seemed to surf around the edges of our conversations.

Noise. Nonsense. Irritation, all of it.

I leaned back in my chair, code forgotten, and grabbed the remote to lower the blinds that cut my office window off from Daisy's desk outside. My neck felt tight, and my shoulders ached, so I leaned back, shutting my eyes, not intending to do anything but relax. Just for a little while...

New Orleans

Joe Andres was a mean man. That seemed to be true of a lot of male folk in the city, especially the ones who paid no never-mind to the laws laid down about hooch. Most days I could get away with walking through the drunken crowds, the reckless fools who didn't give a single thought to the policemen lurking on every corner, itching to find someone easy to stir up mess with. But that was New Orleans, not here in the swamp, where mama had taken us to keep us out of trouble, since she said those Irishmen from the Channel were having a fine time celebrating St. Paddy's Day.

I didn't mind it so much, except for Joe Andres being up at the Simoneaux house. It was nice to be away from the trolleys and crowds, the wicked gleam in ole Ripper's eye and the constant worry that my mama and Lulu would get found out for making drink no one was supposed to have. But having a fool like Joe Andres that close meant I still had to keep at least one eye out for trouble.

I liked my Bastie's farm. There were chickens pecking at the ground on the side of the house, next to the shotgun building with the pale blue door and cream walls where Bastie used to store her gardening tools and the feed sacks for all her critters. That led away from the old creole cottage my granddaddy Bastien had built for her with his own two hands some thirty years ago before the pipe he smoked festered his lungs like dry rot on a dock and killed him by the time he was sixty.

The house was cedar framed; the color of the wood had gone all dark like the belly of a rock settled on the riverbank, and Bastie kept pretty green shutters on the two windows outfitted at the front of the house. There was a porch with five-feet-long steps and handrails, where she kept a whiskey barrel cut in the center to catch the water she pumped from the well. She'd use the washboard inside that barrel to beat and scrub out the laundry on Saturdays all day, if the weather was right.

But in front of the porch, just off the side of the cottage, hung an old swing, big enough for three people to sit on, swinging back and forth so that the rusted chain that hung from the oak above it squeaked and moaned in a sort of rhythm that made me smile. On that porch Bastie told me all her stories—how she'd worked with her mama in Atlanta, tending to some rich folk's babies as her mama cleaned their fine house. She talked about caring for those babies, a girl and a boy, Linda and Luke, like they'd been her own, until she caught the eye of my granddaddy Bastien, who she swore was the most handsome fella she'd ever seen her whole life. He took her away when she was twenty and brought her here to Manchac, where his people had lived for years. He'd spent most of their marriage working on the cottage and planting everything he could for his bride, promising her this small farm would be something straight from the heart of a fairytale.

I sat on that swing this morning, worrying and fretting over Dempsey, looking out through the line of crepe myrtles Bastie had planted to keep the outline of Simoneaux's fancy house distant; she'd wanted a place hidden from the world, and with all those trees, dozens and dozens of them, and the lush fit of gardenia bushes and climbing roses that ran up and along the fence line, my granny had managed that well enough. But I could still make out the pitch of their roof and the small cottages peppered away from the big house. Dempsey said his daddy used those for his friends when they came to fish the Manchac, but Bastie had said once they'd been used for slaves, folk who never did have even a single choice where they lived or how they did their living.

"Run this up to Mr. Foster's place, Sookie. Aron will take you, but you got to meet him down at the crossways. He's at that loose-tail woman's house." The heavy basket was in my arms before Mama stopped speaking, and pushed me off the swing and down the drive, and I headed in the direction of Clarice Dubois', a girl my Uncle Aron had been sweet on since he was ten and too stupid to understand that following after a girl too old and too rich for him was a fool's errand. Mama didn't like Clarice, said she wore too much rouge and swung her hips on purpose. But then, Mama didn't much like when her brother got played a fool and Clarice Dubois was aces at that game.

Behind me, my mother cleared her throat, finishing off the annoyed sound with a low, long sigh that made me get my feet moving faster. She never asked me and Sylv to do a thing. I reckoned she didn't have to, but the order she gave just then came at me in a bark, something she said through the tight grit of her teeth. I was used to it, didn't bother complaining that the cross ways was at least two miles down past most of the empty fields the Simoneauxs let out to farmers. I hated walking past those fields and half-wished I'd answered the knock that had come at my window the night before.

Dempsey wouldn't trouble my granny and knew better to ask for me at the front door when Mama was at home. He'd knocked at my window a few times, whispering my name like he hoped no one would hear him. I did—far as I could tell I'd been the only one—but still didn't answer. Sylv's warning had been clear and had me thinking things I didn't like much. Things like telling Dempsey to stay well away from me. Things like he didn't belong with us, but just thinking that made my stomach go all heavy.

Walking down the drive, glance veering to the Simoneauxs' place and further down to their empty fields, made me wish I'd met Dempsey at the treehouse this morning, like was usual any time we were home for the weekend. But I hadn't, still keeping my brother's warning in mind.

"Don't drag your feet, neither." I swear Mama's frown had only gotten worse the further away I walked from her, and when I looked over my shoulder, caught the small snarl of her top lip, I figured I'd need to save myself from her anger if I didn't move faster.

My mama didn't hate me, I knew that, but I also knew I had the look of whoever my daddy had been, and that always had been a sore spot between us, not like I could help it.

"Nothing for it." Bastie had blown off my question, the same one I'd asked a dozen times before I'd made twelve. "You don't need to worry over that." But every kid needs a family, and ones like me, who grew up not knowing much about their daddies, needed them the most. Maybe that was why I took to Dempsey. Maybe I saw something of that missing family in him, because he knew his daddy and still didn't much have one.

Bastie told me not to worry about who had made me. Mama wouldn't ever pay any mind at all to me, all the times I'd asked her. But hanging out in Manchac and working in the city, you hear a lot of gossip. Me and Sylv didn't look a bit alike. He was the spit of his daddy, a man called Dante' Lanoix, who mama married when Sylv was two. Bastie said Mama and Dante' had been sweethearts in school, but that he'd gone off to the Army when she had Sylv swelling her belly and came back changed. We got his name, and Mama got some money from the government when the scaffolding Dante' climbed at work gave way, and he fell forty feet off a building. Mama buried him next to her daddy and then never spoke about him again.

But I was a Lanoix only by the name. Only because Dante' didn't much mind that Mama had already been pregnant with me five months when he came back after the war to call on her. He'd only wanted her and took what came with having her.

My daddy could have been anyone—some sweet stranger who flattered Mama until she got on her back, maybe told her how pretty she was on the rare times she laughed and smiled. Maybe he could have been one of the men who tipped their hats to her as she walked through the Square on Sundays, ready for Mass in her pretty, yellow, dropped-waist dress and her hair finger waved all soft and close around her face. Likely though, if the gossip was true, my daddy was a white man Mama lost her mind over just a little. At least, that's what Lulu had said to one of the new maids Ester brought in when she wondered why my skin was so much brighter than my brother's.

I hadn't had a good listen to all that Lulu said, but I know I heard her mention Dempsey's uncle, his mama's brother, Lionel Phillipe, who had stayed with the Simoneauxs years back before Dante' stuck around for good. Back when Mama's smile came easy and honest.

If Lulu wasn't a liar, that might make Dempsey's mama's hateful looks at me, definitely at my mama, hold more sense. That would also mean that Dempsey wasn't just my friend; he was my cousin. But I didn't think about Dempsey the way I do Uncle Aron's boy, Hank. I didn't think of Dempsey any way except how his bottom lip curved up in the middle, making it seem like he's always chewing his lip. I liked to think about his face and the small, faint freckle that sticks out from the others along his cheekbone. And his eyes, those big, bright eyes that look gray and blue and shades that remind me of the Gulf, way out in the deep when the dolphins and porpoise chase small boats, bobbing along the surf. I'd only seen it once, the Gulf, but you don't forget something like that, not ever.

Whoever my daddy had been didn't matter much now. Not to me and not to my mama. But sometimes when I was nodding off in the middle of Mass or when Bastie's low, sweet voice hummed a hymn all soft, like in a whisper, and my eyes got all heavy and I started to fade away, I'd catch my mama watching me like she wanted to see something on my face she wouldn't look for when I was full awake. Most days, that hard stare of hers was followed by a curved lip and a look of outright sick. Most days, it was all I could do from asking what sin I'd committed and how she wanted me to repent. After all, it wasn't me that asked to get born.

But sometimes, I got the notion that Mama was looking for something of the man who made me in my features. My nose was long and small at the tip. The bridge was slender and maybe too long for my round face, but my eyes, Bastie always said, were like melted chocolate to match my skin. Sylv was darker than me, his nose wider, his lips plump and wide like his daddy, and never once had I caught Mama looking at him with anything else but sweet love, maybe a little sadness for the man she'd loved and lost too soon.

So because I knew it so well, I didn't waste much time thinking on the bad mood that came up on Mama when she looked too hard at me as I trotted towards the cross roads. Instead, my attention went to the

95

wide field surrounding the Simoneaux property and the stalks of sugarcane that rose up taller than a grown man.

When we were little things, me and Dempsey would run out in that field, hiding and laughing like fools, chasing each other with the scratch of the tall grass and the thick stalks slapping against our knees, the sweet residue from the sugarcane making Dempsey's britches and my thin cotton dresses sticky with dirt. Sometimes Sylv would play with us, tapping the tips of the stalks just to prove his stretch could reach, that he was bigger and braver than us.

Once, when we were twelve, Dempsey gathered several stalks and took the pocket knife Uncle Aron had given him for his birthday to the skins, cutting away the surface until only the meaty inside, sweet and satisfying, came dripping out in a slow, delicious trickle. We made ourselves sick that day and Dempsey's daddy whipped him good for coming home in such a mess.

The memory stuck with me then, as I cleared the north corner of the field. I'd just about forgotten how that field, empty and still despite the spring wind coming up to push around the stalks and drying grass, and had come closer toward the end of the gravel road. I could make out the street sign ahead and glanced over my shoulder at Bastie's little cottage that looked like a dollhouse silhouetted against the lowering light. It was Dempsey and that sweet juice that took away the fear that always came to me when I walked away from the farm, from the protection of my sometimes home. From Dempsey too. Good sense told me I should have remembered. Remembering, minding what you knew, good and bad, tended to keep you far from trouble.

It didn't that day.

I smelled Joe Andres before I saw him. It was the bourbon-thick scent of his bottle along with the dirty odor of his sweaty body that rose up to spoil the sweet sugarcane perfume in the air.

"Hey gal…you come here a minute."

They always called us gal, no matter how grown we were. Bastie was pushing upwards of seventy and every white man that came across her still called her "gal" and my grown-ass Uncle Aron got called "boy."

I might not have been grown-assed myself, but I knew better than to let some piss drunk white man get his hands on me if I could help it.

Pretending not to hear him as he came out of the field worked for just about a minute. To my side, I caught the stumble of his shadow when he tried to keep up. It was a stupid wobble of a step broken something fierce by how many times he brought that sloshing bottle up to his mouth.

"Hey gal, I said come see me."

That shadow got bigger the closer he came no matter that I was almost jogging. Joe Andres had a fat, jiggling belly and one shot of a look over my shoulder told me he had his dingy white button-up shirt open to show the dirty undershirt underneath. But he was a full grown man and could move a pace when he wanted to.

He wore a tan hat with the brim pushed up and his sweaty brown hair curled up to wet the fabric, making a damp line form against his forehead. When I didn't stop, he took a sip, stopping for a second to guzzle the brown liquid in his bottle before he threw it to the ground. Then, he came at me.

"Get over here, you little bitch."

I didn't wait to hear what else that nasty man would call me. I took off running, moving closer and closer to the cross ways, praying like a nun that God would keep me out of this old man's grip. I was so scared that it felt like someone had turned up the speed of my heart and started burning my insides.

There were a handful of steps between me and Andres, a few more that I kept adding to it, counting on the liquor he'd drank to keep him slower and his fat gut to make chasing me a stupid idea that he'd get tired of doing when he got too winded.

But that nasty white man kept at me, grunting and wheezing and he put his own speed into his steps and I swore I could smell the sick stench of his breath fogging in the air around me, getting closer until it was against my neck.

My moves went sloppy and the buckle from my t-strap shoe popped, slowing me into a stumble, the gravel from the road falling into my shoe until I couldn't move much, until a hop or two to remove it had me falling on my knees just long enough for Andres to catch up.

"You listen to me…" His words were clipped, winded and came out in a rasp and he edged closer, reaching out his thick, short fingers toward me. "When I say you come to me, you better get your tail right in damn front of me. You hear me?"

He was drunk, I reminded myself, knowing that what I did just then, this bastard wasn't likely to remember and then Andres took hold of my arm, pulling me up from the ground to shake me between his damp palms.

"I tell you to…to come…and you…" He shook me hard, fingers curling, grabbing onto the collar of my shirt until he had a fistful of fabric in his fist and two buttons popped from the movement.

He lunged closer and all I could smell was that hooch, thick and warm and wet and the dirty, sickening smell of his sweaty, round body. All I saw was those chapped, fat lips of his coming closer and closer. My sense returned and again I told myself this drunk man wouldn't remember, and I did the only thing I could; I hauled back and socked Joe Andres one good time in his eye.

I think, maybe he was surprised. I was barely a hundred pounds and there wasn't a whole lot of strength in that punch, I knew that, and reckon he did too. But Andres still stopped trying to put his mouth on me. He made a small, shocked noise, something that might have been a belch, maybe the air sticking in his throat but the sound was wet and gurgling, something that would have made me laugh if he still didn't have his hands on me.

Andres opened his mouth, reminding me a guppy sucking on the air around him when he jumped out of his bowl, but I wouldn't let him speak. I jerked back, twisting away from him and I think, maybe, he was too surprised to move at first, that some "gal" had the gumption enough to fight back.

The gravel under my feet dug into the soft surface of my heel, and I pulled away from Andres, twisting my hips to get out of that tight grip, but he held on and I could hear a ripping sound as I moved. Four sharp steps back and Andres held part of my shirt between his fingers. I looked down, mouth hanging open and breathing hard as I pushed down that burning sweet anger that had me wanting to scratch this drunk bastard's eyes out, and noticed that my skin was against the open air and my skimpy undershirt was showing. And when Joe Damn Andres looked down at my bosom, when he threw down the rip of my shirt and took to licking his lips and stepping toward me, I stomped my one-shoed heel onto the top of his foot and didn't wait to see how bad I'd got him afore I was off in a scared rabbit run, back the way I'd come.

The sun was nearly gone now, except for the faint shadow that covered the ground. I ran on and on until I'd cleared most of the empty sugarcane field, ignoring the rich smell in the air and the row of crows watching me thunder down the road back toward my Bastie's cottage.

It wasn't until I was past the cottage, back against the south fence line, past the tool shed and away from the house and the left section of the property where Sylv and I had mustered up the smarts enough to build a small tree house against one of the largest oak trees on the property. The tree house was no more than a few loose boards tied together with fraying rope in knots and what was left of the tin roof Aron had taken down when he repaired the tool shed. But it was secure enough, and we were still small enough that fitting inside wouldn't harm us any. Now it seemed like the safest place to hide from Joe Andres case he still was after me. I was up the tree and in the back of the small shack before I even thought twice.

"Sookie!" It was a whisper somewhere around the back of my head; pushing past the blood pumping hard and heavy into my ears. The sound was barely there, lit with a dim light inside my head, coming outside of the tree house and I was safe, safe, but maybe he was still coming for me. There were too many things working around inside me just then, most of it fear and worry that Andres would find me or worse, that maybe he'd make up a lie that I'd attacked him and the police would come for me. That would be the end of me no matter what I said.

They'd never believe me over that fat white man. Not ever.

Mainly, though, my own brain worked to do the biggest damage. It was more than the terror of being punished for hitting a white man. What went on and on in my brain was the possibility of what could have been—that sweaty, fat body sliding against me; those tubby short fingers rubbing all over me and the smell of his mouth and tongue and that burning liquor left on my skin when he'd finished.

I wanted to be sick, thought maybe I would be; even got to my knees, slumping over the open hole in the board floor in case I threw up. Below I saw the twisted, long roots of the tree, how they went out into the yard, how they reminded me of twisted limbs and broken bones underneath the ground.

My head spun and swam and I couldn't make the shake in my hands quit good enough. When the sound of my name came again, it took a full minute for the noise of it to hit my ears.

"Sookie?"

My whole body went shaky in relief when my addled brain realized it was Dempsey calling my name, not Andres or some devil from hell. When I didn't move or say anything, he climbed up into the shack, just barely making it through the opening, he'd gotten so much bigger than when we were little.

"Hey." He didn't try touching me when he came in front of me, kneeling into a crouch as I backed against the wall, pulling my skirt over my knees. "What is it?"

His voice was so soft, so low just then. It felt like a whisper, like some song I knew but had never heard before. His tall height and the sweet scent of his skin knocked up inside my nose, stretching sensation and sweetness into every pore of my body.

"Sook?"

I wanted to take his hand when he reached for me. I wanted so much to let Dempsey put his arm around me and hug me close so I could wet his shirt with my tears and hold on to him. It would feel good, so good, just for a little bit, to disappear in the circle of his body and lay all my troubles down; to be with him in a world we could fashion together in that small shack resting within the limbs and leaves of my Mimi Bastie's big ole oak tree.

But that would not do. Not with Andres probably after me. Not with him running his mouth over how his eye had gotten all purple and bruised. Not while Dempsey's daddy was likely listening to all Andres had to say and was right now on the phone to the police, making them thunder up our gravel road to drag me into one of those big police cars.

Instead, I jerked at Dempsey's outstretched hand, the stench of Andres' breath still stuck in my sinuses, the feel of his grimy hands gripping my arms and the sound of ripping cloth, and I withdrew back into myself. It seemed I'd sully him somehow just by touching him.

But Dempsey was mule-stubborn, same as me and he cocked up an eyebrow, curious, a little worried before he dropped his hand to his knee. "Come now, Sook, tell me what's got you spooked." He inched closer, the heat of his body a comfort. The sweat had set down my back and though I'd run hard and fast in the small spring heat wave, I felt cold, like my bones were made of ice, and chills had moved over my skin, goose bumps on my arms, making me looked like a plucked chicken.

"I…" Could I tell him? How many times did Dempsey offer to hear me speak whatever fretted me? A dozen? A hundred more that he'd actually done it without needing to ask. He was my friend, always had been, even when his mama and daddy told him to keep away from me and my family. Even when his face was bloody and his lip busted, even then Dempsey still wanted to listen to whatever held my attention.

"Sook," he started, reaching for me again. This time I didn't flinch away. This time I wanted him to touch me, just a little to see if that touch would warm me up. But then Dempsey dropped his hand, nodding at my torn shirt. "Someone do this to you?" When I didn't answer, Dempsey's jaw went tight and his mouth went stiff, as though someone had whispered something dark and dirty in his ear and just the sound of it had his feathers ruffled. "Who the hell did this to you?" He leaned back, coming to his knees to stare down at me with his hands balled up tight at his side. "Was it…God, Sook, was it my brother?"

"What?" My voice was low, awed likely because I didn't believe his question. Malcolm Simoneaux was nearly eighteen and hated the sight of anyone, man or woman, who didn't look just like him and his people. He hated black folk worse than his daddy. Dempsey should have known better to ask, but right then to me he didn't seem like he was having thoughts that made much sense at all.

"It was. That son of a bitch. I knew he was home. I knew he was drinking, if that son of a bit…" He went on mumbling to himself, pacing around in a circle before he said something rude and filthy under his breath and then Dempsey headed toward the opening that led to the ladder below.

"No!" He didn't slow until I scrambled to grab him, pulling on his arm. "Dempsey, don't be a fool. It wasn't your brother. I swear." He came around to face me, mouth still set hard and somber when he stared down at me. "It wasn't Malcolm, cher, *I promise."*

He took to looking me over, hard, but that small word, cher, *worked like a balm on him, keeping the rise of fury from his head. He liked when I called him that which is why I never did it much. But the more Dempsey looked, the more frozen and raw I felt. Was there marks or bruises starting up where that old man had grabbed me, scratches? I was too scared to look, too caught up in the hard look on Dempsey's face. In my stillness, he looked me up and down, over my face, to the top of my head, back down to my face, over my cheekbones, until he stopped to stare at my mouth. I swear there was something peculiar about the look in his eyes then, how he took on the air of someone who hadn't had anything at all to fill his belly. Dempsey stepped closer, resting his hands on my shoulders and I let him, liked how big his fingers felt on my skin, how one palm covered my collarbone completely. But then it was like the moment between us passed when he realized just how torn my shirt was and went all still.*

His skin went pale white just as mine pinked up and heated over my cheeks as his gaze traveled down my neck, to my resting on the beige strap of my frayed undershirt.

"Who..." He cleared his throat, like something thicker than hay had taken root in the back of his mouth. "Who?"

It was the breath I let out that brought his attention back to my face and again his expression straddled somewhere between irate anger and fretting like none I'd ever seen from him before.

There was no sense in lying. Dempsey would believe me even if no one else would. No one who mattered to me anyway. "That Joe Andres was drunk and snuck up on me on the north side of your daddy's sugarcane field." He nodded once, and his jaw worked hard again so I hurried to keep him calm. "Likely he's too drunk to know what he done…"

"What did he do?" The pressure of his fingers on my shoulder tightened.

"Nothing, Dempsey, he didn't get to nothing." When his expression didn't change, I grabbed his hand, twisting my fingers with his and pulled them both from my shoulder. "He tried to grab me and got hold of my shirt but…I…well, I socked him good in the eye."

Dempsey's laugh came quick, like a streak of lightning that makes the darkest night light up. It was a nice sound, something I didn't hear near enough for my liking. "You punched that fat jackass?"

"Dempsey Simoneaux!" He shrugged, ignoring how I fussed at him for the cursing. Couldn't be helped. Dempsey had probably never used such crude words out loud before now.

"Well, I'm speaking the truth. I doubt the good Lord would mind so much me calling a spade, a spade."

The laugh that pulled from me felt nice, but not as much as how I lit up with things I didn't know how to name when he pulled me close and let me rest my cheek against his chest.

I could have counted the seconds of my breath just then; I could have set them inside me like moments that would be precious if ever there came a time when the world had gone all black and dark and I needed *something to remind me of the lightness I'd known. That moment, with Dempsey's strong arms around me would have been the brightest light in my memories. It would have split away the darkness and made me happy for the blindness it caused.*

It wasn't smart to hope for things that would never be. It wasn't my life that was charmed. When you live here, when you are as I was, as all my people would ever be, hope was a funny thing, especially when there was trouble stirring around the edges of our days. Like the rim of the levee just before it breaks, worries were coming. I knew that because they always did and no amount of wishing me and Dempsey could disappear from the world right then would keep the waters from spilling over.

"Dempsey…what if he comes after me?" I spoke that low, against the fabric of his cotton shirt. It smelled fresh, like he'd pulled it right off the line.

"Don't you worry over that, Sookie." He pulled back, lifting my face up with his knuckle. "You don't ever have to worry about anyone hurting you, so long as I'm around."

He was so sweet. Maybe a little stupid about how things worked, but Dempsey sure was a sweet boy. The frown came back on his face when I shook my head. "You can't say that."

"Can so." I liked the way he tilted his head, how there was so many things he thought just then, each one showing themselves in the shift of his mouth; how it moved from frown to smile and back to something in between the two. He moved his hands around to touch my face, holding my head still like there was something he wanted to make sure I heard and knew to the marrow of my bones. I couldn't breathe when he looked at me the way he did then, all serious and

fierce. One look and he stole the air from my lungs.

"No matter where I am. No matter where I go, I won't let anybody hurt you. Not ever."

I wanted to believe him. There was a truth he spoke just then, something he uttered without a sound that lit up his eyes and made those high, sharp cheekbones look pink and bright. He had a nice face, good enough for the pictures, I'd wager. He was handsome and sweet, but not so smart about how our lives would always be.

"I wish I could believe that." He went on holding my face and I stared at the shine in his eyes, how the dim light through the cracks and spaces between the walls around us shone bright in his gray eyes. "It would be nice, I think, to have someone always watching over me."

"I mean it, Sook. With everything I am." His touch got firmer when I shook my head again and Dempsey pulled me closer, my head resting on his chest. "As long as there is breath inside me, I'll protect you."

"I don't need you protecting me."

"Maybe not, but I need to do the protecting."

He circled me in his arms, holding me to him, and I could feel his heart beating in his chest, strong and regular, safe.

"Why?"

It took him a long few seconds before he answered. Around us the night went on as it always had, as it always would. The owls and crickets made on with their noisy business, as the wind swept cool relief through the leaves around us. I stopped worrying about Andres and whether he'd be coming after me. Just then, everything went away, my thoughts, my worry, even the breath in my lungs until I heard Dempsey's answer.

"Because, sweet Sookie. I love you something fierce." And right then, the world stopped spinning. The axis of life became uneven and slow as Dempsey Simoneaux, a boy who'd been my friend, bent close to me, breath hot and sweet against my face and kissed me so slow, so soft just enough that my body felt electrified. Just enough that I knew that at that moment, my world slowly began to unravel.

Nash

The skyline is different. The noises of sirens and the low howl of dogs, and animals skirting along the tree lines, they're different too. There are no coyotes in Brooklyn and few moments that are quiet enough to hear the damn things if there were. But sometimes on a Thursday morning at four, my body shakes me awake, and there I am, twelve years old, holding my sister's hand, listening from the hallway as the cops explain to the sitter about the accident.

"He was drunk. He's been arrested. She didn't make it."

There wasn't anything I remember more clearly from my childhood in Atlanta than those words.

It took a village, literally, to keep me and Nat out of the system, even though the village was full of blood-sucking mercenaries. There were enough aunts and uncles, enough cousins, that took pity on us after our grandfather died four years later—or, to be honest, took more to wanting the government payouts supposing watching over us gave them—to let us stick together until we could get the hell out of Atlanta as soon as we finished high school. Most of the time, I manage to keep all that past low down, hidden someplace where I keep all the things I don't want to remember—like the memory of being fired for the first time, or the first girl who told me I wasn't good enough for her. Those things got locked away with the memory of a parentless childhood. It stayed there and I never touched it. Until it comes on its own at four a.m. on any random Thursday.

"He was drunk."

That bastard lived in the low down.

Four-fifteen and I watched from the roof deck of my building as two kids argued on the sidewalk outside of my building. A guy and girl—Latin, from the look of them. The yelling sounded like Spanish, anyway. I caught *puta*, understood what that meant, and shook my head when the guy started in with excuses his *chica* wasn't feeling. The sky was dark, cloudy. Despite the noise and overhead fog, I could still catch a scent of rain peppering the air, kind of bitter, and it set something cold and weary in my bones. The yelling got louder, pulling my gaze away from the dotted cityscape and small stars lighting up the night. He was on his knees now, voice high and pathetic, reminding me why I didn't mess around with anyone for too long. There was always drama. There was always stupidity that weighed you down, and I'd never met anyone worth all that drama. This poor jackass was begging for her to stay, begging for the drama to slip around him like a noose.

Four-seventeen and suddenly I realized I wasn't alone.

"You following me?" I asked her, itching for something to do with my hands as Willow came close. She wore colors I'd never seen on her: neutral, boring, surprising. Wasn't like her to wear beige or keep her hair neat and braided so tight. But I wasn't going to care about her or what she did. Convinced myself of it, didn't I? The hell did it matter, her wearing boring-ass clothes?

"No," she said, stepping closer to the edge of the roof. She held her arms crossed, and I wondered why she looked so sad, she who was usually always smiling. "I just wanted some air." She moved back, stepping behind me to sit in the wicker chairs set in a semi-circle around the Home Depot fire pit Mickey had bought last fall. It had cost him thirty bucks. Discounted for being a display. That was a little shopping tidbit I'd floated his way when he talked about charging us an extra fifty a month for "maintenance" on the roof deck.

But the pit and the chairs, even the bickering couple five stories below faded from my attention as Willow rested against the chair, feet propped on the arm of another one, her head tilted as she watched the black sky above us, and sighed.

"Everyone likes me."

I told myself I shouldn't bite. She was casting a line and wanted me to nibble. What kind of thing is that to say anyway? I should have turned my back on her and went down the stairs, leaving her to her sky and sighs and moods.

"It's a family trait. My people are just universally liked."

"That right?"

Hell. Look at me, biting at Willow's line.

"It is. My parents are do-gooder types. They recycle and volunteer and love to go hiking in the mountains just to pick up trash left behind by other hikers. They go to Africa every summer to help build wells. I go with them, most of the time, and for the most part, people like us." From the corner of my eye I glanced at her, spotted how her face seemed calm, like she was talking to hear the echo of her own voice against the night. But her body was rigid and she moved her foot in a quick tap that told me she wasn't calm in the least. Those crossed arms, too, folded tighter as she went on. "We've never been told to mind our own business or to go back where we came from."

Willow stood then, moving back to the edge of the roof but keeping her distance from me. Her voice was soft, a little beige like her clothes, and when she continued, her attention was on the couple down below who'd abandoned their fight for making out against a light pole.

"You probably think I'm some privileged little white girl who's never had a bad day in her life, don't you?" I only glanced at her, letting my lone arched eyebrow answer her question. She took that expression for what it was, shaking her head like she wasn't surprised. "Yeah, I thought so," Willow said. "But the thing is, Nash, my parents brought me to Africa and Yemen and Costa Rica and a thousand other places because they wanted me to see that privilege doesn't give you a pass. It gives responsibility, or at least it should. My Granny Nicola started it all, making cakes and pastries for her family, then her friends. Ten years later she was manufacturing ten thousand cakes and hundreds of thousands of scones and turnovers a month. She made our family wealthy. It wasn't my parents' money, or mine either, because none of us had earned it. Being born into wealth doesn't make you rich. For my family, it meant we had to spread the good fortune we'd been given. We have to pay it forward."

Hell, did I really have to be listening to this self-reverential, poor little rich girl bullshit at four in the morning? "You got a point?" The question was rude, but needed to be asked. She looked tired—there were small bags under her eyes and her face was drawn and shadowed, as though she hadn't slept in a week. Had to be something more to it than bemoaning the burdens that rich white folks bear.

"I got a point," Willow said, stepping close enough that I saw her eyes were rimmed red. "No one has ever avoided me in my life. Not growing up, whenever I've set my eyes on something important. Something that needed to be done. All the times I've hassled people to donate to one cause or another, pried their hands away from their eyes so they'd actually seen what was going on, or shamed some rich fat cat into building a dozen wells for villages on the other side of the world, not even those people avoided me." She turned toward me and her mouth looked tight, as though she fought her anger and did a piss poor job of it. "You're the first. Ever, in my life, and that really bugs me."

For a second I only watched her, pushing back that huge need that rose up in my chest, the same one that wanted me to touch her, to bring her close enough to taste. But that wouldn't help me keep her out of my way. It wouldn't do anything but give her another reason to keep knocking on my door. So I went with being an asshole.

"First time for everything, sweetness."

Willow dropped her arms, and her face went all red and blotchy. "Why are you such a jerk?" Those eyes though, they were cold, steely and it hit me square in the chest when I realized I'd pissed her off. Kinda liked how it looked on her.

Still, I didn't appreciate that know-it-all shake of her head or how her anger seemed to make her think she was right about me. "Look, you don't know…"

"I know you're avoiding me. I know that anytime I see you on the sidewalk or in the lobby, you head in the other direction."

Willow stood right in front of me. There was an eyelash on her left cheek and I fought to keep my hands in my pocket so I wouldn't brush it away. Even in boring beige, she was beautiful, something I tried like hell to deny over and over in my head. Something, it seemed, that was impossible to do.

"There is something happening here, and you're running from it."

That had me laughing, a quick, cruel sound that tightened her mouth until there were small lines around her lips. "It ain't like that."

"Something happened to you." Just as she said that a quick breeze floated around us, pushing her bangs into her eyes. She reached up to brush them back. "Something happened to me, too. I don't know what it is, Nash, but there is something between us."

"That isn't what's happening here."

"If there was nothing happening, you wouldn't be avoiding me." She stepped closer, and I refused to back up, to show weakness in retreating, but I couldn't hide how shallow my breath had become. She spotted it. "If there was nothing, you wouldn't be so nervous when I get close to you."

I did step back then, I had to, and I thought she might follow. Willow was a pushy sort of female, the kind that didn't back away just because you wanted them to. She got inside your head, claws sharp and deep, and wouldn't let you go without a fight. Part of me liked that about her. The other part of me, the one that reminded me I didn't need a damn thing but my brain and ambition to get what I wanted, that voice was loud and obnoxious.

But you don't get rid of a claws-deep woman just by pushing them away. You strike, you injure, and just then, I wanted to hurt Willow so deep that she'd have no choice but to drop me like a toxic bomb.

"I'm nervous because you're insane. Certifiable. I'm not into you." I put a little gravel in my voice just then, ignoring how wide Willow's eyes had gone at my insult, how she let her mouth drop open like a guppy out of its tank. "There is nothing happening here."

"I am *not* crazy."

Just then, she didn't look convincing, and I understood why. This was the woman who believed in auras. She was the same female who pulled me into her boho madhouse because one glance at me told her there was something wrong with me. I wouldn't admit to her she'd been right about that, but who she was, how she was, I understood why she was so insulted. I was willing to bet it wasn't the first time someone had called her crazy. It sure as hell pissed her off.

It hurt just a little to see that frown, but my plan had been to keep her away. My plan had been to remember the work I'd spent years doing, to keep focused because I was nearly there, had nearly made it. My plans didn't include some white-assed hippie chick who promised things with a look, who expected the same from me.

I needed her angry. I needed Willow to hate me. "Whatever you say, nutjob."

I expected her to rage, to fight back. To come at me swinging. Instead, she didn't flinch, or even frown at my insult. It was almost as if she had expected me to be an asshole. And hell, I wasn't ready for how cool, how cruel, how correct she could be. It only took a small brush of her hand under her chin and that sad, disgusted frown to show that she could see through me.

"You're such a coward."

It was a gut punch I hated feeling, one I tried hard not let show on my face. "What did you say to me?"

"You heard me, and you know it's true." She was in my face with three small steps, taunting me, accusing me. "You're running. You felt something between us. That night in my apartment, then in yours. There is something happening, I have no idea what it is, but you feel it too."

"No. I don't!" Willow stepped back when I yelled, but she didn't cower. I desperately held on to my lie, despite feeling like I was being outmaneuvered. "Sorry to bust your bubble, nut job, but no. The only thing happening is I have a crazy ass neighbor who keeps leaving cupcakes at my door. The same crazy neighbor who pulled me into her apartment the first night we met because she swore she could see my *aura*." I made sure to accent that word as sarcastically as possible. "So yeah…like I said…crazy."

Willow stood her ground, that same impassive frown pinching her features, her eyes hard and sparking. She didn't buy my excuses, and that look of hers was nailing me to the wall despite my noise and the shit I was trying to spill. Willow might be a little weird, she might be a lot in her own world, but she wasn't afraid of a damn thing—not me, not my loud yelling voice or the thing that pulsed between us, the very same thing I refused to admit was there.

"You'll figure it out. Eventually," she said, stepping

back. "One day you'll get over your issues and admit that I'm right."

"I damn well won't."

"And when you do," she interrupted, cocked up an eyebrow, curious, a little worried before her expression changed and her lips twitched. "Maybe then, Nash, you'll stop running from whatever it is that's got you spooked."

It was another gut punch moment. I'd only ever heard that expression once in my life, and it had never come out of Willow's mouth.

"I just hope I'm still around when you're ready to admit it."

She left the roof then, reaching for her braid. It was loose, and her hair was hanging in a huge mass down her back by the time she made it to the stairs. I could only watch her, heart pounding like a drum inside my head. The only other time I'd heard about being spooked was some girl named Sookie in my dream, and there was no way Willow could know about that.

Was there?

Willow

Effie Thomas was a librarian who liked to tell patrons to "shut the fuck up" anytime they got a little too loud in her library. She'd been admonished at least a half-dozen times when she first landed the gig, but she was damned good at her job, and by the time she'd made head librarian, no one had the nerve to tell her to stop yelling at noisy patrons.

We were dorm mates for two semesters at NYU, sneaking booze we weren't old enough to buy and kissing boys we had no business knowing. I loved Effie like a sister. Or, at least, like I supposed you should love a sister, if you had one. Effie was also somewhat of a dabbler in transcendental meditation. "Hogwash," my mom would call it, but Effie, despite the filthy insults she flung at loud mouths in the reference department like a monkey with shit at a zoo, Effie happened to be one of the calmest, most well-adjusted people I knew.

But I was a little desperate, a lot annoyed, and figured that my mother's standard "walk around in nature" remedy for de-stressing wasn't going to cut it this time around. I'd let Effie direct me if it meant I could find my center again.

"Breathe in, Will. Through your nose, releasing through your teeth." Effie sat up straight, her knees facing mine as we rested cross-legged on the plush rugs draped around my living room. She had her hair elegantly wrapped in an up do with jewel toned scarves twisted around her braids. It was an elaborate, complicated arrangement that Effie had never shared with me, likely with anyone. Her tank top was a little threadbare but so soft, and she wore red yoga pants that clung to her lush thighs like paint. She was beautiful, with wide set eyes and skin the color of wet sand, lips that puckered naturally. Effie was by default quiet, but could shatter the windows of any room with a cool, mean glare or that filthy mouth of hers when riled.

"You paying attention?" she asked, poking me with one slender finger, the nail long and painted something she liked to call *Bitch Red*. "In and out. Easy breaths, and when you are relaxed," she exhaled, and I smelled the hint of clove on her breath, "then and only then do you start your mantra."

Ah. That was a problem, or it might be.

"You have it, don't you? A mantra?" I opened my eyes, pushing a sweet smile on my face to lessen the blow that might come when Effie discovered I hadn't quite chosen my mantra. Not like I hadn't been thinking of and discarding idea after idea... I shrugged, and the tall woman lowered her shoulders, tapping three of those nails on the hardwood floor at her side. "You serious?"

"I couldn't decide..."

"It's vital, Willow. Damn, girl, how many times I say that to you? *Vital.*"

"I know...I'm sorry." Effie laughed at me when I dropped

120

my face in my hands, rubbing my temples. "Nash has got me so…"

"Sprung?"

I jerked my head up, staring at Effie, mouth open a little. "That's probably the perfect word for it. *Ugh.*" When I fell back, lying against the sofa pillows I'd tossed around my floor, Effie came to my side, elbow to elbow with me as I watched the ceiling, not seeing the small cracks in the plaster or the dust bunnies collected in the old chandelier. "I never get stupid over men. Not ever."

Her laugh was warm, and as we lay there, side by side, I was reminded of late nights in our cold dorm when we'd huddle close together because the furnace never worked right. Effie sounded sweet, a little too amused, which told me plainly I was about to be teased. "Well," she started, pushing me over so she could rest her head on the same pillow as me, "there was Micah Wiley sophomore year."

"Not fair, you went stupid over him too. Every girl with a pulse went stupid over Micah."

Effie snorted, waving those nails at me as though my accusation had zero merit. "Please. What would I want with some football player? He had nothing between his ears."

I moved my head slowly, eyes squinted as I watched my friend. "Who the hell cared?" She laughed again, shrugging away her denial. "No one cared if he could quote sonnets. It was that body…"

"True enough."

A flash of memory circled in my head and it brought me out of the moment. Eyes tight, I tried to block out the voices, the deep, rich sound that I knew I'd never heard but that sounded so familiar. Something I heard only in my dreams. And that face—warm, dark amber eyes with flecks of gold, bright and kind. A mouth that I...that someone I didn't know...so wanted, dreamed of. My thoughts were complicated with guilt, something that didn't make a bit of sense. There was no one for me to be unfaithful to, and even if there were, the man in my dreams wasn't real. If he had been once, he would be old by now, older than my parents, because that was the world he lived in. Not mine.

"You need a mantra," Effie said, lifting up on one elbow to look down at me. "It focuses your thoughts. It's the center that you concentrate on while your mind bends to the will of the universe. The mantra is key, Will. I've only ever..." she paused just then and the silence brought my gaze to her face and the hard set of her mouth as she frowned. "What the hell has you looking all dreamy-eyed and simple?"

"Nothing...it's..." It was everything—the dream and the emotions that Isaac stirred in me, but it was the memory of a man I'd never known. It was Nash, too, and the stupid way he ran—from me, from life, from everything he saw as a complication. "I can't stop thinking about him, Effie, and it's pissing me off."

"Girl, please. He's just a man."

122

I blinked at her, unable to make her see reason with that stupid gobsmacked expression I no doubt had plastered on my face. "Honey, he's *not* just a man. He's…Nash is…God is he just…"

"Unavailable?"

"What? No! I'd never move in on someone else's guy."

"I dunno, Will, sure seems to me like you're chasing after something you can't get. You sure that's not it? That you only want him because he's one of the few things that has been out of your reach and that scratch you can't itch is what's driving you crazy?"

I gave her the skank eye. "Are you crazy? Damn, Effie, you know me better than that."

"So what, then? He's hot? How hot can he be, really?" When I cocked an eyebrow, my friend's doubtful frown loosened into a grin. "What? Like Jesse Williams fine?"

"Better."

"Shemar?"

"Better."

She held up a hand. "No damn way."

"It's not just those eyes or that smile…"

"Liar." She ducked when I tossed a pillow at her head, laughing at me and the stupid blush I knew she could make out on my cheeks. "So you're into him? I get that. 'Bout damn time."

"I've been trying to start a business, you know."

Effie tilted her head, waving me off like I was a little pathetic. "Yes, tell me how hard that is, Ms. Moneybags."

"Not fair." I moved my braid around my shoulder, twisting the ends between my fingers as habit. "Besides, I'm not using my parents' money. I got a loan."

"Will…"

Effie's gaze shot to me, followed me around the apartment when I slipped into the small kitchen to fill the kettle for tea. "Do me a favor and don't start in with the 'you're being stubborn' lecture, okay?"

"But you are."

"Not the point." I dug the tea tin from the cabinet, ignoring Effie when she stretched, mumbling something under her breath that sounded a lot like judgment. "You and my dad, the pair of you think I should just take advantage of that money, but the business wouldn't be mine if I did. This way, it is mine. Completely, utterly mine. Plus, this way I know what every small business person feels like when they have to come up with a business plan and try to land capital. Pride and experience. It's essential, Eff."

She sat on the sofa, crossing her legs under herself as she watched me. "I wasn't going to lecture you…except about not finding your mantra."

The kettle sounded and I dropped two tea bags in each of our mugs after filling them with water, bringing Effie's hers as she fiddled with the trim along the arm of the sofa, those red nails pushing against the purple fabric.

"Well," I started, sitting across from her in the plush chair my mom had handed down to me. It was a chevron pattern she'd gotten bored of last summer, and the gray color corresponded nicely with the purple and white of the lap blanket I'd draped across its back. "There was one thing that kept cropping up in my head. I think it was something I'd dreamed of and can't forget, even though I also can't quite remember exactly where it came from."

"The same dreams you were telling me about? With the redhead and the janitor?"

"No. It's different, somewhere older, something I can't remember nearly as well…"

"The dream doesn't matter, sugar. Just the mantra. What is it?"

When I tried to recall the dream, the details got fuzzy. There were only minute flashes of memory that seemed clear—there'd been a night wind and a purple sky. There'd been a boy, the one whose eyes I was seeing through, and a girl I—he—loved, more than anything, and there had been a promise that stuck, something around which their world—and mine, by extension— pivoted. Over and over, it had planted itself inside my heart.

"With everything I am." I said over the rim of my mug. The warmth from the hot liquid heated my skin as Effie looked back at me, waiting for an explanation I wasn't sure I could give her. "I don't know what it means." I took a sip, watched her do the same. "Will it work?"

Effie polished off her tea and smiled, motioning back toward the floor and the assortment of rugs and blankets and throw pillows assembled that made for a comfortable place to focus and meditate. "It's a start at least."

We settled back down on the floor facing each other, and at Effie's urging I let the words collect in my mind, pushing them past my lips, soft but focused.

"With everything I am," I said under my breath, like a whisper meant only for my ears. Maybe it was remembered hope. Maybe it was a promise made decades before that meant something then. Whatever it was, I took it for my own, not really sure who it should be meant for—the man in my dreams or the man who liked to pretend I didn't matter at all.

"With everything I am," I thought, letting the silence move around me, letting my breath and energy and the collection of thoughts and moments lull me into another time, another space. I'd found my center, and it brought me to the past.

Washington, D.C.

Isaac's face took my attention for most of the weekend. It was a sad state, really, and one that hadn't gone unnoticed.

I shifted my skirt, laying my forehead on my arm as I hid among the stacks, wondering how I could have been such an idiot to let it go so far. I was here only because the library felt safe to me. There was a warmth to this place that had nothing to do with the stacked stone fireplaces in the four sitting areas or the ceilings that pitched high, fifty feet or more, and several stories that seemed to stretch out into the clouds visible through the glass at the top of the ceiling. The place was old, nearly as old as Lincoln University itself. And books? Thousands upon thousands that took up ten floors, every shelf stacked with hundreds of books, some right off the presses, some older than my folks.

It felt like a castle, and me, tiny speck of a girl that I was, I felt safe here, away from the raised eyebrows of the city where women still weren't so commonplace around our university or any others housed in D.C. Here where it didn't matter if you were rich or poor, black or white, male or female.

Where there weren't bastards who lost their temper and struck out.

"Don't let anyone keep your eyes on the ground, my little pepper." Dad had said that so often it had become something I repeated to myself as a reminder of what was expected of me. My parents expected me to be great, but I demanded perfection of myself. It was stupid really, but I wanted to make them proud. That perfection had been expected by Trent as well. And like the fool I was, I let him go on thinking it was all right to demand that perfection from me. But his idea of perfect and mine weren't the same. They never would be.

My lip still throbbed, and when I wiped away blood, my anger rose something fierce. It became a ridiculous pulse of rage that I tried to keep down, deep inside my chest where all my worries and sorrows lived.

It would not do to let my anger overtake me. If it did, then he had won; he had made me into something I didn't want to be. Weak. Hysterical. Out of control.

But it was damn hard reminding myself of that fact.

My parents would be upset—not at me, of course. But upset that I had allowed myself to be so upset, to fall short of expectations. Trent had been sure to remind me of that. There were always expectations.

"Your father won't want Senator Mansfield to catch wind of this unpleasantness, Riley. You know that as well as I do. With my father working on the President's staff, there's just too much riding on getting the Voting Rights Act passed, and we've all worked so hard. Your father, too. It would be a shame to let any other concerns worry your father or our office when they should all be focused on other things. Important things."

He was a coward. Trent was also full of himself. My father wouldn't care what Trent's father thought of him putting his hands on me. My father was a big man with a quick fuse when tested, and I was his only daughter. He'd throttle Trent without thinking twice about it. But then, that was the problem, wasn't it? Dad had worked tirelessly helping Mansfield get the Voting Rights Act on the President's desk. It was monumental. Essential. I needed to remember that before I went off telling him that Trent Dexter had smacked me when I told him I wanted to end things between us.

My folks were expecting me home over the weekend. Mom's sister was flying in from Europe Sunday morning. But I couldn't let them see me like this, split lip and weak with anger and shame. My parents had survived Hitler's terror both on the battlefield and in the concentration camps. They were relentless and strong. I couldn't let them see me being anything less than what they'd always been.

My face felt sticky and wet, and I sniffled so loud that the sound went around the library like a calling card advertising that I was being pathetic, crying over some bastard in the fourth-floor Politics and Religion stacks.

It only took that small noise for Isaac to find me. He moved slow and quiet, stopping at the beginning of the row to look to his left, squinting to see me in shadows and darkness.

"Miss Riley?" His voice was soft, as though he wasn't sure of what he saw when he looked down the aisle. Then he must have spotted my red hair as it hung around my face, and moved toward me with a welcoming smile. It was only when I wiped my face dry with the back of my hand that Isaacs's steps slowed.

He squatted in front of me, arms resting on his thighs as he moved his head to the side, looking like he just wanted a glimpse of my face still hidden behind my tangled hair.

"You didn't show. I waited for you. Almost time to close up." His voice was soft, the guilt of disappointing someone else, too, swam like piranha in my stomach.

"I'm sorry." I sniffled, using my nails to comb the knots from my hair. "I got into…there was something that came up and then I just…" I waved a hand, motioning around the books. "I ended up here."

Failure was not an emotion I generally felt. It simply wasn't allowed in my father's home. You worked hard, you were rewarded. You didn't work hard enough, and you tried again. I had not forced Trent's punch, and I damn well knew it wasn't my fault, but that didn't make the sensation burning me up from the inside any less painful.

Isaac didn't say a word. He didn't have to. He simply waited for me to say something else. The silence around us became too much, the weight of it too heavy for me to stand, and I forced my head up, to look right at him. I watched his eyes flick quickly to my busted lip, his gaze steely.

I waited for ten full seconds as he stared at me. His focus was strong, felt like a wave over my features, and I fought back more tears, wanting so badly to let him comfort me, but fearing to seem any more weak and pathetic than I already was. The silence between us was uncomfortable, as was the fierce anger that began to shift his expression. There was rage brimming behind his eyes, and the disgust and hatred moved his nostrils into a flare. Unbidden, the collection of tears hanging onto my lashes dropped onto my cheek. It was then that he seemed to calm.

"I'm a mess." It was an excuse I threw out that he ignored, moving to lift a knuckle under my chin.

"You're so beautiful, Miss Riley."

My breath caught. No one had looked at me the way Isaac was: like I was remarkable. Like there weren't a dozen ginger-headed girls with dark brown eyes running around the city. Like my pale skin and a million freckles were exotic or interesting. Like that busted lip wasn't there, didn't belong. Isaac looked at me like he saw me, really saw me, and it took my breath away.

My body shuddered when he palmed my face, and I blinked, wincing when he brought out a handkerchief to my wet cheeks and still bleeding lip. He fixed me up without me asking, so gently, like it was something he'd do regardless, and I felt the tension in my gut settle, release, and vanish the longer Isaac went about cleaning me up.

He made me feel safe, protected in a way no one but my father had before.

"A man does this to a woman," he said, brushing the hair behind my ears, "and he deserves to be put down like a dog." Isaac paused, and I could smell sandalwood on his skin, chased by the smallest hint of bleach. "You say the word, and I'll put that dog down."

Something happened to me then, a fierce rush of something that made me want to do nothing but cling to Isaac, damn his arguments about our differences. I wanted to kiss him then, to hold onto him until we were breathless. He wanted to avenge me, to protect me from the danger I couldn't protect myself from, and some small part of me, a part that was ancient and primal, found this singularly attractive. Oh, how I wanted to give him permission; I wanted to be protected. But the world we lived in, even in D.C., as Isaac had always claimed, did not allow the freedom to attack and not be punished. Especially for someone like Isaac.

"No," I finally said. "Trent is not worth the trouble it would cause for you."

"He can't go without being…"

"He will be, don't worry." I inhaled, and my chest constricted with scent of Isaac's skin and the proximity of his body to mine. "I'll take care of it."

It was then that I saw something from Isaac I hadn't seen before. His stony resolve crumbled, and whatever excuses had always *kept him from wanting me, from allowing me to act as though I wanted him too, fell away when he began to lower his hand, and I held it still against my cheek.*

His skin was warm, and I could just make out the sharp bite of his calluses against my face. He had an arch along his top lip and eyes like a perfect circle, a play of amber and gold vying for dominance in his irises. Not hazel really, but somewhere in the middle, someplace that said Isaac came from people divergent and varied.

"Riley…" he said, a warning I didn't want to hear. My gaze didn't falter; I may have stumbled with Trent, but I knew what I wanted, what was best for me, and that was not some overbearing, suit-wearing bully. And Isaac, sweet Isaac, took my lifted chin for the invitation it was, made a sound deep in his throat, and just like that, with a single tilt of his head, stopped fighting and kissed me.

The world went away, and I heard the song of hundreds of voices inside of me that sounded so familiar, yet were unlike anything I'd ever heard before. Maybe it was that active imagination of mine working in overdrive. I had wanted Isaac's touch for months, had daydreamed about it for hours, and now that it was here, I realized that my imagination was dull and pathetic. Reality was so much better.

He moved his mouth over mine, tentative at first, but fueled by my reaction and the awesome magnitude of what this felt like, he moved more confidently, more surely. Isaac wanted me and took what I offered freely—his lips soft, directing, his tongue teasing and satisfying all at once, careful of my broken lip, yes, but oh, so absolute.

He moved his hands, fanning his fingers into my hair, holding my head steady, and I pulled back, feeling the smile against my mouth.

"Miss Riley," he said again, but the words were like a prayer, and I decided just then, with Isaac watching the strands of my hair slip through his fingers, that he could me call me anything he wanted as long as he kept touching me. "You could tempt an angel with this mess of fine hair. I like it. It suits you."

I responded, pulling him close, wanting the taste of his mouth again. He delivered, leading me in the movement, mouth and lips soft and sweet, a little desperate, a lot greedy, and my breath grew labored, fanned out against his face and I lifted with him, following as he pulled us to our feet, as he pressed close to me and my back came up against the books on the stacks that surrounded us.

My mind was full of the outline of Isaac's hips and thighs as we pressed together and the sturdy, guiding strength of his hand as he held a palm against my lower back. I felt like a decadent sinner, taking and taking with no concern for consequences.

But the heat of the moment and the shadows that hid us would not keep our secrets forever. As quickly as we had come together, a voice sounded at the end of aisle, a low, amazed curse, and we pulled apart to see Lenny's grim face.

"Time to lock up, man." Lenny didn't look at me. He kept his attention on Isaac, watching him as though saying more would cause the world to shatter.

"I hear you. Give me a minute."

One beat, then two. Then the slightest nod of his head, and Lenny turned around, stalked off without a backwards glance.

Isaac took a moment, watching after his friend, and then he turned back to me. Before he could say anything, I spoke up.

"I'm...I'm sorry," I told him, hoping he didn't think I regretted wanting him, or what we had done. A quick jerk of his head and I smiled, eager to take that worried look from his expression. "No, Isaac.... I'm sorry we got interrupted."

A slow, easy smile spread against his face, then Isaac's gaze drifted to my mouth, and I thought he might kiss me one more time, but he frowned, pushing his eyebrows together as he ran a fingertip against the cut in my lip. "Did I make this worse?"

"I didn't feel a thing but the hum of your kiss."

"My kisses hum?"

"Absolutely."

He watched me then, eyes sharp and focused, and I wondered if he'd ever tell me about all the thoughts I could read on his face; all the secrets he protected so fiercely.

"This thing between me and you, it could lead to a lot of trouble for both of us."

"Isaac, I'm not worried. Trouble comes even if we plan for it. It comes when we don't."

He shook his head, smile sweet, those amber-glinted eyes sparkling like he thought I was naive or simple or a dreamer who wouldn't be told to give up. Isaac gave me one last kiss, the first of what I prayed would be a thousand more, a million more, and then he pressed his lips to my forehead.

"Come on then, I'll walk you to your dorm and make sure you get inside

134

safe."

And for the first time in hours, right then with Isaac, that's how I felt—safe.

Isaac and Riley cleared from my head as the fog of meditation ebbed, until I realized where I was and what I was doing. Then, the realization hit me hard, a slap of comprehension and clarity I hadn't felt before. I could still feel those broad hands against my back, those thick, full lips working hard over mine. Isaac had felt so familiar. He'd felt so real.

He'd felt just like…

"Oh my God," I said, pulling Effie from her own thoughts, spurring her loud shudder and gasp with one loud oath.

"What now? Man, I was in a good place…"

"I'm sorry," I told her, jumping up from the floor to rummage around for a jacket. "I've got to find Nash. I have to tell him."

"What?" Effie said, following me as I found my tennis shoes and slipped them on at the same time. I was to my door, had it flung open before she stopped me. "Tell me. What do you think you discovered?"

"I know why I feel something between us. It's the past, Effie. Nash and me, I'm sure of it—we knew each other in another life."

Nine

Nash

Roan had a limp, something I knew had gotten worse since I first met him as a punk kid at Howard trying to pass Chem 101. He'd taken time from his teaching duties to tutor me, and something had clicked. He became the cool cat too old for students to notice, but to me, he was a man without limits. The kind of man I wanted to be. I kept in touch with him even after he retired, and he stayed my mentor through the years. It was Roan, in fact, who had given me the push to plant roots in New York. "Opportunity," he'd said, "lives with the masses."

I'd listened, and while I waited for Nations to make a little noise, Roan kept his birds, spending most of his time on top of the pre-war building he owned downtown. It was a run down, shabby place that he hoarded, didn't want company or tenants, preferring some quiet and solitude after years in academia, so I knew where to find him when my life was turning to hell.

The pigeons cooed and sang like it was Showtime at the Apollo and Roan was Steve Harvey, laughing at their noise like it was the sweetest music he'd ever heard. He was somewhere upwards of 6'2, a wiry old man who wore his salt and pepper beard a little long, a little unkempt, but his clothes, which reminded me of some once-was player still keeping himself sharp and his swag on point, were pristine: ironed jeans with starched creases and a designer sweater, wool pea coat and a page boy cap pulled low over his busy eyebrows.

"Nephew," Roan said, laugh low, amused at the small tease he'd shot my way. I wasn't his kin but he still liked to call me that, and when he did, the word always made him laugh. Roan waved me onto the roof when I peeked out of the stairwell door. "Come on."

"My man." I greeted him with a quick slap of our palms touching before he gave me a one-arm hug. "How those feathery rats of yours?"

"Watch your tongue." He still smiled despite my insult, those light, almost green eyes of his, lighting up as he messed with one of the cages; two pigeons jumped on the railing in the center, flying closer to the other side. "What's up? You lost? Haven't seen you in going on two months."

"Been trying to perfect the code. Duncan is getting restless."

Roan nodded, one corner of his mouth twitching up as he continued to adjust the broken side of the pigeons' cage. "Seems to me, from what you say, that Duncan is always restless."

"He's ready to start making money." This time Roan shook his head, nibbling on his bottom lip like he had to fight to keep something rude from coming out of his mouth. That never lasted for long. "Go on," I told him, laughing as he shrugged.

"It's not my business…"

"That's never stopped you before."

He smiled outright then, pulling off the gloves he wore so he could push his hands into the pockets of his coat. Roan leaned against the low brick ledge that divided the roof into sections. All around us that brick was covered in graffiti, artwork from gang members or punk kids he'd scared off some years back when he bought the building. He'd never bothered fixing the place up, and now, if I came here to see him and that paint was gone, it wouldn't seem like Roan's place at all.

"This Duncan cat, you've mentioned him a few times, and seems to me, every time you have, it's to say something about how he wants to make money."

It was the truth, but that had more to do with Duncan and what he always wanted to talk about than me projecting when I complained to my old tutor. "Well, that's kind of his job, I guess. After all, money makes the world go round, man."

"No." Roan pulled all expression from his face and the deep wrinkles around his mouth and eyes hardened just then. "Greedy men, sad men, that's what they think. Money don't rule the world, Nash. At least, not a world worth living in anyway."

The air was cooler than it had been the day before, and I tugged up my collar as Roan pulled out another pair of gloves, these leather, not fit for messing with dirty birds or the mess they made. "I guess you got a point." I hated the sound of my own voice, how the missing sleep had turned it to gravel, how the dreams and Willow had distracted me so that I couldn't focus, couldn't relax.

My mind buzzed and simpered. It felt woolen and sharp with so much chaos, so many things twirling in my conscience thought, it was hard to quiet it enough to rest. And even when I did, my attention got split between the life of the girl who was so familiar, so comfortable, and the echoes of images I didn't recognize at all. Something with libraries. And the scent of sandalwood... and a hint of bleach.

Whatever I felt must have been written on my face. Roan stop messing with his gloves and tilted his head, sizing me up like he thought I might be sick. "Boy, what is wrong with you? You look dog tired."

"I am." That confession came out with a sigh, and I closed my eyes, stretching my neck and shoulders. When I looked back at Roan, he was smiling. Never a good sign. "What?"

"It's a woman." He nodded, that stupid, smug smile taking over his whole face. "Don't I know it. Man, just looking at you, I can see that much."

"You're wrong, man. I got no time for females." But even as I denied it, Roan's laughter got loud, loud enough that the pigeons stopped their cooing.

"The hell you talking about? Everyone has time for

women, and if they don't, then they damn well should find the time."

I shook my head, not bothering to watch him laugh like a fool at my expense. Roan had never had a wife as far as I knew, though the secretaries in the Science Department sure liked to flirt with him. But that was Roan. He'd been a college professor, a scientist his entire adult life. He had no idea what it was like to build something that could go global.

"In case you forgot, I'm trying to build a company...get funding so I can leave Brooklyn and move on up."

"Okay, Mr. Jefferson," his laughter still showed up in his tone. It was the first time I'd seen him look so pleased with my worries. "Whatever you say, but just remember, money won't keep you warm at night, and it won't give you a family."

"I got a family."

"A sister you see once or twice a year?"

"And you, old man."

"Ha!" He leaned back, hand over his stomach as though the idea of him being my family was ridiculous. "Then you are in a world of trouble. I'd be a piss poor family member, Nash. You know that."

But what I'd had of family hadn't been much better. A father who got drunk and destroyed our lives; aunts and uncles who took care of us because they got a check from the state to do it. I hadn't seen much in the way of families at all, but what I had seen hadn't impressed me much. "No worse than what I had."

With a sigh, Roan dropped the teasing smile. He'd never

asked for any details on what had gone down between my parents, but I'd told him anyway. I'd probably told him more about my life than anyone else.

He bent forward, elbows on his knees, and I swore I could make out what he'd say before he opened his mouth. Roan was wise. He'd lived a life I'd probably never understand, and every second of it showed up on his face, in the haunted touch that made his eyes shine. "You can't keep reliving the past, son. You've got to let that go."

"Easier to say, old man."

"It's simple." He sat up, not smiling, not doing much more than giving me a cool glance that told me he wouldn't argue with me. "If you want a life, a real good life, you gotta earn it."

"The hell do you think I'm trying to do?"

"Taking over the world with money isn't what I mean. Money, hell, that comes and goes. You make it, you lose it, but at the end of the day, when you're old and ornery it's not money or the things it buys you that will make you happy. It's the people who are at your side, the ones that are there because they are yours and you are theirs. That's real, Nash. That's the realest you'll ever hear from me." He paused, moving his jaw a little as he watched me, and it seemed to me it was Roan's looks, the things he didn't have to say, that kept me silent. It was his expression and what it told me that kept me quiet. "Your woman, what's her name?"

"I told you I don't…" It was pointless to deny. She might not be mine. She might not be what I told myself I wanted, but Roan could read me. Even if I didn't admit it, she had infected every part of my life. I didn't bother lying to him. "Willow. Crazy white chick with hair that goes on forever and ass like you wouldn't believe." I took a breath, knowing I couldn't pretend that was all that drew Willow to me. "She also is funny and weird as hell, and I can't get her out of my head."

Roan nodded, working his fingers over his beard like he needed a minute to decide what advice to give me. Finally, when he nodded again, some silent decision that seemed to satisfy him, the smile returned to his face. "Good. You go to her, and you tell her all the things you think make sense. You tell her you'll do whatever she wants to keep her. You tell her you're no good without her."

"I never said I was sprung."

The laughter was loud again and I hated that it was me and my miserable life that seemed so funny to him. "Hell, Nash, you are. Maybe not bad, but you're getting there." Roan stood, slapping me on the shoulder. "There's worse things in life than bein' all sprung over a woman."

"Like?" I asked because I couldn't imagine anything worse.

Roan's eyes sparkled then, lit with something that brightened his dark skin. "Not being with one at all."

Nash

The lobby was dark when I finally made it back to our building, and the silence, the eerie quiet, put me on alert. There were only two people near the elevators, and I might have not noticed anyone at all, except one of them was Willow. Her back was to me, so she hadn't seen me, and I just stood there watching her twist a strand of her chaotic hair around her finger. Then came her laugh—sweet, high-pitched, and I noticed with a start that she was laughing with the guy standing next to her. That's when the alert I was already on flared, and my temper made me a little hot.

She wore an oversized sweater and tights, boots that hit above her knee and a chunky scarf that made her looked like she'd prepared for a hay ride in the country and not a Friday night sitting in front of her T.V. or, whatever it was that crazy chicks like Willow did when they weren't reading auras and basically messing with the calm of complete strangers.

"So," the guy said, as he leaned against the wall right next to the elevator. "You think that'll work for you? Next weekend?"

"Yeah. Sure." She sounded so excited, so upbeat.

Funny thing about jealousy; it stings a lot more when

you're the one feeling it, which made no damn sense in the least. I wanted her out of my hair. I wanted Willow to stop blocking my focus and keep clear of me. From the looks of it, she was working on doing just that. So why the hell did me seeing some burly looking guy that was too pretty to be anything more than a punk standing a little too close to Willow, speaking with a tone that he definitely wouldn't use if he was hanging with his boys, bother me so much? There was too much sweetness in his question, and it made me want to tussle with him until he stayed the hell away from her.

"All right then, *lucita*. I'll see you next weekend." The asshole nodded at me as he walked away, but I didn't bother to return the gesture. I was too damn focused on ignoring Willow as she watched me reach in front of her to push the up button.

"Nash?" she said, standing next to me as we waited for the elevator to hit the lobby.

"What's up?"

I could feel her eyes on me, that cool, calculating stare like the sun against my face, but I took a breath, not looking at her as I pushed down the need to ask her who the hell that guy was and why she'd been talking to him. I hated feeling this way—out of control and unable to handle myself, even if I kept silent. But damn, it bothered me that Willow was getting attention from anyone else— and it bothered me even more that it had worked my nerves.

"Nothing's *up*," she said, looking up at the display as the numbers above the elevator got lower and lower. "So I guess you're still denying the obvious."

My breath was loud as I exhaled, regretting that I hadn't taken the stairs the second I spotted Willow in the lobby. But it had been a long night coming back from Roan's, and the lack of sleep and the stress of everything surrounding me had worn me out; my body felt like dead weights locking my feet to the tile floor as I stood there.

"Willow, I'm not in the mood."

"Oh you don't have to tell me." She looked to her left, and I glanced at her, held back a head shake when she moved her gaze up and down my body. "Your aura is off again." She waited a beat, and I could have timed her next question down to the second. "You want me to..."

"No, I don't." I stared down at her, frowning when she looked a little hurt, but I was too damn tired to care too much that she hated my answer. "I'm tired. I just wanna crash."

The elevator bell sounded, and I waved Willow in, tired but not a complete ass, and she slipped inside, automatically pressing the buttons for both our floors. The ride up was slow, but then it always was. Mickey didn't invest too much money in maintenance to anything in the building, and the elevator was no exception. It was always getting stuck or stopping in the middle of different floors, or, if it had been a really long time since it had been serviced, it would take a solid three minutes to move between floors. By how slowly we moved, I figured the ancient elevator was due for a tune-up.

"I've been meaning to talk to you." Her voice was slightly breathless. I wanted to ask her about it, urge her on, but couldn't take the risk.

"Thought you did that the other night."

She moved next to me, flinging her hair over her shoulder, and I caught a whiff of her shampoo. It reminded me of honeysuckle and sweet pea flowers, something I hadn't been around since I was a kid back in the south.

"You know that wasn't planned." She looked down at the end of her loose braid as she raked her fingers through it, unraveling her hard work. "I'm…sorry if I was pushy the other night." She glanced at me, holding my gaze for a minute longer than I'd intended. "I was, wasn't I? Pushy, I mean."

Something in my brain told me to give her something that would take the worry from her eyes, but I was nothing if not stubborn. Even though Roan had promised I'd regret being all alone with my money and success, I wasn't ready to give up on that American Dream quite yet. I had to play cool, let her know that I wasn't interested. But, damn it was hard.

"You were fine. It was late."

"Nash…" I recognized the tone in her voice. It went all soft and sweet and Willow's hand touched the back of my arm, standing closer than she should, but not close enough for what I wanted, dammit. I closed my eyes, wincing a little when she grabbed my hand.

"I think I figured out what…"

But Willow didn't get a chance to finish her sentence. The door slid open, and I stepped through with her right at my heels, trailing behind me, intending no doubt to continue the conversation in my place. But leaning against my door was the most beautiful woman in the world. She was thinner than when I'd seen her last, and when she saw me, her smile went megawatt, and I sort of forgot about Willow for a second.

"Hey," she said, glancing between me and Willow, her smile never dimming.

My crazy neighbor dropped my hand like my fingers stung her, and I could feel the tension snap as she stepped away from me. I could have explained. It would have been the decent thing to do, but my jealous ego was still smarting from Willow being chatted up by that flirty Puerto Rican down in the lobby.

I played the prick and decided to take advantage of the situation.

"Hey!" I said in my warmest, most delighted voice, and leaned in to plant a kiss on my visitor's cheek as I moved to unlock my door. "I'll see you later," I tossed over my shoulder to Willow, resisting the temptation to catch her reflection in the hallway mirror next to my door. "Come inside, sweetness…" I trailed off, and ushered the woman inside, not looking back, too much of a coward to watch the look of hurt on Willow's face.

Nash

"I've seen you do some shitty things before, but I gotta say, that was the shittiest."

Natalie followed me around the living room, her voice raising as I discarded my keys and wallet on the coffee table. "Ah, Sis, it was perfect timing. It's better that she thinks I'm taken."

"Damn, Nash, is this you pulling that 'I'm too busy and important' nonsense? Because, if it is, I gotta say, little brother, that it's played out as hell. You aren't the G that you think you are."

"Nat…"

"I come here to see you because you've ignored my phone calls and texts for weeks, and here I find you blowing off some pretty young thing that clearly is into you." I tried to play off the quick jerk of my gaze at my sister, attempting to divert that stupid hopeful look I knew was in my eyes. I looked a little too encouraged, a lot too pathetic. "Oh…so I'm right? You want her to be into you?"

I slumped in my recliner, leaning back with my hands covering my face. Natalie sat next to me on the sofa arm, waiting. I hated when she did that, like she was so damn convinced I'd unload all my issues on her and wait for her to fix my problem. I didn't feel like hearing her nag at me, I'd had enough of that for one night from Roan. Instead, I shot for deflection.

"What's this little brother mess? Little brother, my ass."

"I came out first."

"Yeah, a whole four minutes before me. That's doesn't count."

Natalie shook her head, ignoring my assertion to glare at me like I'd earned it. "You gonna tell me what's going on with you?"

"You not here just for me. I know that."

I never won when we stared each other down, but I tried hard just then, matching my twin glare for glare until she rolled her eyes. "I have a new designer to check out."

"Uh huh…"

"But I wanted to check up on you, too." She smacked my arm when I shook my head. "Stop changing the subject. You gonna tell me what's going on with that girl?"

"No." She should have known better. Things hadn't changed that much since I last saw her. My twin had been gearing up for a new gig on a sitcom for a major network, doing the set design. By the labels she wore and the jewelry she sported, I got the feeling things were going pretty good. "New purse?" I said, nodding to the Prada bag on her arm.

She smacked me in the arm again, lowering herself onto the sofa when I laughed at her. "Tell me."

And so, I did. Everything. About Willow and my aura, about the dreams that felt so real. I unloaded everything to my sister just like I'd always done; we'd shared the worst of our drama and not once had we looked down on each other. Wonder Twins and all, that wasn't just some DC Comics fantasy. Nat was my down-for-whatever sister. My drama was hers, and right then all of mine was tied up in Willow.

"You like her." I shook my head and Nat laughed, reminding me of Roan's smug ass. "It's true. You're very into her."

"Whatever," I said, slipping into the hall to grab a pillow and blanket as my sister sat on the coffee table. "I got no time for anyone." I stripped of my shirt and flopped onto the sofa, watching Nat as she looked me over. "What?"

"We can table this for tomorrow, but for now, I gotta tell you something."

She had that worried, shifty-eyed thing happening, something that always told me that bad news was coming. Nat had gotten the same look on her face when she told me our father had contacted her when he got out of prison, and when she had gotten pregnant and didn't plan on keeping the baby. Bad news always followed that look.

"Damn, Nat…what the hell is it?"

She adjusted on the table, tapping her index fingers together, a nervous annoying habit she had. "Hear me out, okay?"

I sat up, pulling my feet on the floor while I held the pillow over my lap. "Are you pregnant again?"

"What? Oh God, Nash, really?" She flipped the bird at me, scowling a little. "Your nephew is the only one I'm gonna have, ever. You know this, and he's happy with his parents in New Orleans, okay? Give me a little credit for learning from past behavior."

"All right, my bad." I tossed the pillow to my side and waited. When she only looked at me, I folded my arms, clearing my throat. "Just come out and…"

"I've been spending time with…Dad. For about a year now."

Something loosened in my chest; it felt hot and bitter, stinging as I took in a long breath. Natalie watched me close, her eyes cautious, concerned. She had spoken to the man responsible for our mother's death. The asshole who took everything away from us.

"What the hell is that supposed to mean?"

We sat there for a few seconds, watching, waiting, as the threat of an argument moved around us like a fog, choking every good thought, every emotion that would make me admit how much I'd missed her. This was a game changer, something I couldn't easily stomach.

"Before you start getting all worked up and yell at me, I'll tell you he was in treatment on the inside. He's been sober thirteen years, Nash, and he got his GED while he was locked up and is working on his bachelor's at a small college out in San Francisco."

Nat stopped tapping her fingers and had instead taken up a

little bounce with her knee, moving without knowing she was doing it, nervously watching me as I let her words sink in.

Finally, when she stopped moving her knee, I sat back, hand on the back of my head because it felt like the only thing that would ground me to the earth. "And?" I spit out.

"And what?" I tilted my head, glaring at my sister until she stood, slipping off her shoes and moving them next to her purse at the bar. "You gonna give him shit for trying to better himself or me shit for wanting to have a relationship?"

"Hell, yes."

"My God, Nash, he was sick. Addiction is an illness like cancer or diabetes."

"Except, when you get cancer, it's only your life that's in danger."

"Nash…"

"He killed her, Nat."

"He did. And he's sorry for that. He really is. But nothing he can do now will bring her back. We have to come to terms with that."

I shook my head, ready to yell, to scream until she saw reason, but I knew better. Natalie was bullheaded. If she latched onto something or someone it stuck. Even, I guessed, if it was the man who took our mother from us both.

"You can't just forget…"

"No, you can't, but sugar, you have to learn to

forgive." Nat's voice was strong, but she didn't yell. It was a calm tone, something she'd perfected when we were kids and temper and anxiety had turned me into a bad seed. It was her nurturing way, and that firm, confident tone never failed to pull me back from the edge. But this wasn't me buckling to peer pressure from asshole kids putting on me to lift beer from a convenience store cooler. This was the man I'd always hated, inching his way back into my sister's life.

Still, Nat adopted that tone and just the sound of it had me tamping down my anger. She leaned forward, taking my hand. "You've got yourself all twisted up over the stuff that happened to us. You're still letting it rule your life."

"I am not." I jerked my hand back and leaned against the sofa with my arms over my chest.

"Really? So pushing away women, not wanting to rely on anyone at all, thinking that your life will be perfect with enough money? That all comes from losing everything you had as a kid. It comes from not trusting the one person who should have never let you down."

"Yeah?"

"So maybe if you let it, that mess will keep you down. That happens, little brother, and the man who killed our mother, also killed the person you were back then. You hold on to that, and Nash, that kid stays dead."

She knew she'd had me. I tried to tell myself I was too tired to argue. I tried to move the reason and logic around in my head so that I made sense, so that my reason was sound. But Nat always saw things differently than me. She always saw the potential, always had hope even in the grayest parts of our lives.

"Man, whatever." I stood, stretching as she moved in front of me. "We'll talk about this tomorrow." I nodded toward the hallway. She's stayed with me a half-a-dozen times and knew the routine. "You take the bed." I laid back down on the sofa, fluffing the pillow as I stifled a yawn. "For now, let me sleep."

New Orleans

After I didn't come back home, and Mr. Simoneaux's old Chevy had circled our driveway for the third time, Mama and Uncle Aron came looking where I'd most likely be— the tree house. We'd seen the headlights from our hiding spot; whether it was him looking to see where Dempsey had gotten off to or maybe Andres telling some lie about me, making the man bring him around to see things over, I wasn't sure. But Mama made her irritation known.

"Why you hiding up there, girl? You do something to that hateful man?"

"No, Mama. Not me. I ain't done nothing."

"You always running your mouth, sassing folk…" Then she shut herself up when I climbed down and she noticed how I held the too-big shirt Dempsey gave me over my chest. She didn't fuss about how I'd missed the delivery, then, not when Dempsey climbed down after me, then

took my hand and went to move in front of me a little, as if to run interference between me and my kin. Both Mama and Aron looked at me holding Dempsey's button up over my chest like it was only a flimsy excuse to cover myself and then traded a look that was both worried and a whole lot scared.

"Ms. Lanoix, it was me, honest. I'm the one he's looking for." Dempsey had a way of speaking to grownups. It was how calm he could make his voice. It was deep, deeper than it should be at only seventeen, maybe that was what put people at ease. "I forgot about cleaning up after myself again when I got done fishing this afternoon. Left all the bait and tackle on the dock. He's probably looking to skin my hide."

A few moments passed with nobody saying anything. Mama was no fool, she knew when someone was trying to pull something over on her, but maybe she thought I wasn't worth the trouble of finding out what that something might be. The more we stood there, me looking at the ground and Dempsey looking at Mama liked a wupped pup, the more the anger seemed to leach out of her and resignation set in. Finally she signed, and gave Dempsey a soft look that she'd never once given me. For Dempsey, though, it came easy enough. "Fine then." She told him with one head shake that he needed to keep after himself. "Mind your business, Dempsey Simoneaux, and don't bring your daddy's belt anywhere near this property."

"No ma'am. Wouldn't hear of it."

It satisfied her enough that she seemed to forget how late the night had gotten or that it was the first time she didn't settle Dempsey on Bastie's sofa or at least on the floor in Sylv's room. Uncle Aron, though, wasn't so easy to take Dempsey at his word.

Mama had just made it through the front door when Uncle Aron pulled a cigarette from his front pocket, eyes steady, gaze moving between me and Dempsey as we watched him. He let out a long, slow breath and smoke puffed and billowed around his head in lazy, round rings. "The two of you, by God, will do us all in." Another drag and Uncle Aron nodded for us to follow, leading us toward the fence line and the broken path that led the back way from Bastie's property and the south end of the river. "Tell me now," he said, leaning against the fence post, flicking ashes that burned orange-red then faded to nothing as it landed on the black ground. "What's all the fuss about?"

And so, I told him about Andres and his searching, drunk hands, about him tearing my shirt and me running like loon after I popped that fat white man real good in the eye. It took only a few minutes, with Dempsey adding how he'd come to find me in the tree house looking more vexed than a kitten, claws deep on the bow of a sinking boat.

Aron was smooth, slow, with everything he did. There was a little white at his temples and he wore his mustache neat and trimmed. He kept himself looking sharp with fine pressed suits and a fedora for whatever job each day would bring. Tonight he wore a pair of dark slacks and a shirt opened at the collar. But the fedora was sharp and pristine and the suspenders he wore had gold clips and teeth. It was date night, and by the look of his slow grin and missed-button state of his shirt, date night had been a good one.

"Well now." Another drag and my uncle threw the cigarette to the ground, stamping out the small flame with his heel. "Seems to me it'd

be best if the pair of you keep to yourselves this lovely night."

"I can sleep in the tree house." Dempsey shrugged as though there was nothing to be debated. Most nights when we stayed at the farm, he slept in the tree house just to be out of his family's sight. "There's a blanket up there, I'll be fine."

"That won't work," Aron replied, taking off his hat to smooth back the tips of his hair that had gotten mussed in whatever activity he'd gotten into. "Your daddy is fool enough that he'd come up that ladder and drag you out by your ears." He thought a second, flopping the hat back on his head. "And Joe Andres might sober up enough to remember who gave him the shiner I bet he's sporting." He glanced at me, a hesitant smile stretching across his face.

Dempsey grabbed my hand again, squeezing it tight as though he wanted me to not worry over the "mights" Aron laid out for us.

"Nah, I reckon its best you both clear out." He glanced back toward the cottage then looked at us again, lowering his voice as though he was sure someone was listening. "Can I trust you two to walk out to the fish shack and stay there?" We both nodded, not bothering to look at each other. "And can you promise me, Dempsey Simoneaux, on your honor, you won't be thinking of things you ought not think about with my niece in the same room?"

Dempsey widened his eyes, blushing a little before he nodded quick. "Good. You keep her safe and don't get up to anything funny. I'll be down to check up on you in the morning, but mind what you're doing cause I won't be telling you exactly how early I'll come get you."

"Of course. We'll…it'll be all fine," Dempsey promised then lifted back the thick brush hiding the small opening to the trail, motioning me to go ahead first. Luckily the moon was out, and though it was slow going, we could see the

path to follow.

We walked in silence for a few long minutes until Dempsey didn't seem to take the quiet and started up whistling "Black Water Blues," likely because he knew how much I loved Bessie Smith. I just started in on a chorus, singing about having no place to go, when Dempsey stopped me, covering my mouth with his hand as he pressed right behind me. He leaned down and the scent of his breath, like peppermint, came soft against my cheek.

"There," he whispered, nodding to our right beyond the cover of the trail. By then we had walked past my Mimi's property line and crossed over back into the Simoneaux land that edged along the river. My heart was pounding like a scared rabbit, and when Dempsey tried backing away, I grabbed his arm, pulling him tighter still just to keep myself from running or my fingers from shaking something awful.

The river was low this time of year when the hurricane season had yet to start. There would be heavy rains, and storms that would come—one was brewing in the gulf, coming in from Alabama. It had been on the radio and was all my Bastie could talk about and fret over for a week straight. But the boat passing around the riverbank right now had no problems cutting through the dark water.

There were voices and the trickle of water moving as a paddle dipped in and out of the water. I couldn't make out who they were even as we sidled closer toward the river, staying beneath the heavy limbs of the cypress that skirted toward the end of the trail, but there definitely was more than one voice echoing quietly over the water.

"Poachers, looking for gators from the sound of it," Dempsey

whispered in my ear.

"They not in season?" I only asked to keep Dempsey leaning close to be heard. I did so like the way he smelled and how much heat his body made as he came close to me.

"No. I don't reckon. If they were, those boys would be out during the day hunting." The small boat floated further up the river, and Dempsey took my hand, pulling me away from the trail and toward the small shack some fifty feet back off the water.

He nodded at the broken cinderblocks Aron had fashioned into a walkway and Dempsey helped me navigate it, stopping to offer me his hand and picking me up a little by my waist to make sure I made it from the path without slipping.

The small front door was made from three thick planks of pine with three smaller pieces nailed across, and as Dempsey grabbed the knotted twine of rope looped into a small hole in the wood that serves as handle, the small hinges that had rusted from the weather and moisture in the air made what seemed to be an earth-shattering screech, but probably wasn't all that loud.

"That Aron is clever."

"Not so clever." I nodded a thanks to Dempsey as he held open the door, but I didn't step inside straight away; instead, we both leaned inward, looking over the small bucket in the corner upturned, I reckoned, to act as a seat and the two fishing poles leaned against one corner of the tiny shack. "He comes out here when he's had too much whiskey, and Mimi won't let him in the house. Drunk fool will throw a line out that window at two in the morning, thinking he'll surprise the catfish when they're half asleep."

"Does it work?" There was a little laugh in Dempsey's voice, like he already knew the answer to his question.

"Comes home with dozens, more than that when he's good and drunk."

"Then I won't fault the man for his drink if it means your Mimi will fry up some catfish for us."

Dempsey smiled at my shaking head then followed me away from the shack to sit near the bank. "There's a purple sky tonight." It was something Bastie liked the best about the spring. The sky on the Manchac was always clearest at night, but in the spring the weather was the brightest, like God settled the seas and calmed the wind so that we could have a clear sight of the most beautiful of his kingdom.

"What did your Bastie say about it? I forget."

"Purple skies come when God is in court. He comes close to us, and the purple we see is the hem of His royal cloak."

Dempsey shook his head, smiling to himself as we both looked up into the dark sky. It wasn't only purple, but blue with swirls of gray swimming in the darkness around us. If I looked away from Dempsey, I could only make out his silhouette from the corner of my eye. He looked dark as coal in that purple light.

"If God is visiting, He might not like to see what's happening here."

Dempsey was right. The way things were turning, how restless and mean folk had gotten—how our own lives had found the same restlessness, wouldn't make any God happy looking down on it.

"Maybe He only sees the good among us."

Dempsey went quiet, slipping his hand to mine to move his palm over the top of my fingers. "Then He only sees you, Sook."

And then Dempsey, who swore he loved me, leaned close, pulled my face toward his and showed me for a little while that I wasn't the only good one in that small corner of our world.

Twelve

Nash

When I was young, my father wore a Bulls ball cap. It was red and black and had Jordan's number twenty-three taking up much of the right side. He'd won it from a work raffle. Five bucks had gotten him a Bulls swag pack and a chance at airfare and two tickets to the Bulls/Celtics game that season. He'd spent twenty bucks that day: five on the ticket and fifteen on a case of Bud he'd polished off before his lunch break ended.

I only remembered that because he'd been fired for drinking the Bud, and my mother threw the cap out the second-floor window when he came home that night. I'd found it the next morning on my way to the bus stop, stepping over my father, who'd passed out on the front porch and stayed there the whole night.

That morning, I'd looked down at him, face pale and hollow, lips chapped and white, and realized for the first time in my brief nine years, that my father was a loser. He wasn't the cut-up he pretended to be when he and Mom drank during the Falcons games, laughing and teasing each other when the dirty birds won. He wasn't the guy that would stay sober for a couple of weeks, meeting me and Nat at the bus stop, fixing our dinners when Mom worked late or took a

163

night class. He was the guy who'd passed out on the porch with a brand-new Bulls cap twenty feet away from him near the garbage can. He was the asshole who made my mother cry when she thought we were asleep.

More than anything, I was petrified of turning into him.

It was the main reason I'd kept to myself, had stayed clear of any drama that might contribute in any way in making me more like my father.

"You gonna sleep all day?" Nat called, pulling me from my thoughts and what remained of my sleep and damn Sookie and her drama that locked me down each night. There had been the boy again, Dempsey, and the asshole who'd tried attacking her. It felt like metal had lodged itself in my chest when I thought of that little girl—something about her made me rage with anger, something made me sick with guilt. I couldn't place her, couldn't do more than blink away her face, the fear she'd felt and the sweetness, how that boy had made her feel when he… I was losing it. I was losing my damn mind.

The scent of bacon and pancakes hung in the air, making my mouth water, and I got up from the sofa, a little disoriented by the thick blanket on the floor and the pillow on the other end of the room.

"Bad dream last night?" Nat asked, pouring a mug of coffee for me as I dropped onto the stool in front of the island. I shrugged, and my sister shook her head. "You were fussing all night. Woke me up twice."

She'd brought dark roast with her, and the smell, the taste, reminded me of milk coffee my mom let me make when I was ten and wanted to drink with her before she left for work. It made me feel grown to watch her move around the kitchen, getting ready, packing her lunch and complaining about all the things she'd never finish up before she had to leave for her office. Now that coffee was an elixir I needed to be more human and damn sure more awake.

"You wanna talk about the dream?" Nat leaned on the island, pushing a plate in front of me, and I dove in, shaking my head as I shoveled a forkful of pancake in my mouth so I couldn't talk. "You're such an ass sometimes, Nash." I looked up at her, eyes squinting to glare at her, but she only smiled back, laughing at me because she knew I was aware I could never get her to back off with some punk-ass frown. "Boy, please. Put away the grump face and tell me about the dream."

I swallowed, grabbing a paper towel from the roll to clean the syrup from my face. "Nothing to tell, really. It's stress. I'm under a deadline and distracted. That's all it is."

"Didn't sound like…"

"Jesus, Nat, I'm fine." I didn't mean to snap at her, or make her my voice go all loud and bitchy. By the rigid lines along her mouth I got the feeling Natalie didn't appreciate my tone, no matter if I meant it or not. "I'm sorry…it's just, that girl?"

"The one you wanted to make jealous?" She smiled when I shook my head. "What about her?"

"She's…the distraction, and it's messing with me bad. It's a damn fog I can't clear away."

Nat polished off her coffee, staring out the stretch of windows to my right, her long red nails tapping against the handle. It took her a minute to gather her thoughts, to form an opinion about how much of a mess I was at the moment, but then she rinsed her cup and leaned against the sink, watching me eat, staring hard as though she needed to consider her words carefully before dishing them out.

"Maybe that's what you need, Nash."

"A distraction?"

Natalie shook her head, resting on her palms in front of me. "This girl. From the way your eyes go all bright and round when you talk about her, and how you looked at her last night, how hurt she seemed when she saw me, I don't think she's the fog."

"What the hell else could she be?"

Nat's smile came back just then, and it loosened the tension that had set up inside my shoulders and chest since I saw Willow with that guy the night before. It was kind of uncanny how she could do that for me, but I loved her for it. "Girl like that, she isn't anyone's fog, Nash. She's the light that clears all the bad away. You might want to admit that before she realizes what a mess you are."

Twice in two days I'd gotten the advice to pull my head out

of my ass. Roan spoke it because he was old and thought he knew best. Nat did it because she thought I'd never realize what was in front of me without a little push. I didn't even want to stop to think if they were right or not.

It was both their voices I tried to block out as I got dressed that morning, as Nat went on and on about me coming to visit her out in Cali, though I knew she only asked because she wanted to "accidentally" run into our father while I was in town. I wasn't an idiot.

"Maybe next year, when things are a little more settled with my company," I'd told her, holding open the door for her as we left the lobby.

"You said that last year. And six months before that. It's been almost two years since you came to visit me. That's three times now I've flown out here to see you, little brother."

"You said you only came to town to check out a new designer. Don't play like you came here just to see me." But that frown was tight and the glare was lethal. Nat might have added me to her itinerary, but I was not afterthought. "Sorry."

It really had been that long, though I would have sworn she was wrong. Stuff gets messed up in life, promises are made, then broken, intention paves every path you make, even the one that leads to hell. I'd spent so much time focusing on my own stuff that I forgot there were people who needed me. People like Nat, who lived on her own in California. People like Roan who pretended he didn't need anything but a good book, his birds, and a windless day. No matter what I'd tried to make of my life, no matter how many times I promised myself I didn't need anyone, I forgot that people still needed me.

"Hell, Nat, I'm sorry. Really." She lost the small wounded look on her face, and her expression softened, head tilting as she watched me. "I honestly don't think...I mean, the business and investors... God, I've been working so hard on getting ready for this meeting next week that I forget to eat or sleep or even check up on you." She smiled then, waving her hand to hail a cab as I shook my head. "I got to be the worst damn brother in the world."

"Nah," she said pulling her bag up on her shoulder. "Just sometimes remember the world doesn't need conquering. Plenty of fools have tried and failed at that." Nat's eyebrows went up, and she looked over my shoulder, smile lethal now. "And try to remember that even if you manage to rule the world, the view from the top is a little boring when you're sitting up there all alone."

"Sis..."

"You think, maybe, when you're ready, when you come to see me that you'd be up for seeing..."

"No." I hated to have my sister leave with my frown and that sharp bite in my voice, but there are some things you can't squash so easy. Natalie shook her head, like she was amazed by me and how tight my grip was on the past, how close I kept my anger. But sometimes, hating my father was the only thing that kept me warm at night. "I'm sorry. You...you know I got you, no matter what. But this, Natalie? I just...I can't..."

"I know," she said, stopping me to pull me close and hug me. "I know. Just, instead of 'no', say 'not yet,' okay? For me?"

She held me a little, right there out on the sidewalk, and for the first time in weeks, my entire body relaxed. I hadn't felt that since the night in my apartment when Willow worked her wild juju on me. My sister pulled away, touching my cheek, and pushed the smile back on her face. "I'll see you, Nash." She kissed me then, pulling me into another hug that threatened to break my bones, before I opened the cab door for her, and she was off, back to her life away from me.

It was only when I turned around to head toward the station that I noticed Willow on her cell, glancing away from me, then back up again. I wanted to stop her before she walked off. I wanted to tell her I was sorry for being a punk, for trying to make her jealous. I thought about just grabbing her and kissing her and doing my best to forget all those walls I'd built to keep from failing myself or anyone else that came along.

Willow's face was drawn, her skin paler than it had been last night. She carried a white box under her arm—more magical cupcakes I guessed—and from the way her hair looked more tousled than normal, I guessed she'd spent the night in her kitchen baking, because it helped when she was restless, because it distracted her from the things she didn't want to face. Same as me, Willow deflected.

She still had no clue that Natalie was my sister, and now she had just seen me say goodbye the "morning after"...

I wondered just then if Willow would talk to me, or if I'd messed things up with my childish jealousy so bad that she wouldn't have anything to do with me again, and I would have messed up any chance I had with her, whether I wanted it or not.

But before I could make a move, Willow's phone rang, and she looked down at it, turning away from me, disappearing down the street before I made it to the front entrance, and something knotted deep inside my chest, something I didn't think I could loosen on my own. Something I knew I'd put there by being a coward.

Thirteen

Willow

There were baking dishes littered around my small kitchen, and the entire apartment smelled like cupcakes and the sweet decadence of frosting and dark ale. I'd attempted Irish Car Bombs again and had spilled a bottle of Guinness on my floor, the sticky mess collecting to pool into the grout line on my tile floor.

The oven had sounded ten minutes ago, five minutes after I should have opened the door and the latest batch was a burnt mess.

"Stupid Guinness," I griped to the oven and the dark brown cupcakes that had cost me ten bucks to make. That definitely wouldn't make the cut. I pulled on the room temperature beer, letting the half-empty bottle empty down my throat. "Stupid me."

My sofa was large and comfy, a hand-me-down piece Effie had given me when her second job as a spa owner had finally turned a profit. It seemed everyone wanted to meditate and get a facial on the same day. My friend capitalized on it. But me and the cupcakes? No. Today wasn't a good day for my little business, and I thought about my great-grandmother just then, wondering how many burned batches of cookies and brownies she had to go through to get her recipes perfected. I wondered if the weight of her life ever kept her from concentrating on getting the job done.

At my right, on the hall table that led out of the front room, sat a picture of my great-grandparents on their wedding day. Their smiles were bright and lit up their entire faces, and I glanced between that picture and my own reflection in the mirror above the mantel. My face was shaped precisely like my great-grandfather's, but my eyes, they belonged to her. I tried to smile, thinking of the cookies I'd delivered to the homeless shelter a few blocks down from our building. The director had been kind, had thanked me over and over, and I watched myself in the mirror, gaze shifting back to my grandparents' picture and back to the mirror as I thought of that day at the shelter. But my eyes didn't gleam quite as bright, and my smile, no matter how closely it resembled my grandfather's, didn't seem as wide.

I kept watching, zoning out, forgetting the shelter, forgetting that picture, and Nash's face slipped to my conscience and stayed at the front of my mind. His mouth, his smile, that sweet, beautiful smile…the sound of his laughter and the rich, full sound of his voice. Before I knew I'd done it, my face ached a little with the smile that wouldn't leave my features, and I shot my gaze back and forth from the picture to the mirror and slouched against the billowing pillows arranged around the sofa.

Nash. He was the only thing that made my eyes sparkle like my great-grandmother's. He was the only thought that made me look

exactly like my grandfather.

I turned on my side, stuffing the pillow against my chest as I recalled the precise arc of his face, the exact bend of his mouth and the soft brush of his tongue. It was only then that I let the day go from me. I put away thoughts of burnt cupcakes and smiles that didn't match my great-grandparents'. It was only with Nash's face frozen in my thoughts that I thought my dreams would stay in the present.

I was wrong.

Washington, D.C.

We existed in our own world. Away from my classes, from my family, from his friends, Isaac and I became an island, distant, exotic and wholly decadent. There were moments when just the stretch of his smile would send a thrill to my stomach and other places tantalized by that look, and I was left breathless and weak. Other times I nestled against his chest with those wide arms around me, his mouth at the shell of my ear whispering promises that we pretended were real and honest and true. They felt that way, in those stolen moments.

I met him every night after his shift ended, with Lenny keeping watch and the library free from anyone who'd care what we were up to. The curve of his top lip and the tiny space between his front teeth were small imperfections I found delicious—irresistible—and Isaac knew it. He knew me, in just those few short weeks; he had discovered how to hold my neck so that our mouths met at the perfect angle. He knew that a kiss on the base of my throat would have me frantic and eager and

desperate for his mouth. Isaac knew that I didn't like being called "baby,"
Trent's pet name for me. He knew my brother was my best friend and that in my
eyes, no one's father was better than mine.

And that's where the problems started to surface.

"No matter what you say, no man is gonna be too happy about someone
like me…"

"Don't you finish that sentence." My face was flushed and my lips still
swollen from his kisses, when I pushed him back. It was the same argument we'd
had for a week, and it stemmed from my parents wanting details about why I'd
broken up with Trent.

"Someone like me, coming to knock at his front door, telling him I'm
there for his little girl?"

"You don't know him. My family isn't like that, especially not my
Dad."

But he hadn't believed me, not then, not even when I told him my brother
had come to see me, not batting an eye over why I'd decided to remain on campus
during the summer break instead of staying with our family at the lake house.

Ryan had come to my dorm, a care package from my mother under his
arm, and had gotten downright nosey about how I'd been spending my time.

"It's a man," he stated.

"What?" He watched me shove the box into my room and waited in the
hallway to walk with me to the park. "You've been drinking, right? Long night
at Gadsby's that you haven't recovered from? I know how the ice well fascinates
you."

"Listen to me, little sister, I know you better than anyone. If you were

just busy with studying and school projects, you wouldn't have missed Sunday out on Lake Deer Creek. Not with the Crafts joining us. You love Joanie Craft and haven't missed a chance to race her to the pier since you were twelve."

"I'm not twelve, Ryan."

"Obviously," he said, holding the door open for me as we left the building, "but that whole not-being-twelve thing didn't stop you last summer. She complained the entire weekend about not being able to have a rematch."

*He hadn't been wrong. No amount of studying could quell my competitive nature, especially not against Joanie Craft. She was a sore loser, and I'd wanted to beat her two years running. But then Isaac borrowed Lenny's Bel Air and we drove down the **G.W. Parkway** for hours. The roads twisted into loops along the backdrop of lush green forests that seem to stretch on for acres and hilltops that billowed up and down among all that thick greenery. They were supposed to be building a state park in the area, but the day had been a little overcast, and the road was nearly empty. It had been a perfect afternoon. Isaac parked along a dip in the tree line, hiding the Bel Air behind thick-hanging limbs that brushed the ground. I blushed to think of how we spent those next few hours hidden behind the greenery, with the birds serenading us and the breeze blowing through the open windows.*

I hadn't thought about Joanie Craft or our swimming races all afternoon. There had been Isaac kissing my neck, quoting Zora Neale Hurston, telling me with his mouth and fingers what he thought it felt like when "love makes your soul crawl out from its hiding place." He

loved her work—so did I—and we got drunk on Hurston's words, on the slow,
honeyed sound of Billie Holiday working her own poetry on the radio, on the scent
of sweat and sweetness of each other in that car. There had only been Isaac and
me and the sound of his heartbeat against my ear as we watched the purple sky
becoming inky black.

"So?" Ryan had said, the question hidden in the inflection of his voice.
"So, maybe *there's a guy."*

There was a little tease edging around his laugh, and I knew I'd be
harassed relentlessly. We cleared the main campus water fountain and neared the
park benches, a row of thirteen to symbolize Lincoln's greatest accomplishment. It
was on the last bench that I sat, with Ryan's focused stare waiting on me to
elaborate.

"Do I know him?" Ryan stretched an arm behind me on the bench, and
I concentrated on two pigeons flying between the spray of fountain water across
from our seat. The day was warmer than it should have been for early summer,
but there was a breeze that made it bearable.

"Not unless you're familiar with the cleaning crew in the library."

Ryan's smile dimmed, and an eyebrow shot up. "Cleaning crew?" I
nodded, silently inviting him to ask the accusatory questions. "As in, janitor?"
Another nod and my brother went quiet.

He knew what that meant. There weren't many white men doing service
work at the university. As part of their cultural policy, the university had made
work-study enrollment possible, had even offered audited classes to their employees
who wanted to improve well enough to become fulltime students. Students of any
race could subsidize their tuition with student worker jobs. Lenny was one of those

students, and Isaac was working toward that as well, aiming to start at Lincoln the next semester. He just needed to perfect his application and work on his admissions essay. But it was common knowledge that many of the student worker service positions were held by black students.

It was one thing for my family to champion equality—they had, my entire life. My Jewish mother had seen her entire family wiped out in concentration camps; my father had been one of the soldiers liberating her camp. Intolerance wasn't something they forgave easily. It's why they had devoted themselves to working toward civil rights. But their only daughter, their little girl, falling for a black man? In D.C., at the height of the civil rights movement? Well. I wasn't sure how they'd react. The longer Ryan's silence stretched, the more uneasy I felt with my belief that who I loved, no matter who they were, didn't really matter to my family.

After what felt like hours, Ryan sat up, joining me in my distracted focus on the pigeons and their fountain diving. When he spoke, his attention stayed on the birds. "Is he a good man, Riley?" Then he held up his hand, stopping me before I could answer. "What am I saying? Of course he is. You wouldn't fall for a jerk."

"No," I said, coming close to admitting what had pushed me and Isaac together, but that would bring Trent's obnoxious behavior front and center right at a crucial time for the Voting Rights Act. "No, I couldn't be with anything but a good man." I paused, turning to face my brother, and he glanced at me, his face relaxing when I smiled. "He...he makes me feel safe, Ryan. He makes me just so damn happy."

I didn't have the words to explain to my brother the thousand small things that Isaac did that made me laugh, made me think. I only knew that our conversations went on for hours, even before he first kissed me. I only knew that he asked me what I thought about issues and actually listened to my answers, that he would tell me what he honestly thought, and didn't try to change my mind when our opinions differed. We read together at the library when there was no one around. Sometimes he read pages and pages out loud with that rich, booming voice, and it sounded like heaven to me. Isaac liked to hold my hand even when we walked down the street, even when his pinky curled around mine drew the attention of total strangers. He made me laugh; he made me think, and I liked to believe I did the same to him. But Ryan didn't seem to need to know any of that. Ryan loved me. He was my best friend in the whole world, and he likely could see that I was truly happy. The rush of it colored my face.

"Well, then," he finally said, smile wide, eyes brightened with laughter again. "That's all that matters, isn't it?" The pigeons flew off and my brother ignored them, took to shaking his head as though the questions he had didn't matter in the least. Ryan nudged my arm, a playful gesture he'd always done when he wanted to tease me. "Imagine that, my kid sister in love. Wonders never cease."

"Very funny." He stood, leading me away from the bench and past the fountains. "You never know, maybe you'll luck up and find someone someday," I quipped.

"No way, sis. One O'Bryant in love is more than this city can handle."

The phone had not stopped ringing for a solid week. The summer still moved on,

but Trent hadn't moved on with it. As August approached, word was the President was about to sign the Voting Rights Act. That meant Trent would lose the leverage he had that kept me from announcing to my family and the world the reasons why we had broken up. It had been nearly a month since he'd hit me. A month since the first time Isaac kissed me. It made no sense for Trent to be so relentless, but then, Trent wasn't used to being denied anything. His image was more important to him than anything, and like most bullies, he didn't mind who got hurt as long as he got his way. I very well might have been the only one who'd ever told him no, and I was pretty sure his vanity hadn't accepted it, even a month later.

"I'm going to take the phone off the hook," I threatened Trent when I finally answered the phone after an hour had passed and he kept calling with no let up. I didn't much worry about him coming to my dorm; Mr. Thomas, an older Texan around my father's age who took shrapnel to the knee in Japan during the war, took his security guard duties seriously. He wouldn't even let Ryan sit for too long in the lobby unless I was with him.

"You're being a little ridiculous, Riley. This childish behavior of yours has gone on too long, and Senator Mansfield is sponsoring an important dinner. I'm sure your father has mentioned it."

"He might have."

"Of course he has." There was a confident ease to his tone that made him sound too familiar, too sure of himself. "I'll need you to accompany me. My father doesn't know that you and I have quarreled, and he'll expect you there with me."

"You and your father can expect all you want, Trent. I'll be

there, but I won't be with you."

I hung up before he could make a complaint, in a hurry to meet Isaac at the library after his shift. He'd gone to see his sister, up from Atlanta, in Richmond while she visited friends, and I'd not seen him in nearly two days. My fingertips tingled, the closer I came to the library. I'd missed touching him, kissing him. I missed everything that only Isaac could make me feel.

It seemed like the silence was exceptionally heavy around the library when I entered, though I wasn't sure if it had anything to do with Trent's call, or just my missing Isaac.

We'd spent almost every day together over the past month—at the library, necking in the stacks, sometimes taking Lenny's Bel Air to New York to attend poetry slams or hear really good jazz. Isaac came alive in New York, where there wasn't nearly as much attention given to us. We were one couple among many that looked a little out of place, who came and went as they pleased regardless of their surroundings.

Now though, something odd and unsettling buzzed around my stomach as I moved through the silent lobby. I spotted Mr. Welis reading a paper as he leaned against the front desk, a small mug of coffee on the desk top.

"Miss O'Bryant, good evening."

"Hi, Mr. Welis." We rarely spoke, Mr. Welis and me, only a handful of times when he'd ask what I thought of Isaac's chances of getting into Lincoln. The older man wasn't a stranger. To my surprise, the older man never glared at me the way Lenny did sometimes.

"You looking for someone, Miss Riley?" He had a nice smile and beautiful eyes, nearly green, which looked nice against the dark complexion of his

skin. He was lighter than Lenny, but not as light-skinned as Isaac, and handsome for an older gentleman.

The question threw me off a bit. Generally, Mr. Welis would smile a little when he spotted me and Isaac together. Mostly, though, he just ignored us altogether.

"Uh…no," I said, listening to my gut to keep Isaac's name out of our conversation. "Just going to study a little before the library closes."

He nodded, his smile a little bigger than I thought it should be, but before I could give it any consideration at all, he turned back to his paper like we hadn't spoken.

I moved further into the library, expecting to hear some noise, anything to lead me to wherever Isaac was, but all was quiet. Lenny mopped the second-floor tiles, but he didn't hum or whistle like he normally did while he worked. And Isaac wasn't anywhere to be found—not on the first-floor kitchenette or by the elevators where he usually met me when I arrived.

Something felt wrong… off somehow. For the first time since I'd begun hiding out at the Lincoln University library, it didn't feel like home. As I moved back toward the sound of Lenny's mop moving, I realized the reason the place didn't feel like home was because Isaac wasn't there.

"Lenny?"

He didn't stop his work, instead focusing even more intently on the movement of the thick mop head smearing water and foam across the marble tiles. His back was facing me, and I noticed for the first time that there was a long scar that ran down his neck and disappeared into *the starched collar of his blue button up. There was no telling how he'd gotten it. Isaac had told me the most awful stories about his childhood in Georgia—how he and Lenny had both struggled growing up in the south.*

"Lenny?" I tried again, this time loud enough that my voice bounced on that marble and back against the floor-to-ceiling windows around us. He turned, frowning a little before he forced a nod in my direction. "Where's Isaac?"

"Couldn't say." He lifted his shoulders, shrugging like he didn't believe I had any right knowing what had happened to Isaac. "Best you go on out of here before I have to close up."

He was dismissing me. I'd spent the past month falling in love with his best friend, laughing and joking with both of them, and Lenny was dismissing me like he didn't know me?

"Hang on just a minute." He stepped back when I faced him, glaring, my growing fear and anger at being disregarded getting the better of me. "Don't do that, Lenny. Don't you talk to me like I'm nothing. He was supposed to meet me here." He moved and I followed, step for step, until he gave up trying to get back to work. "Tell me what happened."

Lenny was good at guarding himself. Isaac said it came from years of getting out of trouble anytime Lenny disobeyed his mother or acted out at school and didn't want to get lashing for it. But there was something hiding behind his bored, practiced expression that made me even more worried, because he was doing such a good job of it.

"Lenny...please, tell me. What happened to Isaac?"

He pulled a folded handkerchief from his back pocket, rubbing it along the back of his neck, though he didn't sweat and I suspected he only did that out of habit, as some odd way to help him think. His face was pinched tight, and the muscles around jaw flexed and moved as he continued to work that small square of fabric along his neck.

"He'll whop me for sure, but damn if I can't stomach seeing him so out of sorts." He glanced at me, forgetting the handkerchief when I narrowed my eyes. "Mr. Welis said someone had reported him. That he was...ah...well, that he was following after some of the students and making them uncomfortable. Said some fella told him Isaac had been seen following his girlfriend back to her dorm. So they canned him. Didn't want there to be no ruckus."

"Oh, for Pete's sake." Trent. That bastard. He just couldn't stand the thought of not getting what he wanted and was willing to ruin lives to get his way.

When I glanced back at Lenny, I could see that he knew. That he and Isaac and even Mr. Welis probably knew exactly who had made the report and why, but there was nothing they could do about it but follow procedure. My blood went from icy cold with fear to a rising anger in the space of a few heartbeats. "This is my fault," I told Lenny, livid that Trent had orchestrated this. "Trent...my ex...whatever he was. I know he did this."

"That's what Isaac reckoned too, that it was that fella...the one you used to go around with. He's got a far reach, that one."

"Lenny, where is he?" He automatically started shaking his head, even picked up his mop as though he'd determined to ignore me. "Please, I just want to check on him."

"He's fine. Just waiting out the end of the week and trying to

head off to New York and see if he can't…"

"Head off to New York?"

Lenny paused, cursed to himself as though he hadn't meant for the slip of information to worm its way from his mouth. "You didn't hear that from me."

"Lenny, please. Just tell me where he is." He rolled the mop and bucket away from me, starting on a new section ten feet away, throwing up his hand to stop me when I tried walking across the wet tile. I like to think of myself as a strong woman, someone who may look fragile and be willing to act the part of a polite, well-bred young lady. My go-to way of dealing with horrible things was to keep smiling, to always have a kind word, to look for the good in things even when they were rotten, but still one who could hold her own in a storm, or not fall apart if the unexpected happen. But right then, I felt all hollowed out, empty. I could only stand there and stare at Lenny and that mop of his moving across the floor, too devastated to even cry.

Finally, when I didn't move, he looked back at me, and I must have cut a pretty pathetic figure because suddenly his resolve splintered. "Oh, hell, Miss Riley, I can't stand that look." He held the mop handled between his fingers, head shaking as he watched me. "That little cottage out on Lakeside? I reckon he told you about his uncle's little camp out there?" He had. Isaac promised to bring me there one weekend when he wasn't working so hard, but we'd never found the time. I nodded, walking backward as Lenny continued. "Fools, the pair of you. And don't you go telling him I told you all his business."

"I won't!" I turned, started to sprint away and slipped a little on the wet floor, laughing at Lenny's loud curse. "Sorry!"

"And don't you be driving out there by yourself!" I threw a wave over my

shoulder and heard Lenny continue. "I mean it! You get a ride or you take the bus, but don't go off on your own!" His voice got fainter, and I doubted Lenny believed I listened to his warnings as I took the steps two at a time, my mind set on one goal and my heart feeling like it might leap from my chest.

Ryan didn't question anything I said because that's what family does—stands with you and helps you when you need help. He sat next to me in his Impala, twisting his fingers on the steering wheel like he hoped the small distraction would keep him from speaking.

He lasted a whole two minutes.

"Speak." It was all the permission he needed.

"I'd say this no matter what guy was in there, sis."

"Uh huh. I know you would."

To my left, Ryan's stared glassy-eyed, as though he was willing me to stay put for fear of what waited for me in that small cottage on the lake. Isaac was there. There was a shadow blocking most of the lamplight from the side window—I'd know that shape anywhere. Those shoulders I'd touched and held half a dozen times. That strong, wide back I'd run my fingers over. That thick, long neck, I'd kissed and cradled until the sun dipped low onto the horizon.

"I just…" Ryan's breath was warm, fogging the windshield when he exhaled. "You're my kid sister."

"Ryan, we're not kids anymore."

"Yeah, well, to me you're still that soapy-faced two-year-old

jumping out of the tub when Mom went to answer the door."

I smiled, remembering how often Ryan loved to tell that story. He came off good in it. Me, not so much. "Here we go again…"

My brother ignored me, grip loosening on the wheel. "You slipped on the floor, nearly knocked your head on the tub."

"But you caught me."

Ryan nodded, looking out beyond the windshield, and I wondered if he watched Isaac like I did. "I caught you."

He moved his hand onto the seat next to mine, and I looped a finger around his, same as we'd always done when we were kids. It never got old, the closeness you feel to a sibling. It never was enough.

"I can't stop you if you want to…"

"It's too late, Ryan." I tightened my finger around his. "I already fell."

He waited to start the engine until I was on the porch with my arms around my waist and my nerve slipping between weak and endless as I decided if I wanted to knock. Isaac had to have seen me leave the car. The Impala had thick doors and closed with a thud that ricocheted around the lake. My approach wasn't silent and neither was the sharp tap against the door when I knocked. The strong scent of roses blew through the air when a breeze moved the dry, fallen leaves from the oaks around the porch, and I tightened my sweater closer to me, not sure if it was fear or the chill in the air that made me cold.

I counted my breaths as I waited for the footsteps on the other side of that oak door to quiet, and when they did, I stopped breathing altogether. Would he be angry that I'd found my way here? Did he blame me for Trent's lies? Would he send me away?

There were bright lights and colors swirling in my head that felt like something I forgot and couldn't quite place. There was music lost in those small seconds as I waited on the other side of that door, like something I loved had been stripped from me, and I'd never be rid of the loss, or perhaps the edge of possibility. Everything held and waited with those footsteps, and when the door opened, when Isaac's impassive, steady expression shifted, even minutely, I believed that what I'd lost stood right in front of me. It was the strangest sensation—he was there, inches from me, and it felt something like longing and need and long-released hope had just all vanished from me in an instant. He was here.

I couldn't wait for him to touch me. I didn't want to. He'd been mine a long time ago and here he was again. It was stupid to feel that way, I knew. It made no sense, but seeing Isaac after just two days apart had felt like years—decades— and I wanted to smash the time between us. I wanted to forget it had ever been there.

"Riley…"

I wouldn't let him send me away. I couldn't. Isaac's body went stiff when I lunged at him, grabbing onto his neck with no intention of ever letting go. It took him three of the longest seconds of my life before he surrendered his fight and held onto me, those massive arms around my waist, the sensation of him inhaling my hair and my feet coming off the porch as he held me close.

Isaac set me down and looked over my shoulder, pausing without moving his hands from my waist, and I followed his gaze, smiling at Ryan as he watched us.

"He's waiting to see if you'll send me away." Just then, Isaac's

grip lowered, resting on my hip, as though he had me, like he had me and had no plans of letting me go. His breath was warm against my neck, and I glanced up at him, my body feeling buzzed by the look in his eyes, how he didn't seem able to keep from looking at me like I was real and there and his.

I waved to Ryan, and Isaac offered him a nod before he opened the door and led me inside. I heard the car pull away, and then there was only us.

The cottage was nothing more than one large room with river stone fireplace and hand-scraped hardwood floors. There was a small kitchen tucked away in the back of the cottage, and the rich scent of coffee percolated from the back of the room. Two large chairs were situated in front of the fire that crackled beneath a thick wood mantel holding several small picture frames, each one with the thinnest layer of dust. A large bed was pathetically hidden behind a thin curtain. I did my best not to stare for too long at the mattress or think of the untucked blankets and how the entire place smelled of sandalwood and shea butter soap.

"You…you were fired." I looked up at Isaac as he leaned against the largest of the two columns, thick masses of hand-sawed beams that held up the entire cottage. His gaze was heavy on me, and I fiddled with my hair, pulling it over my shoulder to braid it absently, an unconscious habit. Isaac only nodded, watching with his mouth tight and drawn, like he wanted me to say my piece uninterrupted.

"I guess you figured it was probably Trent." The name came out low, like a curse, and I couldn't keep my lip from curling a little when I spoke it. "I'd bet anything it was him." Another nod and I stepped closer to him. "Are you…" My tongue felt thick and knotted. "Do you blame me?"

"Riley," he finally said, standing away from the beam. "Come here to me."

I didn't hesitate, and his arms were around me, my face against his chest before anything else could pass between us. This was where I belonged—safe, protected, loved. The idea shocked me, made me huddle closer to him. Did Isaac love me? He'd never said it, but I felt it just then, in the fierceness of his arms, in how tightly he held me, as though he wouldn't let go. As though he would never let me go.

"You think I blamed you? You, of all people?" His voice rumbled against my ear, and I hummed, loving the feel of it. "How is it your fault when that dog runs his mouth?" Isaac pulled back to look down at me but kept me in the circle of his arms. "That bastard hit you. He hurt you, body and soul. No one deserves that, least of all you. I wanted... I wanted to....but you wouldn't let me. Your heart is too big. I don't know if you were protecting him or me, but you wouldn't let me take out my anger on him, even though he deserved it. And I figure if you can let go of what he did to you, then who was I to hold a bigger grudge? So I did what I could to be there for you when you were down. And soon, all I saw was you."

"But if it hadn't been for me..."

"This is what I've been telling you, Riley, for months. This is the world we live in. It's the way of things." He said it so simply, not as something that was a sad, pathetic thing, just a statement of fact.

"But that's not...it's not right."

"Maybe it ain't, but that don't change it. Maybe nothing will. Maybe time will, who knows? But in my gut I know who I can trust. I *know who looks at me and sees me, not some damn idea they have in their heads." He moved his hand, running a finger along my bottom lip. "This thing we got...I told you, it won't be easy."*

"Nothing good is ever easy, Isaac."

There was a pause as unasked questions hovered around us. I considered what life would be like with Isaac, that no matter how committed we might be to our relationship, we could not exist in a vacuum. Struggles would follow us wherever we went, and would spill out to our families, our loved ones, our friends.

He waited. Although Isaac was the one who moved with caution, the one who refused to assume that the easy road would be ours to travel, he waited for me to come to a decision. He wanted me to say yes, but wouldn't ask the question. He would not lead me anywhere, but would be waiting for me when I arrived—if I didn't turn back.

"Isaac?" He nodded again and brought me closer. His cheeks were wide, his features strong, and he closed his eyes, as though he relished the feel of my fingertips over his face. "Will you love me? No matter what happens?"

Isaac pulled me against his large body, his hand around my waist. His voice was quiet, but filled with strength, with conviction. "Always."

No one had touched me like Isaac. He had a way about him, something real and honest that was assured by his long, perfect fingers down my back and the slip of his tongue inside my mouth. There was no fear, not when those fingers gripped me tighter, when he slowly lowered my zipper and held my hand as I stepped out of my dress.

He watched me then, and even though a different Riley might have been shy, I liked the way his stare felt against my bare skin. It was me he wanted, only me; only I could sate his hunger, redeem that desperate look that had caught him in a silent pause.

Isaac still held my hand, arm extended, with that hard, greedy gaze working over me. He made me feel needed, wanted; he made me feel necessary. And when he pulled my hand to rest it against his heart, I held my breath, waiting to hear what he thought, hoping he wanted me as much as I wanted him. "My sweet…my beautiful Riley."

He stepped back, my fingers trailing away from his chest, and tugged off his shirt, dropping it to the floor, instantly forgotten. Isaac picked me up and carried me to the bed, divesting me of everything that kept me covered, and everything that kept him hidden from me.

I had never seen a naked man before. I'd never been naked with a man before. But there I lay on Isaac's large bed, covered by his long legs and muscular thighs, my small frame underneath him, open to him as he took control and showed me what it meant to be loved.

"You and me, Riley, there's nothing but this. Nothing else but this, how we are right now."

Isaac never spoke much of his feelings: the things that rocked his soul, the many worries that kept him up at night. Maybe he didn't know how to say he loved me, but just then, with Isaac's warm, solid body right against mine, skin to skin, touching me like no one ever had before, I decided words weren't all that important.

"Nothing else, my love. Nothing else at all."

And then he came to me, and took possession of me, and moved so deeply and so fully in me that there was nothing else at all.

Later, when even the crickets had set their song to something *low and tired, I lay next to Isaac, feeling boneless and surreal. He felt like a mountain against me, the hard planes of muscle, the sharp twist of ligaments and bone that pressed into me, hard where I was soft, but tender and sweet. His breath had gone slow and even, and I knew he slept, his eyelids fluttering as he dreamed. Yet even while he slept, he held me, set me to fit just under his chin with the slick feel of his sweat moving with mine. We'd moved together like a dance, bodies gliding to fit a perfect rhythm, a perfect life that once again made me feel a loss that was not mine. Next to this man, my man, there was only peace, only the sense that we were beginning…we had only started to know what that meant.*

Nash

It was the dream. The waking dream again.

There was something tied up in that dream—a memory, a life I knew but had never lived. That was the only explanation.

The dream crawled inside my skull like a centipede. It stayed there, burrowed itself so deep inside my brain that imagination got squashed. Nothing was fantasy anymore. What had been figments of my imagination had grown to something real, something I couldn't beat away. Something I couldn't ignore.

It had me jerking awake. None of the others had done that. Not when Sookie ran from some asshole trying to hurt her, not when I knew the danger she headed toward was starting to take shape.

This one was different. This one was realer than anything I'd ever felt.

The woman, somehow my woman? She'd been so real. So much. And I shuddered, I called out in the idle of that dream and woke with sweat dotting my forehead and slipping down my back, and ready, so damn ready to finish what was started in that dream. It made me want something that wasn't mine.

The dream stayed with me during the investors' meeting, as Duncan talked about projections and media outreach. He spoke, and I watched his face, focused like I understood the meaning behind the noise, the unrecognizable words his mouth made. I knew he was expecting me to weigh in with some technical spin, but it was all I could do to keep from completely drifting away.

Lucky for me, he liked the sound of his own voice. Even Duncan and his slick CEO arrogance didn't distract me from the dream. The sound of his pitch, that salesman shine he thought might impress the investors, didn't do a damn thing to erase what I'd felt. What I'd seen. What I remembered.

The dream stayed even as his nagging turned into a whining drone that made my teeth ache.

"What the fuck was that? You just tuned out. You weren't engaged at all."

No. I hadn't been. Still wasn't as I fed him some line about a migraine.

"I'll catch you later, man. I gotta jet."

He didn't buy my excuse. Duncan's eyes narrowed, and I swear I felt his stare hot on my neck as I stood waiting at the elevator. I kept my head down, wondering for the umpteenth time how I'd gotten messed up with someone like Duncan in the first place.

Ah. Right. I had a program and no cash. Duncan had deep pockets and was looking for someone's coattails to ride. One plus one is always two.

Didn't much care if he bought the migraine excuse. I felt something right at the base of my skull. A pressure, a dull ache, but I wasn't sick. I was high.

My brain went into autopilot as I left Manhattan, grabbing the A train to get me to downtown Brooklyn. And the whole way home, with the rocking of the train, the funky smell of the city getting fainter with every stop, and the even worse body odor of all the compressed bodies, the ache in my head—threatening to turn into a migraine for real—growing the closer we came to my stop, that weird memory nagging at me.

That shit wouldn't let me be.

Over and over in my head, as I huddled tight behind my jacket in the unseasonably chilly weather, the memory came clear as a raindrop.

Me and her. Me and the woman I didn't know. Me as a man I'd never been.

The smell of roses. The hint of dust and coffee.

The feel of worn book bindings and the scrape of metal chairs on wood floors.

The taste of honey on my tongue.

The woman wrapped around me, holding tight, like I was her lifeline. Her red hair between my fingers, her nails pulling at my collar. Feeling needed. Feeling free.

A gust of wind blew off my hood, had my eyes

watering as I jogged the rest of the way toward my building, barely acknowledging the people grouped around the front entrance. But then the sound of kids screeching cut into my brain, and I finally noticed that Old Man Walker was handing out Jolly Ranchers from the top step for his grandkids and the others bouncing around; he couldn't get the wrapped candy out of his pockets fast enough.

In that small chaos, compounded by an arguing couple from 3C coming out of the elevator, brushing past the cluster of kids in their red and green puffy coats and their sniffling noses, heels clicking on the tile floor and crackling over the candy wrappers littering the hall, I forgot about the dream. If only for a second.

Until I saw Willow at the mailboxes.

Until I realized I couldn't walk away from her.

She didn't look much like the woman in my dream. Her hair was not red, but light brown. The redhead's had been thick and bone straight. Willow's was wild, all over the place, as though she could never get it under control.

The woman in my dream had been thin with barely a hint of curve to her shape. Elegant, graceful, like a ballerina. Willow was all dips and bends, luscious, her legs strong with well-defined muscle and a wide, wondrous ass.

Suddenly the rest of the world receded, and there was nothing but the movement of Willow's hair as she dug the mail from her box, the rhythm of her limbs as she swatted at that thick mass of hair, the swoop of her jacket hem against all those round, perfect curves as she turned, her attention on the envelopes in her hand.

The smell of her skin, the jasmine in her hair, seemed to billow around me as I stood motionless in the lobby. She was everywhere, familiar and yet unknown. A stranger/not stranger I had held at arm's length, but still far more real than my dream, than the memory it was trying to evoke.

Willow stopped short as she noticed me, pausing with the mail held against her chest, a frown appearing on her face. I knew that expression from the last time I saw her, when I lied and told her I didn't want her, when I had spoken promises that even then I knew I'd never keep.

"Nash." There was a bite in her voice, the clip of my name, as if she was trying to sound disdainful, yet her voice still held an undertone of something that, if it had a flavor, would have tasted like honey.

And then the dream, that sweet, stinging memory, crashed over me. It wasn't the first. It wasn't the last. There was no girl called Sookie, no boy named Dempsey who loved her. This time, I'd watched, not knowing who I was; a voyeur in someone else's life, but someone who felt so real to me. Someone I knew better than myself.

Déjà vu and fantasy and nonsense I did not understand hit me like a fever, and I was lost.

The redhead kissed my neck. The hint of her soft, liquid tongue against my skin, tugging on my ear, wanting me with a fierceness no one ever had before, overwhelmed me, and I had to close my eyes to keep from being dragged under.

"What's wrong with you?" Willow's voice reeled me back in, and I opened my eyes to see her sweet, concerned expression and the curve of her mouth, the fullness of her bottom lip.

Then Willow... she took the back of her hair in one hand, twisting it into a braid—the smallest gesture that I'd seen her do a dozen times—and suddenly I realized: the woman in my dream had done the same thing. The same motion, the same movement. Just like Willow.

A sharp intake of breath—that was me. Willow had backed up a half-step, her face confused, conflicted, and despite what I'd said before, I reached out and slid my fingers tentatively to touch her face, guiding her chin up so I could look into her eyes.

"What are—"

She made the smallest noise, something that sounded like a moan and a laugh at the same time. It transformed, deepened to a growl when I kissed her. Yet even as my mouth found hers, as my tongue slid along her lip, begging an invitation, one thought consumed me, something I didn't believe was left over from my dream. One thought that made me brave, made me hungry: *this woman belongs to me.*

Fifteen

Nash

She was winter. The cold, cool stretch of emptiness that you think will consume you. The frigid bite you think won't ever leave your bones, the one you try to pretend isn't there, but can't keep out of your head.

She was fall and the scent of a fire, the crackle of heat, the coming of change you try to pretend won't come, but does anyway, that you wait for the whole year, that you wish away when it finally comes.

She was summer and the scorching warmth of sun and sin, the slick feel of lotion and the spray of ocean water, the salt of that spray on your tongue and the cool, crisp relief that comes over you when you dip inside the bottomless water.

She was spring, the fresh sweet smell of jasmine and the honeysuckle temptation of light and love and beautiful rebirth that cannot be ignored. Willow was the phantom spark of all those things I loved and hated. The things that tested me. The things that healed, all wrapped up in that tempting silhouette, in the sweet surrender of her body pressed against mine and the whisper of a tease in every syllable that formed my name from her full, thick lips.

"Nash." It was song, sweeter than Coltrane, hurt worse too, my name, the hidden tone of promises and pleasure I stopped telling myself I didn't want.

Four seasons, laid out before me: Willow's wild hair fanned against my pillow and her waiting body—pale skin and a trail of freckles that crossed her chest and dipped with the curves along her stomach.

"Nash," she said again, reaching for me when I came to my knees, looking down at her, wanting her with an ache nothing had ever worked up in me.

There were two small lines along her hips, lightning on her skin and the round bends of her breast, the sweet arches along her hips and down her thighs when I touched her there. That look, though, went deeper, settled closer than the scent of her skin or rise in my body when I watched her shimmy out of her clothes and crawl on my bed, waiting, ready for me to react.

Now I was and I had to breathe deep, to separate the want someone else held in my dream and the urge to take what was mine and mine alone; what I wanted for myself because of the sensation only Willow moved in me.

"Take off your shirt," she said, and I did, working one shoulder at a time out of that cotton, discarding it because it kept me from her. She touched me, nails against the lines and letters over my body, her mouth, her tongue warm and soft on my neck, over my chest, traveling like a wanderer, searching, seeking.

We came together like colors, moving into a gradient of light, of motion that reminded me of the sea, waves and water, sand and shore. We were sweeter than those Coltrane chords, went deeper than each note.

"You taste like honey," I told her, moving closer, lips and tongue on her flesh, in the dips of her body. The invitation open, ready as she pulled me close. I took another bite, moving her apart with my knee, holding her tight until there were small marks from my fingers against her pale skin, and she shuddered, gripping, clawing at me like she couldn't get close enough.

"Nash…" she breathed, and that melody spurred me on, had me forgetting control and patience and all the swagger I thought made me smooth. I was nothing but feeling, touch and taste, and desperate, desperate with the want of her under me, with me slipping inside, deep, sweet.

Free.

Later, when my body cried out, when I thought I couldn't move enough to even leave her body, Willow cuddled next to me, fit like a puzzle piece against me. We didn't sleep. There was only the sound of our breaths and the slowing race of my own heartbeat pulsing in my ear.

Her skin was the softest I'd ever touched, sweeter than the honey I swore I tasted from her neck when I kissed her, and it reminded me of things I thought I'd figured out when I was a punk kid.

"You're smiling. I can feel your lips stretching against my forehead."

"I am. Sated. High as hell off you." I moved back to catch her gaze, smiling when I saw she looked half-buzzed as me. "You remind me…" I touched her arm, let my fingers move over her elbow, to her wrist. "You remind me of what I always thought I knew about women when I was a kid."

"What was that?"

It was probably stupid, but it was real. Everything I felt with her, right in that moment, everything I said, it was the realest I've ever been. Willow wouldn't let me hide, so I decided not to try.

"The way a woman looks, the secrets she keeps, that mesmerize a punk kid with no clue what happens behind those doors, behind those pink curtains. It got me wondering, all those years, when the girls in gym class disappeared before me and my boys had finished our game on the court. Why'd they leave so soon? What did they do in that locker room that took up so much damn time?"

"Did you ever figure it out?"

She liked my smile. She'd said that a half-dozen times. I saw what Will thought of me, how she went all still, all quiet, when I threw a smile her way. There was something in the press of her lips, how the very tip of her tongue wetted that full bottom lip in the middle, like she wanted to taste me on her mouth, like my smile reminded her how much she wanted me right there.

I didn't answer her, just flashed that smile slow, subtle like I knew she wanted it. Just the right side twitching up, my lips protruding like they waited for her to take up what I offered. Willow's gaze shifted, moved over my face like there was something she looked for, maybe something she wanted to find that I wouldn't give up easily. And when that glance stayed too still, too focused on my mouth, I relaxed the muscles around my lips just enough to slip my tongue along my bottom lip. Her focus shifted, followed the change of movement, and gave away what I knew she wanted.

"No." The whisper of the word pulled her attention back to my eyes, and I fought like hell not to smile again. Couldn't give away all my cards. "Not then. Not all at once either. That came with time. High school, college, all the females around then, all the bodies and scents and senses I'd never felt before, all those mysteries I wanted like hell to figure out, it was sensory overload, and, little punk I was didn't have a damn clue."

Willow pulled her long hair over her shoulder, let the slip of loose braid move along her bare shoulder until she held the breakaway wisps between her fingers. Like feathers, like movement and grace I'd never seen anyone manage before, that woman could blink, pass a look over her shoulder and bring any man to his knees. But I had not lied. Lessons got learned in college, when every female that came at me made it easy to uncover certain secrets. I had to learn, and back then, eager as I was, those lessons got taught quick.

Willow's hair reminded me of pebbles wet from the river, the color darkening with each press of the current. "I learned, but even then, all the stuff I figured out, never prepared me."

"For what?" She gave me a little of that knee-bending glance, and I pulled my attention to the thick tendrils of hair she loosened from the braid to weave between her long fingers. She held her breath when I took the hair from her hand.

"For the one and many." She wanted me to clarify. She wanted answers, and I had them, but I liked the way she smelled. I liked how warm her skin felt when I brushed my arm against her back. I wanted to live in that moment just for a little while, to suspend our reality until there was only the feel of our skin together. Something that was wet and warm and somehow right all at once. "Women, to a boy, are scary, so fucking scary that we don't know to catch hold of that fear. It burns in our guts, and it's that sensation we run from. Every man, no matter what kind of man he turns out to be, is a scared punk at ten, at sixteen, at eighteen, when it comes to women." Will shuddered, the thin hair on my arm brushing along her spine when I slide my fingers between the wave of loose braid that fell on her shoulder.

"We don't understand why girls get us all twisted up inside, make us feel like we could either scream or get sick or explode all at the same time. And then, you get a little closer to the many things that keep a man spent over a female, things that as a kid has you running scared. As a man, though, when they let you closer, you get a little clarity. A little realization, and damn, do you want to unravel those mysteries. You get a touch, a small one, and if you're really lucky, next comes the taste. That only makes you want more, and maybe if you got game, if you're cool, know to handle your business, then you get another taste, a deeper one. The touches get you closer to a taste, until you think you've found it all out—what a woman has, what you can do with what she has."

"And then?"

"Hell. Then? Then she unravels another mystery, and all the mess you think you knew about women is nothing. Then you realize you know nothing about them. Then you realize there is so much more to know until you know the truth."

"What truth is that?"

"That you'll never understand it all. That every woman has a level of mystery no man could possibly discover. There are many. That many starts with one. It starts with the held things she won't ever tell you, no matter who you are or what you can do for her. The one and many that you spend your life trying to discover. It's an addiction, really. Like drinking something that tastes so fucking good, something you believe will fill you up but only makes you realize you could never be full. It makes you drunk. That touch, that taste, the bodies, the smell, all the things that make a woman so tempting. You want to drink…it all up."

"Nash…" My name came out like a purr and Willow brought her fingers back to my chest, circling around the thin hair there, moving over my skin, and I felt every touch she made. "Do I make you drunk?"

I pushed her close, my mouth hovering over hers, our bodies pressed firm, nearly back to where we'd been just minutes ago. The smell of sex and sweat filled my senses, and I lowered my voice, not caring just how real I got right then.

"Sweetness, no woman alive could make me drunker." Then I kissed Willow, deep and long, and got so high I could look down and not see the earth.

Nash

We slept for an hour, rolling over half-asleep at the same time, pulling at each other when our bodies woke, when our minds likely stayed frozen in whatever dreams made us shake and move in our sleep.

"You changed your mind," she said to the darkness, a slow, soft stroke of her nails against my arm as I curled around her.

"You were right." That small stroke stopped, and the mattress shook with her small laughter. "Don't get used to it. That's a freebie."

"I can't see it right now, but I'm willing to bet your aura is red."

"Red is good?"

She stretched, looking over her shoulder to squint at me. "Red can be good. It means virility and passion and...love." She looked away from me, pulling her hair off her neck. "It could also mean anger and violence."

"I'm damn far from angry or violent."

"I don't know," she said, sliding closer to me. The feel of her soft skin and that wide ass against me was almost too much. She knew it. She knew the power she had in the small maneuver of her body next to mine. "That seems like something that might do some damage." She laughed, arching her back so her ass rested full against me, teasing and rousing until I was nearly ready for her again.

"Demon woman, my body can't...not yet."

It was good to hear her laugh after so many weeks of irritating her, of telling myself she wasn't what I wanted. There was a quiet in this space, something that I didn't know, had never felt before, but that felt somehow right and real and what I wanted. Willow's laughter reminded me of wind chimes, soft and sweet and constant, something that filled my chest with sensation.

"Nash," she said after her laughter had gone quiet and sleep had nearly taken us again. "Are you listening?"

"Yeah." The word came out a little sleepy, a lot still high from the spell Willow worked over me. "Yeah, I'm awake."

"I figured something out the other night, before...well, everything."

Something warm and numbing moved into my head then, something that had me dropping my guard and forgetting what I'd probably have to give up if I wanted to be with Willow. "What did you figure out?"

She moved then, slipping the comforter over her chest, holding it there as she looked down at me. "I think...I'm pretty sure we knew each other in another life."

"In another life" echoed a little in my head, like the vibration from a chord when it's played loud and piercing. Willow hadn't misspoken, and she wasn't joking. She hung onto that comforter like it would protect her, like it would keep her safe in case I told her she'd gone straight out of her mind.

"Wait...what?"

"Think about it..." She moved closer, tugging up the blanket and nudging me to sit up. "Since the day I met you, I've felt this...this thing, and I know you have too." She moved her head, tilting it until I glanced at her and let her hold my gaze. "I'm not wrong, am I?"

It would be stupid to shut out the things racing through my head—how she made me feel, how much I wanted her again and again, all the things that tied us together in that moment. But there were other things too—memories that had kept me from sleep, memories that felt so real, so familiar, and somehow had always kept Willow in my mind when I thought about them. But did that mean my entire belief system would be changed? Did that mean I'd have to start believing the fairytales our relatives had always told us?

I liked Willow. What I felt for her scared me a little, but that didn't mean I was ready to buy into her out-in-left-field juju.

"Oh, there was something there. I'll give you that one, but I don't think it means that you and me knew each other. That's doesn't mean I'm ready to stop believing in evolution or that this life is it for us."

Willow moved her head, the smallest shake that might not have been anything more than a twitch. But her eyes widened, and I noticed the way her mouth twitched, not like she was about to smile. That was her fighting to reel in her irritation.

She didn't pull away from me when I reached for her. Instead, Willow held my hand in her lap, tracing the lines and dips in my handprint with the tip of her nail. When she spoke, it was to my palm. "There's something inside me. I can't explain it, but it's there. It's this little monster that whispers to me when I sleep…every damn time I dream."

I was familiar with the sensation. There was a loud, angry voice screaming things to me, telling me to feel something, sometimes to not feel anything at all. It was the same voice reminding me that I didn't have time for women, that I was fine all on my own. But that didn't mean Willow needed to know that. "What does it say?"

I saw the answer in the movement of her irises, how that slow, eager gaze gave away everything she wouldn't let her mouth confess. But Willow was a master at distraction, eradicating the focus on things she did not want on her; her expression told me all I needed to know of how she felt.

"That doesn't matter." She moved away from me, dropping my hand to lean against the wood headboard next to the large window. There was moonlight peeking in through the glass, and I thought, idly, that Will was born to bath in that light. A goddess living in shadows that kept hidden the secrets no one was worthy to unveil.

"So? The monster? That asshole keeps you up at night?" The half-smile was quick, only twitched her mouth into something that resembled a smirk before she licked her lips, moving her attention onto the traffic out on the street and the group of kids passing a half-empty bottle between them. "What's the monster doing to you, Will? He giving you the blues?"

"Not so much. It's not the dreams themselves. It's not what happens to her…"

"Her?"

"The girl in my dreams."

"So there's a girl and no monster?"

"The monster is the…the voice. It tells me to pay attention. It tells me that everything matters—the fire…the screams and the…*God*, the emotions. The emotions are the worst."

She mentioned the dreams like she knew I'd had a few of my own. Willow couldn't know what had happened to me the night she'd tugged me into her apartment. I had never mentioned it. But as she spoke, the spell of her thoughts, the reminder of her dreams, weaving something ethereal and holy into the room, I realized she had known about my dreams. She'd known and had kept the knowing to herself.

"Will…that shit isn't funny." I slipped from the bed,

tugging on my shorts as she watched me, feeling my chest tighten and my face heat.

"You know I'm right. You…I hear you, Nash. When you dream. Sometimes you scream. Sometimes…sometimes I know what you'll scream before you make a sound."

The black T-shirt in my hand fell to the floor when my grip loosened, and I watched Willow, trying not to think too much how she looked unreal, supernatural, sitting against my headboard with moonlight soaking into her skin. If I'd ever believed in angels, it had been right then. But I didn't believe in angels. I believed in facts and figures and a lot of logic.

"That's not possible."

"And yet here we are. Feeling…things." Willow got to her knees, grabbing the sheet to wrap it around her shoulders. There was something about her expression that left me feeling nervous—curious—but I couldn't speak. Not with how she looked at me. Not when I knew she had something to say. "Every night for a week straight I tried to rescue…" There was a name bouncing on her tongue. It was right there in her features, in the way she frowned, how the smallest line between her eyebrows tightened the more she concentrated on not uttering that name. Then, Willow sighed, leaving the bed to rest against the cracked paint window, head back, face tilted up, but she tightened her eyes closed. "I tried hard. Every night…every night I fail."

I didn't know what she meant. I only knew that I'd had

dreams that felt like memories. I'd dreamt of Sookie and Dempsey and D.C. and love that went on and on, emotions that threatened to drown me. But there was no way Willow had dreamed the same dreams. It was impossible.

"I understand that you think certain things are possible…like reincarnation." I sat next to her, pulling her hand against my palm. "A lot of people think that's an easy way to explain déjà vu or the sensation of knowing someone, being somewhere that you've never visited."

"And you don't?" I hated the way she frowned, how her fingers straightened in my hand. "It's not as simple as past lives."

"What do you mean?" She dropped my hand, slowing her movements as she looked at me, crossing her arms like a shield in front of herself.

I'd heard the explanation a thousand times from classmates at MIT and during a few student worker lab jobs I had to help pay my tuition. But I didn't think Willow knew anything about genetics or theories that hadn't quite been proven.

"You walk into a place you've never been or see someone that you know you've spoken to before but never met. It's natural to wonder about, because sometimes it isn't as simple as coincidence. But it's not your memories. It's not déjà vu. It's called epigenetic memory." Willow moved her eyebrows together, and I knew the question she wanted to ask just by the confusion that twisted her expression.

"My mentor at Howard was a scientist. Roan. He was a chemist, but he had a lot of interests; he liked to dabble. Genetics was one of those softer sciences, according to him, that he liked to mess around with. Some things stuck." She went on watching me, arms still crossed, and for a second I wondered if she'd already forgotten that I'd just left her screaming, that I'd touched her and held her and changed our worlds with a few touches. I wanted to get that Willow back, the one that didn't hesitate to touch me. The one that felt and let those feelings move her. But she'd asked, so I pressed on.

"Like the survival instincts that get passed down or those bad memories that trains future generations to fear certain places. It's all genetic. It's written into our DNA."

"The memories?"

"That's one theory, yeah." Her frown deepened and I shot her a smile, banking on the way she'd told me my smile made her feel to push the cloud from us. "Maybe you don't like heights or fear water because your grandfather did. Maybe you feel that familiar sense in a place because once upon a time someone in your gene pool died there or was hurt there. Our life experiences affect how often certain proteins are created from our genes, when the genes are 'read.' A certain experience can trigger a negative or positive reaction."

"You make it sound so impersonal."

"Not at all," I told her, keeping the small grin on my face. She unraveled her arms when I tugged on the sheet, and I breathed a little easier. "It's absolutely personal. It's your family." She might have let me touch her again, but even me moving my thumb across her knuckles didn't take the tight line from her forehead or pull the frown from her lips. "But, then, there is about ninety-eight percent of data we don't know about DNA and genetics. There's a lot of room for error."

"So it could be much more than survival instincts."

I was careful then, moving my head to watch her, cautious but still smiling. "Maybe. Or maybe it's just oxytocin kicks in and you get a rush of warmth and connection because something triggered it. There's just no real way to know for sure."

"So a rush of warmth? Like…like love?" She kept her face impassive, without any real emotion at all when she asked that, and her reaction surprised me. Willow was an earth child. She loved auras and juju. She bought organic groceries and recycled. She protested at marches and volunteered at shelters. No one that does that is missing emotion. No one like Willow lives without love.

"Something like love. Isn't it?"

"I…" Again she curled her arms in front of her chest, this time tighter, brushing her fingers up and down her arms as though she was cold. "I couldn't tell you."

"Come on, Will. You told me your folks have been together forever. You said they get along really well. You told me…" I stopped talked when she shook her head. "What?"

"They make it impossible."

"Your folks?"

She nodded and kept rubbing her arms. I wanted to pull her close, warm her against my chest, but she suddenly didn't look interested in being comforted.

"Every day of my life. They couldn't go long without touching. They'd be sitting there on the front porch, maybe at the kitchen table doing nothing at all…not touching, not looking at each other, reading the paper or doing a crossword, nothing spectacular. He'd hum, she'd whistle, and out of nowhere, for no particular reason at all, he'd stop, grin at her and keep silent. But I knew, anyone would know. It was right there in his eyes. Just looking at her made him smile, and that smile told the world he was thinking, 'My God, I love her.'"

"What's so impossible about that?"

"Because it doesn't happen like that." She pushed off from the window, tugging the sheet higher over her shoulders. "Not for anyone but them. Not for normal people. They set the bar pretty damn high, the way they love each other; that's all they know—how to love each other when it's a Tuesday, when it's quiet and still. How to say *I love you* without a single sound." She shook her head like she was frustrated, and I could only watch her, wondering how she could make something like loving someone seem so ridiculous. Wasn't that my job? "That's not normal, and when I bother to think about it, I realize that I probably won't reach that bar."

Until that moment I didn't realize I hadn't been the only one running from life. Running from something good and real.

"You don't believe in love?" Willow moved her mouth, lips pressed together, answering my question with a single look, one I hated seeing on her face. "I can't believe that."

"And I can't believe you don't believe it's possible that we knew each other before." She stepped closer, the sheet falling from her shoulder. "Nash, if there's still ninety-eight percent of data undiscovered then it's possible you're wrong."

"Possible," I said, not liking how she doubted me. "Just not probable."

"That's not…" She took a breath, and her eyes went cool, glistened against the moonlight moving in through the window. "It's ridiculous that you hold on to beliefs that haven't been proven."

"Says the woman who claims to read auras." I hadn't meant to make my voice so loud or insulting. But it was out there, right along with the cool air that circulated around my apartment as Willow stood across from me, shivering. "Look,

Will…" She held up a hand, quieting me when I moved to interrupt.

"This isn't in my head. I've…there have been so many dreams, and God, Nash, they're real. They're so real." She stepped close, and I let her, too caught up in her words to move. "There are people in my head that seem like family. They seem, God, I can't even explain it right, but there are people, and they are you and me, Nash. They are us, and they're not us, and there are a lot of ignorant people trying to split us apart, and there are promises—my God, the promises—and they all feel so real. They feel like truth." She'd gone breathless, and her eyes glistened the faster she spoke. She exhaled, shivering a little and started to cry. "Nash, they tell me that everything I feel for you isn't some random accident. *With everything I am…I…God…*"

"Willow…" Her name came out of my mouth like something amazed, something broken in two, as though the disbelief I felt was a pathetic thread that loosened every second she spoke. I'd heard that phrase before, somewhere in a dream. It was tucked away with Sookie and Dempsey and the promises they wanted to keep. I could relate. Looking at Willow, seeing how glassy her eyes had become, right then I knew exactly how Sookie had felt when Dempsey kissed her. But how could Willow know? That phrase, those dreams, there was no way she'd heard that from the nights the dreams were too much. There was no way she had the same dreams.

"Will," I said again, stepping closer to her. She moved back, and it felt like punch in my gut. "Please don't be upset."

"How can I not be upset you don't…*wait.*" She moved her chin, tilting her face toward me, as though something had just occurred to her. "You talked about genetics and DNA…Nash, what do you believe?"

She held her breath, like whatever my answer, she was prepared for it destroying her.

"Willow…"

"Please," she stepped back, breathing in through her nose. "Tell me what you believe."

I'd had the argument a half a dozen times with everyone, even Roan. He didn't believe in the supernatural or an afterlife, at least I was sure he didn't. Roan had always told me to make decisions on what I saw. The things I could prove.

"I believe in science, Will. I believe things that can be proven, things that are bolstered with evidence. I believe in the things I can see, the things that are right in front of my face, not in things that ride on feelings and hunches and wishful thinking."

For a long while she only watched me. I read her expressions and the thoughts that seemed to move around her face as she kept quiet, sorting through whatever it was that kept her attention inside her own head. Finally, tears began to collect in her lashes, and I stepped away from the window, reaching for her. "Will…"

"I can't…Nash, I believe in everything. I have to.

This life, it can't be all there is. It's just not that cut and dry. I've seen things—felt things—that you wouldn't believe. My belief, it's important, and I can't just… if life can only be narrowed down to facts and evidence and something you can point to and say, 'there it is,' then what I feel in my bones is a lie. And it can't be a lie. It can't be."

Disappointment choked me as tears spilled down her cheeks, as she shook her head like she couldn't believe me, as if I had erased her.

"This doesn't have to be a deal breaker, Willow. It's just silly…"

"No," she said, voice high, shrill. "Whatever else it is, it's not silly. Not what I believe, and I could never…" The room had gone still. Only the sound of our breathing and the rustle of the sheet sounded as she moved away from me, picking up her clothes that had been discarded around the room. "I can't be with someone that doesn't have any faith, Nash. I can't be with someone whose life is so damned narrow."

I wanted to stop her. Something old and angry inside me burned in my stomach, knotted hard as she dropped the sheet and tugged on her clothes. Even as she reached for me, kissed my cheek, I wanted to pull her close, do away with the work she'd made covering herself up again. But Willow was too determined, too sure, too angry, and I could only watch her as she walked away, wondering what faith had taught her to slam the door on something she wanted.

Worse yet, I wondered what logic told me the same thing.

Nash

Everything felt old and empty. Stale, like a hangover.

It was nearly four a.m., and Willow was everywhere and nowhere at all. My bed still felt warm where she'd been. My body was cooling, starting to go numb every spot where she'd kissed me.

The streetlight outside was yellow, a dreary color that reminded me of a rainstorm, of sickness. I hated the dim light it shot through my room, between the slip of window from my partially open curtains. The pillow on the other side of the bed held three long strands of hair, Willow's hair, and I grabbed the thing, tucked it under my chin, just to catch that jasmine scent, just to remind myself she'd been there.

Only then did I sleep.

New Orleans

There were things that weren't done in the city. Not by folk like me. Not when there were so many eyes looking this way and that, waiting to see what we'd do and who we'd do it to. There was nothing for it, just the way of our world. Some bad men liked to keep us under their thumbs. They liked to remind us all that our kin had been owned by theirs not all that long ago. They liked to tell us how we were nothing, how our kids wouldn't be nothing, just because they were small, stupid people with no notion of good sense. They were mean because it was in their nature. It was how they'd been reared, and how they'd die. God help us, they were raising little ones to be just like them.

When there are eyes looking, judging, you need to be smart about the company you keep. Back on the farm was one thing; there was no nosey spying because the company we kept told everyone right where they'd be. But here in the city, where illegal liquor and cheap dope came easy as dying, boredom led to the devil's business, and damn us all, business was good.

Some things just weren't done. They weren't fittin' at all. Like Sylv nosing around the Chambers cottage at all hours of the night because Lily let him put his hand inside her shirt. Or the way Ripper Dean took any girls with a half-decent smile right off the street without anyone's bye or leave. Sad fact was ole Ripper didn't care if that was fittin' or not. Or, the thing that made those staring eyes widen and those fat running mouths go off a mile a minute, when Dempsey Simoneaux, a white Cajun boy whose daddy had a special hatred for black folks, brought me, the light-skinned daughter of a woman who sold illegal hooch, a bunch of white and yellow roses he picked right from his mama's prize-winning garden.

Things like that happen, especially in the city, and folks tend to notice.

"You are a damn fool." I wanted to say I was sorry for putting that look on Dempsey's face. His smile got a little shaky then, and he lowered his arm, fist full of those pretty roses. But really, he should have known better.

Three white men I'd seen a few times around the Simoneaux place watched as I tugged on Dempsey's arm and pulled him around to the alley just in back of Mama's shop.

"I got these for you, Sookie. To make you feel better."

"Don't tell me why you got them. Lord, Dempsey, I know why you did." It couldn't be helped. The roses really had the fullest blooms, and their scent, thick and sweet, blocked out the nasty smell of garbage and trashed liquor bottles that littered the ground next to us. I took the flowers, despite my fussing, and held them in front of my face, smelling that sweet perfume. "You should have waited."

"No time like now." He stepped closer, resting his palm on the brick wall at my back and I wondered if he'd dare to kiss me, right here, where anyone could look into the alley to find us standing close, our mouths just inches apart.

No. That wouldn't do.

It was only him reaching forward, the space between us getting smaller and smaller, that made the fog that had come with the smell of those roses lift from my head. Dempsey leaned, eyes already closed, and I pushed him back with the flowers against his chest.

"Oh no you don't, Dempsey." He moved again, taking the flowers out of my hand to stand right in front of me, and I shook my head. "No indeed. You stop right there."

"Why would you want me to do that?" I hated that smile, just a little bit. I hated it because before it had loosened my strength that night in the fishing shack. It had me forgetting that I had no business kissing boys like Dempsey. By the end of that night my lips were swollen and beat with a throb from all the kissing. That smile told me that Dempsey wanted to make my lips throbbing and swollen again.

"Come on now…just a little kiss. I did bring you flowers."

"Uh huh, from your mama's garden. You had to steal them. She wouldn't give the Wise Men a single flower for Jesus's birth, much less her son. Especially when he wants to give them to a no-account colored girl like me." He really didn't think sometimes, and it had me fuming. God knows the trouble he'd be in now. "She's gonna whip you good."

"Ah, sweet Sookie, it's worth the beating…or it would be, if you kiss me." He was taller than me by about three inches, and it was that long stretch of shadow that distracted me, that and the thick scent of his hair, the clean smell from his soap that come off his skin as he moved closer. Dempsey got his kiss, a slow, wet one, before my good sense returned, and I pushed on his chest again.

"That's enough. Go on, get out of here before your daddy's people see us together."

"I ain't worried so much about that." He moved closer, but stopped short when I shot him an ugly frown. Dempsey leaned on the wall next to me, pulling one of the flowers from the bunch in my hand. "He don't much care for Joe Andres, and so when the fool told my daddy that you'd attacked him…" He went quiet when I let out of muffled noise between my breaths, but waved off my worried frown. "Daddy had to drag it out of him. Damn idiot didn't want to go around telling people some girl got him good."

"How is it they haven't come looking for me?" My throat felt tight and I worried something fierce that Dempsey might have sassed his *daddy just to keep the man from nosing after me. But looking at him quick, there wasn't nothing that told me he'd been beaten. The same sweet, wide smile met me just then. The same thick top lip twitched a little when he smiled. The same gray-blue eyes shined, lit with something like laughter as he looked down at me.*

"Because, Sook…" There was a giggle between his breath that made me loosen some of my worry as Dempsey's smile grew wide. "For once in my miserable life, my daddy believed me when I told him you weren't to blame."

"Wha…how is that possible?"

"Like I said, he don't much care for Joe. He was likely to believe me when I said that fool was too drunk to remember passing out in the north field. My daddy believed me when I fibbed a little and said I'd seen him falling over the half-cut stump of that oak that got struck by lightning last summer."

It was unbelievable. Dempsey's daddy didn't agree with him about anything. Dang sure didn't seem the type that would believe his son over one of his loud, drunk friends. But the longer I watched Dempsey, the wider his smile became, and just like that my worry didn't feel like such a heavy thing.

"So, your daddy isn't going to change his mind? They aren't gonna come looking for me?"

Just then Dempsey's smile went a little weak, like he'd only just realized how worried I'd been, how scared the threat of his daddy's anger had made me. Until I spoke it, if I'm telling the truth, I didn't know how worried I was myself. But Dempsey's lowering smile and the way his tall body ate up the space between us as he stood in front of me had me not remembering that I'd been so scared.

"How many times do I have to say it, Sookie?" He moved closer still, and I swore the air around us started to sizzle. There was heat that I didn't

reckon came from the humidity in the spring air. The noise of the city fell away then, just with one look from the boy who didn't care about things that were fittin', things that those staring eyes would eat up like a juicy steak. "Long as I'm breathing, I'll look after you." He held my face, tilting my chin up, so close, just inches from his mouth. His breath was sweeter today than it had been Saturday, and I wondered for a second what he'd eaten that made it seem so. "Promise," he said, like a whisper only half remembered.

And just when Dempsey pressed his lips against mine, the noise of the city and the stench of the alley came back, like the ripping of a bandage on a sore not healed.

"What the hell is wrong with you?"

I'd never heard Dempsey scream so loud, all flustered and surprised. Not even when he wanted to kill his daddy for breaking one of his ribs, but just then it seemed his anger would bubble over.

Sylv pushed Dempsey away from me, standing between us like some sad buffer to keep my friend from me. "You need to get on, Dempsey. Right damn now."

"The hell I do."

They stood there squaring off, like a dozen dumb men do in the city every night. But this wasn't a fuss over a woman they both wanted or money won and lost in a round of dice. This was my brother, who had always liked Dempsey almost as much as me, wanting to keep us both safe. This was Dempsey thinking only he could do that job.

When Dempsey showed no real sign that he'd back down, Sylv shook his head, lowering his shoulders like some sign that he wasn't really mad. "Man, I mean it now. This thing here between you two, it stops right now."

I didn't much like my brother making decisions for me, and I gave him a look, mouth tight from the quick flash of irritation that rushed up inside me. "Don't you tell me my business, Sylv."

"Think I need to, since you won't listen." He didn't bother looking my way as he spoke, seemed too wrapped up in watching Dempsey like he needed to be ready for a tussle when it came.

Dempsey was honest. Always had been, even when his face was all bloody and his eye had swollen shut, and my Bastie had asked how he'd gotten that way; his answer had come without him taking a breath to invent some lie. "My daddy beat me for helping mend your fence, Mrs. Bastie." Part of me thought he didn't know how to lie, so when he looked right at Sylv, all the anger gone from his face, I believed him. I think so did Sylv, and maybe that was the problem.

"Sylv, I'd never let anyone come near her. Not my blood…no one."

My brother let out a long, slow breath, like he wanted everything Dempsey said to be true. They'd been friends a long time. Maybe they weren't close like me and Dempsey were, but Sylv liked him fine. That's why I knew it hurt Sylv to tell Dempsey he wanted him gone. Maybe he didn't really want to see the back of Dempsey, but in Sylv's mind it was the only way to keep us all safe.

Our world wouldn't understand. Not now, not a year from now, and with my brother shaking his head, with him giving Dempsey a look that seemed like good riddance, I realized that maybe Sylv was right. There were men on the other side of this alley hell bent on seeing the end of my family, of all families like *ours. They'd want Dempsey to keep away and would likely go about making that happen in any way they could. It's what his daddy had been trying to beat into his head for years.*

Sylv shook his head, took a second to rub the back of his neck like the argument with Dempsey worked something hard into his body. "That's not a promise you can keep. Is it?" He was right. Though Dempsey wanted me safe, maybe thought he could manage it, being here in New Orleans, being the people we were in New Orleans, left no guarantees. Sylv seemed to know just then that Dempsey could make no promises. We all did. "Didn't think so."

I broke in. "Sylv, don't you go stepping on toes." It was a sad try at getting my brother and my Dempsey to calm. But Sylv had the notion in his head that he was right. He was my mama's son. He was my brother. He wouldn't back away until he had Dempsey admitting the truth.

"He can't even keep that no-good daddy of his from beating on him. You think he'll be able to keep you out of that man's way?"

"I would." Dempsey's try was weak, his voice small, but his eyes were bright again, lit with a fire that I thought might shoot out his fingertips.

"You'd want to." Sylv stepped back, finally looking away from Dempsey to glance around the alley, watching, holding his breath like something lurked just beyond the spot where the alley and street met. "Don't mean you could."

"I can protect her," Dempsey tried again, head jerking toward the sound of feet moving on brick behind us.

"That's not your job." Mama's face was drawn, a little sad as she walked toward us, hands moving around in the apron she wore as she dried them.

"Mrs. Lanoix."

"This thing, Dempsey," she interrupted, *"it's just gone on too long. Sookie is becoming a woman. Time for her to be thinking about starting a family of her own with a man of her own."*

My face flamed and something low and heavy started to build in my gut. Mama had never talked to me much about marrying anyone, but the past few months she'd mentioned me fixing myself up a little. She even had Bastie sew two new dresses for me, and Mama gave me a pair of her small-heeled shoes, with gold buckles. I'd reckoned she was gearing up to push me at some business, maybe have me work in some rich folks' home. But this? No. That was something she'd kept quiet about.

"There's plenty of men in the city that like the look of her." She didn't even glance at me when she said that, as though I wasn't even there, like I didn't matter. *"Men with jobs and homes. Men that will take care of her."*

"I…I can…"

"You can what?" Mama stepped closer, arms folded over her chest as she glared at Dempsey. *"You gonna marry my little girl? You and Sookie gonna live up in the tree house where the owls shit and sleep?"*

"Mama!" She still didn't bother to look at me, keeping all her attention on Dempsey, striking hard while his face paled, and his eyes went narrow. She kept at him, speaking sense that only sounded as such to herself. *"I'm sorry,* cher, *but that's a fairytale, and we don't live in the make-believe."* She paused for a half-second, and the expression on her face went flat; a long line pulled on

her mouth, but she set her jaw as though what she said would have to be taken for the truth. "It's time you keep away from her. For both of your own good."

"No." Dempsey's breath came out in a whoosh of sound and air. I'd never seen him look so heavy with fear. But the gray in his eyes got bigger, and he took to running his hand along the back of his neck as though he had to hold himself back to keep from screaming. "No. You can't do that." Mama seemed done with him, had tugged on my arm and pulled me back toward the street and away from Dempsey, but he kept on us, following along. When he spoke, his voice went high and shrieking. "You can't put me out. You can't…"

"Cher, how can I put you out?" Mama said, dropping my arm to face Dempsey. "You don't live with us. You need to go back to your own people. Be with your own people."

"You can't…Sookie…" He stopped, reaching toward me. He'd almost touch my hand before Mama slapped his hand away, and stood between us like a stone. Dempsey stepped back and kept his gaze down, as though he didn't dare look at her. Like he couldn't stand to see her face when he begged. His voice came out all ragged. "Sookie…she's my people. You…you all are."

"Dempsey, no…" I said, covering my mouth. He broke my heart just then. His life and ours had gotten tangled up together when we were kids. Bastie had cleaned his busted face, and Mama had fed him when his own people wouldn't. Now she was telling him he wasn't wanted anymore, and the look on his face, the streak of hurt and sorrow breaking his stubborn frown until tears made his eyes look like glass,

was more than I could stand to watch.

Mama pushed me out of the alley so I couldn't see what she did to Dempsey, so I couldn't tell how she'd get him to leave. But I heard what he said clear as day, and each sound he made broke my heart a little more.

"She's all I have, Mrs. Lanoix. Sookie's all I have in the world."

Me and Dempsey came from different worlds. We moved together like otters, floating side by side, letting the world around come over us, like a wave, rushing, passing, and the whole time we held on to each other. But those were the things that children did. That's what we'd done when were kids and didn't know about things like family and anger and the differences that kept people apart. We didn't know about money and poverty and struggling, because all the things we'd needed for most of our lives had been given to us. Struggle had been only as important as what game we would play in the backyard of my Bastie's home. That had been all we fretted over. It had been just as important, just as real as it should have been, to little kids.

But now we weren't kids. We were moving toward something that I couldn't name, and in the middle of all that, there were those curious, searching eyes, and the people dead set against anything that would keep Dempsey and me together. They hated us. They hated who we were and who we wanted to be, even if they didn't understand why. It was the way of things, for good or bad, and who were we to change the way the world had always turned?

I slipped into the shop, wanting to curl up and disappear, wanting the world to blow away until there was nothing left. But before I got my wish, Mama came in after me, slamming the door on Dempsey, on all the prying eyes, on all the swirl of hope and despair and want, and I knew that the world would never go away, but would pull me down right along with it.

Mrs. Matthews had not died, not yet. Mama likened her to an old rooster strutting around, teasing death because she was too ornery, too stubborn, to give the reaper even a hint that she was ready to leave this place. I wanted to be like her one day, when my hair was white and thin and my eyes had gone all snowy blue.

There was a whopper of a storm brewing, the sick breath of it raspy in the wind as folk all around the city made their plans. Some would stay, wait it out, not fearing what would come because something always did, so why run? Some had already left, more vexed by the calmness in the air and the low silence that had grown throughout the city overnight, it seemed. The calm before the storm.

For her part, Mama thought it best to keep me hidden in Tremé where neither Joe Andres nor Dempsey could find me. I knew her worry. It was the same as mine, but that didn't mean I was altogether happy that it was Mrs. Matthew's place, too small already for her and Bobby, that Mama locked me up inside. Everywhere I went, or thought of going, Bobby went too. There was no easing away from my little chaperone, and I had to listen to her ask a million damn questions about my brother and what sort of girls I thought he'd go for.

By the third day and another dang round of "oh Sylv is so…" I cooked up a plan to break away from my annoying shadow and get on with heading back to my mama's shop, worry and danger be damned.

I just couldn't take the questions, the worry, and yet another interrogation about my stupid brother. Who, it seemed, had disappeared right from the face of the earth. He, at least, hadn't been hidden in Tremé. Sylv, I bet, had gone on back to Mama's shop, running orders and cash with Uncle Aron like the world was not rattling and spinning to an end around him.

I could stand a little rattling myself, but it seemed the only dang thing in my future was yet another round of dominoes with Bobby and more readings from the Psalms to ease Mrs. Matthew's worry over her own end coming. And the storm, that had blown in with a vengeance.

Bobby's voice was monotone and thin as she read the Scriptures, like a bristle of dandelions in a storm, but I did my best to keep from judging her. She was, after all, reading to her dying grandmother.

"For the LORD watches over the way of the righteous, but the way of the wicked leads to destruction."

Even in that low, even tone, the verse was a nice thought. The wicked would be punished, so the Lord promised. Men who lied and hurt, like Ripper. Men and women, like Dempsey's parents, who struck out in hatred to reign in their own child with violence. People like Joe Andres who thought the world and those in it were here for their own sick needs. All, according to Scripture, would be handed a dose of justice. They and their destruction would not be looked over. They would not be protected in the end.

Would we?

My mama was making hooch and selling it to drunks and whores. She did make some to heal and help, but was that enough? Sylv snuck into Lily's room when her house was settled and dark so he could kiss her and touch her like it was just something to do because he'd got the notion to do it. Did that make my mother and brother wicked? Did the bad they did get cancelled for the times they were good?

It was a thought that came heavy on my mind as I listened from the front porch of the Matthews' small house as Bobby kept on with the Psalms, reading louder now to be heard over the storm. I wasn't thinking of much but how we'd all be dealt with when our time came. I wasn't even worrying over the wind and rain that fell onto the street around that small cottage in buckets and sheets.

Then, out of nowhere, there came a chill with that wind, and something dark and listless fell over me. A feeling took root inside my belly and stayed there as Bobby's voice went on with no movement in the sound at all. That feeling kept my eyes unfocused and the chill on my skin, the lower Bobby's voice sounded and the heavier the whip of wind and rain came down around me. The feeling that something was going to happen. Something bad.

I blinked, trying to bring myself from the sadness that took over. That's why I didn't notice the hunched form darting toward the house, rail thin but tall. His slacks were slicked snuggly around his thighs and the umbrella he held was broken on one side.

"Sookie!" my brother shouted, giving up on the umbrella and throwing it to the ground when he reached the Matthews' porch. He waved quickly, his long, slim fingers like the flaps of a flag. "Come on here, come now!"

Sylv tore off his wet jacket, holding over both our heads when I met him in the street, huddled close and already dripping as he led me away from the Matthews' cottage, down toward the front side of Tremé.

"Uncle Aron got one of those fast and loose ladies from the brothel to give us a ride out of the city." He pulled me closer toward him when a thick band of rain and wind sloshed against us. "Mama wants to head on to Atlanta. The storm is getting too bad; folks say the levies won't hold and it's gonna drown us all."

"She's a little late," I said nodding toward the line of cars and trucks already backed up, horns blaring with stragglers hanging off the back cabs and bumpers like rats on a sinking ship. "The traffic will be stupid."

"Well, at least we'll be headed in the right direction."

We passed another line of cars, these with damn fools not giving a single care to the corners of the streets where the police huddled together, watching the crowd weaving out of the city.

I didn't like the look of one of them policemen especially. He had pockmarks all over his face and a mean little frown bunched under the sparse mustache he wore. Him I'd seen more than once, sniffing around when Uncle Aron and Sylv walked ahead of me to clear the path from busybodies that might be curious about what I carried in my basket.

"What about Bastie?"

"She caught a ride from cousin Ethel. They're head out toward their kin in Virginia." When I didn't say anything, Sylv glanced down at me, putting his arm around my shoulder. "She's snug as a bug." I snorted out a laugh, and my brother stopped walking, moving his chin down. "What is it? You look vexed."

We started walking again after Sylv caught my head shake but he pulled me closer, weaving us through the crowd, glancing this way and that to keep a lookout for anything worrisome that might be headed toward us.

"I don't like it. Leaving," I said, waving a wet hand at the crowd and weather. "Something's percolating. More'n just the storm." A heavy shudder took over my body then, and I fought to push it down. "I feel it deep inside."

For a second Sylv watched me, pulling me from the street and the screeching tires of a rusted Chevy when it came too close to the sidewalk. "Aw, hell, girl, you just mooning over Dempsey Simoneaux."

Until he mentioned Dempsey, I hadn't exactly put my thoughts on him. He'd slipped in and out of my concentration while I stayed with Mrs. Matthews. It was his smile mostly, and the memory of his sweet, full mouth that kept me wondering how he'd fared since Mama sent me to Tremé. I'd spent most of my nights worrying that his daddy had decided Dempsey was a liar and went at him with a belt for talking against Joe Andres.

"You hear anything of him?" I asked Sylv, not caring when he rolled his eyes like I was stupid for keeping my thoughts on Dempsey. When my brother ignored me, I pulled him off the sidewalk to huddle next to me under a broken awning with sheets of water spilling from an opening between two thick boards. Not like it made much of a difference. We both were soaked. "Tell me what you've heard."

"I ain't seen him." Sylv tried wringing out his jacket, cursing to himself when a big splatter of water fell onto his head.

"You lying to me."

"Damn, Sookie, so what if I am?" He threw down the jacket, giving it a kick for good measure before he jerked me back onto the sidewalk. "The both of you are itching for trouble, courting it like it won't be ruin of both of you."

"Sylv…" I waited, ignoring his stupid try at changing the subject.

"I ain't seen him at all since Mama told him to get…"

"But?"

Two fat hustlers, I suspected some of Ripper's old henchmen, walked in front of Sylv, eyes narrow, gaze heavy on the pair of us as we headed into the thick of the Quarter where everyone seemed to be leaving. But we waved them off, more worried about the weather and getting to Mama and Aron in time than over two fat bullies who I bet couldn't keep up with us if we took off running.

"Sylv," I said when we glanced at each other, silently deciding we needed to hurry down the sidewalk.

He didn't look at me when he spoke. "Bastie said she saw a whole mess of Mr. Simoneaux's white men all gathered together this morning when Ethel came to get her. Policemen too, and not Parish either. They was New Orleans cops."

"Did she see Dempsey?" I watched my brother as he moved through the crowd and didn't like how light his skin looked just then, as though something set in his throat and he didn't want to let it out. That look on his face made something thick and knotted clot the air in my throat.

"No," he finally said, taking my hand to tug me along quicker. "She said she hadn't seen him for a week."

Dempsey was the sweetest boy I'd ever known, and he was the only one I'd ever let get close enough for a kiss. I thought maybe, despite the hurry in our steps and the wild noise around us, despite the trouble we were likely all in because of his daddy, that maybe, if our world had changed, that Dempsey would *be the boy I'd get a chance to be with. Maybe forever.*

We made it two blocks from Mama's shop where the sidewalk was thinner and the crowd moved slower. I followed Sylv without really thinking of where we were going or why the streets were filling up with water. It sloshed around our ankles as we scurried.

"Sylv…" I started, pulling on his arm to make him stop but my brother's arm tightened and his whole body went straight as the blade of a knife.

"Son of a bitch." Sylv didn't curse often. Bastie had always made sure we kept our tongues civil, but just then, watching wide-eyed as a few blocks away Mr. Simoneaux and a half a dozen policemen stormed into Mama's shop, I thought maybe Bastie wouldn't mind so much.

Things went muddy then. Dark and thick, as though the water around us came straight from the Manchac and not the Mississippi. Sylv took off, running toward Mama's small shop, and he got tussled and pushed back as Mr. Simoneaux stood next to a large truck with a shotgun on his shoulder and Joe Andres at his side. As I got nearer and spotted Uncle Aron and Mama screaming at three policemen, wrestling with them as they fought the rising water on their calves and the men screaming about prohibition and illegal contraband, I could just make out the shape of a boy sitting in the cab of Mr. Simoneaux's truck.

"There's that little bitch." I could only guess that I was the little bitch Joe Andres pointed to because as I made my way toward Mama, who was still fighting with the policemen and the rising water, Mr. Simoneaux and Andres cornered me. "What you got to say for

yourself, gal? You gonna tell those policemen how you attacked me? How you tried stealing my wallet when I'd had too much drink?"

He wasn't worth the argument, a fact I thought was plain when I darted around him to follow my Mama and Uncle Aron, just as they broke away from the policemen.

"Run, baby. Run fast."

I didn't know where Uncle Aron was or how I'd gotten ahead of him. I didn't know if Sylv followed or where it was Mama was leading us. I only knew that the rain came so hard and fast now I could only make her out by the black hem of her slip as she dashed ahead of me and those long, red nails as Mama reached out her hand.

We came to some building I didn't recognize, and slipped right in. There were tarps that covered the broken windows and wooden crates stacked up ten feet along the inside. It smelled like mildew and dirt and of the sweat and rain that came off me and my mama's skin and hair.

"Keep still," she said to me, pulling me next to her as we hid underneath a wooden stairwell with more tattered tarps and half broken crates. She moved her head, nodding at the burned smudge in a circle around the foot of the staircase and I wondered, trying to distract myself from the race of my heart and the shake that took over my hands and fingers, if this was where drifters came to rest when nights in the city were cold and rainy.

Outside, the rain drown out most of the noise, but Mr. Simoneaux's voice carried and I heard my brother crying out, begging for something I could not hear.

"If we're still and quiet," Mama promised, her voice in a whisper,

"maybe they'll go away and give on up..." She said it like she meant it. At least for a few seconds. Her rare smile was big and broad, like she thought it might give me a little comfort. Maybe make me feel less hopeless than I did just then.

But my mother knew same as me that they would not give up. Not when they felt they were justified, and men like Mr. Simoneaux and Joe Andres always thought they were justified, especially when they were doing the devil's work. And it must have been the devil's work, else how would it have been possible to start a fire when Noah's own storm was raging outside?

The smoke started to billow before we realized what was happening. Sylv's voice was panicked and loud and I swore I heard someone else—a different voice, not my brother's— pleading for things I couldn't hear.

"They'll come out," Mr. Simoneaux said in a voice meant to carry, and there was a whole lot of laughter in that promise. "Don't you fret, they'll come on out."

The smoke got thicker, billowed wilder, and Mama grabbed me, led me to the opposite side of the room where it was a bit clearer, her eyes wide as she hurried around to the windows, yelping when she tugged down a tarp and saw Joe Andres on the other side with a gun pointed right at her.

"Come on out, gal. Come on now." There was tobacco between his teeth and the same greedy spark in his eye that had been there the night he ripped my shirt open. "Don't you make me say it again."

When I started to cough, because the smoke had gone black

and one side of the building had gone up in a hot, bright flame, Mama pulled me along with her towards a set of rickety stairs that led to a platform in the direction of a catwalk on the second story. A large opening, way high up the wall of the building, probably meant for offloading, was broken and open to the elements, with a large chain bolted to the crossbeam above it. Climbing those sagging stairs two at a time, Mama held tight to my hand, thinking, I guess, that if we got to the roof we could jump to the next building. But from the platform we saw that the catwalk up ahead dropped off in the center with only that long chain stretching high enough to reach the broken window.

"You little enough, Sookie, I want you to climb up there." Mama's voice was wild, broken as she screamed over the sound of the flames, fighting off the coughs that wracked her lungs. She pulled off the kerchief that had bound up her hair and wrapped it around my nose and mouth, trying to smile at me through the smoke, trying to give me some courage. "You can make it, baby. I know you can."

"Mama, no. I can't." I glanced at the broken window, some two stories above the ground. "It's too high. It's just too high."

She shook me then like a rag doll, her fingers clawing into my arms. "You listen here to me, girl. You get up there and climb that chain." I hated the way her voice cracked. My mama was strong, tough as nails. In my whole life I never seen her cry or fret over nothing. Now she went at me like she was desperate, like she was near to begging me, and my mama never begged for a thing in her life. "You might fall, you might make it to the building across the way, but you will not burn up in this building."

Just then, a back draft swooped up the side of the building. There were shouts and voices from below screaming at us to get off the stairs and out of the building. But the fire had gotten too thick and all the lower windows and doors had been engulfed with flames. There was no way out save by going up.

My mother let out a wet sounding cough and gasped, getting to her knees to breathe air that wasn't a cloud of smoke, but there wasn't much of anything in that building except that dark, deadly air. She pushed me, hard, toward the opening and the rusted chain that hung from the rafters above. "Mama, I can't leave you!"

"We ain't got much choice, baby."

She looked up at me then, her face dark, eyes red-rimmed and watering, and it was all I could do to remember what she wanted from me. She'd called me baby. She'd never done that before in all my years. My mama wanted me out of that building. She pushed me toward freedom and breath and safety. My life mattered to her—she wanted me to live.

"Mama…"

"Go, Sookie. You go on now."

I turned to look at the opening above. There was so much smoke I could only make out the streak of dull silver from the chain hanging down. Mama had gone quiet behind me, but I was too scared to look back, trying to desperately screw up my courage while the world fell apart around me. I heard and felt the boards under my feet groan, and in desperation, I jumped toward that chain, locking my legs and hands around it, swinging off the half-fallen platform just as it creaked and broke in two, spilling down into the dark below. Mama went down with *it.*

"No! No, Mama! Mama!"

But she couldn't hear me. I held onto that chain like a lifeline, afraid that if I loosened my grip even the tiniest bit I'd join my mother in the flames below.

"Sookie! Sookie, look here…"

My momentum had swung the chain so that it listed towards the open window. I tried to see into the street below, and moved my body to make the chain move in even wider arcs, aiming for the opening and freedom. Even through my terror and the roaring of the flames below, I could hear screams, some angry, some scared, but I couldn't tell which ones I knew or which ones cared if I lived or died. I did catch sight of Uncle Aron on his knees, that hat scrunched up between his hands as he cried something fierce into the fabric. The chain creaked with each swing I made, in and out, flames and air, back and forth as my body felt heavy and my lungs full.

"Sookie! You look at me right damn now!" That was my brother; he sounded so angry. I could see him across the street, angled so he could watch what was happening inside where I was clinging for dear life to the swinging chain. His face had gone near white. And next to him Dempsey moved his attention to me, looking like he was working something swift and clever to get me down.

But I was so tired. My head throbbed and my fingers ached.

Sylv had blood on his lip, and Dempsey's left eye was again a black bruise.

I loved them. The pair of them. I knew that just as sure as I knew that my mama had always loved me. She died to see me out of that building.

I blinked when one hand slipped from the chain, my gaze falling onto Dempsey's face, to that round, perfect mouth. I reckoned I did love him and not just because of his sweet mouth and sweeter kisses. He'd been my best friend since I was little. I supposed I'd always loved him.

Funny thing about love, ain't it? Sometimes it saves you and sometimes, like right then, even love isn't enough.

The smoke billowed up, choking me, so thick I couldn't breathe. So thick there was nothing I could do but let it swallow me whole.

Nash

I felt like a mourner. The only thing missing was the black clothes. Instead I wore a suit, something obnoxious, designer, that Duncan insisted I let him buy me. Five pieces in this suit, and I recycled and restructured them with ideas Daisy grabbed from Pinterest. Still, a cream button up and green tie didn't exactly say "mourner," but I felt like that's what I should call myself.

The dream had not transferred into events that shaped my daily life. It went beyond the sleeplessness and how their recurrence made me feel and act and see the world. Now it had become something that left me desperate and sad and too damn mixed up by all the feelings I had to make sense of anything other than the sadness that wrapped around me like a noose.

I wanted to let it all go; Willow, Sookie and the second-hand memories that people I didn't know had in D.C. Part of me wanted to believe Willow, that it was the lives we led before that drew me closer to her, that reasoned why I couldn't get her out of my head.

"Mr. Nation?"

Daisy's voice pierced through the fog surrounding me, the one that had me forgetting that I had to get ready for a second investor's meeting, this one to determine if I was smart enough and Duncan slick enough to fatten up our bank account. I only had three hours to pull it all together.

"Yeah?" My answer was sharp and fast, like Daisy had scared me awake in the middle of Mass. But I didn't go to Mass and had never been a Catholic, and Daisy, with her shrill voice and expectant tone, was only doing the job I paid her to do.

"Mr. Phillips asked I remind you of the lunch meeting. It's on your calendar."

"Um…hang on Daisy."

I made no commitments. Not to Willow and damn sure not to Duncan, not even with our lunch, where we were supposed to go over what needed to be done before the presentation. But my thoughts weren't on the presentation or the final work that needed to be done on my code. The program was through beta testing, and we had clients who were willing to test the products, but there was still a lot of work to muddle through before we could go live. That would take more focus than I had, something I knew Duncan would yell at me about during this lunch meeting. But I wasn't ready.

"Daisy, tell him I'll need to reschedule."

"But, sir, he said…"

"I don't care what he said." She was quiet on the other line, but then she would be. The walls were glass, and Duncan was loud when we fought. It wasn't like someone walking by couldn't tell when we argued, something that had been happening a hell of a lot lately.

Daisy had seen it all. She'd even doctored my knuckles last week when Duncan pissed me off so bad that I punched my wooden desk like a total idiot. She didn't like hearing the fighting, and patching up my torn flesh when I was being a Neanderthal wasn't in her job description. Of course she'd argue about me canceling the meeting. It would only lead to drama she likely didn't want to hear. So I cut her off before she could say anything more.

"Daisy, listen…" I stood, stretching my shoulders and arms, "there's a…family situation that's come up, and I'll need to cut my day short. Tell Duncan I'll be in an hour early in the morning."

She waited a half-second longer than I thought was necessary and then cleared her throat. "Yes, sir."

My office was a round, giant thing with a modest desk in the center of the room and two small sofas on each side. As programmer, I didn't do Duncan's dirty work, instead stretching out budgets and timelines until my software was perfect; until it was ready for a live date and multi-million dollar clients. But the long hours and worry and concentrating on how to finalize all the hard work I'd put in for the past ten years had become something small and distant to me since Willow had yanked me into her life. Months had gone by, and everything had shifted with her open door, her wide eyes, and the pull of her small fingers on my arm. She had ripped apart everything I knew, spilling open the chasm of focused peace I'd cultivated for myself with whatever game she'd played on me that first night. She'd loosened something, and that something had ushered in the dreams…the memories…the past that would not leave me be.

Willow had taken off without so much as a glance over her shoulder. Like I was nothing. Like she could drop me, forget that minutes before I had been inside her, that I had made her moan and scream and laugh all at the same time. The jasmine from her hair still lingered on my pillow the morning after we'd slept together. There were a few strands of her hair on the mattress and the hem of my sheet was smudged pale pink from her lipstick. Willow had come into my apartment wanting me, taking me, letting me take her back, and had left traces of herself behind. Then she'd been gone before I could stop her. She'd left, and it seemed like hours afterward I could still feel her everywhere in my room.

And then…Sookie died in my dream.

There was a lot for me to mourn.

"Have you lost your fucking mind?" Duncan's loud question erupted as he thundered through the doorway, the brass doorknob slapping against the glass wall. It happened so quick, with such a force, I was surprised the glass hadn't broken. "You cannot cancel on me. Not again."

He didn't bother to ease into this fight. Duncan had been gripping so tightly to the thin hold he had on his patience that this one canceled meeting had him losing it completely. His face was red, like he'd just contracted **rosacea** and hadn't bothered to treat it. Duncan's already small, beady eyes had taken on a wet, glassy look, and the rims around both were blotchy and red. He looked exhausted, old and out of breath, and I knew it was my fault. I had let everything in my head destroy the company we were trying to build. He took a moment to close the door, and then turned on me.

"You are fucking with my patience and you're threatening everything I…"

"You?" I said it because it occurred to me that Duncan, no matter how upset he was, didn't have any real claim on the work I did. He made phone calls. He took rich assholes out for rounds of golf or for fancy meals I couldn't pronounce at restaurants I'd likely never be able to get a table at. But the work? The idea? The plan for it all? That had been me, not Duncan. "You, man? Your work?"

"Don't start with that again. I've pulled my weight."

It took me a minute, but I stood, slowly, hands resting on my desk because I wanted to give him time to calm, to restate what he'd said. But Duncan didn't apologize or backtrack. In fact, he only got redder in the face and his eyes grew glassier. "Maybe you wanna try that again?"

I wasn't a jock. Despite my size, it wasn't in my nature. I was fit and large, but that was Nation genetics. I looked like my dad and my granddaddy—big and brawny, with not a lot of neck and too much lip. If I needed to, and sometimes you just damn well needed to, I could move my shoulders a certain way or pop my neck at just the right time and look intimidating as hell. But I rarely needed to use it.

Just then, I need to strut a little because Duncan looked a lot like he might lose his entire shit.

He ignored my question, mouth quirking like he wasn't sure how intimidating he could look if he curled his lip and bared his teeth. We weren't dogs, and I had a good four inches on the guy—I also knew that without me Duncan had no deal. He had zero leverage. That asshole didn't scare me.

"You need to check yourself," he said, voice high and cracking, but he didn't seem to notice and leaned forward, copying my stance as he glared at me. "I can make your life fucking miserable."

I stood up, flexing my arms a little when I crossed them. "That right?"

"You better fucking believe it." He straightened then, but kept his hands at his side. The red splotches over his cheeks and across his forehead lightened just a little. "I can call in favors, of which I have a shit-ton. I can pull your business license and make it impossible for you to get rental space or staff. Trust me, Nash, without my help you're just a code monkey with no way to get your product to the public."

"And you're just a rich prick scratching your ass until someone smarter than you, more creative than you, comes along so you can ride their coat tails."

"Fuck you..."

"I don't think so." My laptop shook when I slammed

the lid closed, and I came around the desk to glare down at Duncan. "You can't fucking intimidate me, man. I might not have your connections, but I have a product that a lot of people want, and you have zero legal claim to any of it. You pull my license, and I'll go somewhere else to get another one. You block me from renting, and I call a few favors of my own. You think I went to MIT and didn't network? Man, please. Code monkeys stick together."

I knew I'd flaked out on Duncan. My life, my distractions, my damn dreams had split apart the work I'd done with him like a sledgehammer, each blow fracturing another split, each dream cracking apart what I knew as normal. It was my fault, I knew that, but something had always been unsettling about Duncan. Something had always told me that with him, I'd always have to watch my back. And now it was time to cut some ties.

When he went on glaring, unable, maybe unwilling to answer back from my insults, I decided right then he wasn't worth the drama. There might not be a Nations with Duncan, but I knew for damn certain there would still be a Nations on my own.

"You know what? I don't need this." I stepped back, grabbing my laptop and a few notebooks I kept in the top desk drawer.

He watched me as I moved around the office, picking up chargers and books, a few Post-Its with shorthand notes I'd made to myself before stuffing them all in my backpack and loosening my tie.

Duncan watched me in silence until I had grabbed the

doorknob and opened the door. It was only when I'd stepped over the threshold that he decided to speak.

"You walk out of this building, Nash, and I'll sue your ass. You're in breach. I don't like people who walk away from me."

I laughed then, pulling up my backpack on my shoulder. Outside in the lobby, Daisy and the contracted programmers we had hired to pound the code paused their conversations and hung up their calls to listen to us.

"Sue me for what Duncan? I got nothing to my name. I don't have a damn thing to lose."

I left him standing in my office, that face still angry and red. A nod to a few of the staff that had been with me from the beginning, a couple who followed me into the elevator, and I left Duncan's building, leaning against the wall wondering why I didn't feel worse. Wondering why I'd been able to lie so easily. Duncan may not realize it, but I did have something to lose. Something I thought could never be mine again. But it had nothing to do with investors, or programming, or even my precious code. It was something a lot more personal.

Sookie had been scared. Up there on that chain, watching the people she loved most in the world stare up at her, frozen in fear, in terror, I realized I wasn't sure if I'd ever loved anyone like that. Nat, maybe.

My mom, once. But now? Did I love someone enough that losing them would shatter my world? I wasn't sure.

I thought about that the entire way home when the homeless man on the train farted and snored as he slept against the broken subway window. I kept thinking about it when I gave my seat, the last one on the bus, to an exhausted-looking pregnant woman who seemed like she held a bowling ball under her shirt and the damn thing weighed a ton.

Love was for suckers. I'd always thought that. It had been a mantra I kept on a loop in my head anytime a female got a little too attached. Anytime I had the inkling to get that way too.

Until Willow.

Until that night in my apartment. Until the entire room smelled and felt like her. Until a week had passed since she walked out of my apartment, and I couldn't shake the feeling that I'd lost her. Had I even had her to begin with? I had no clue. But damn if it hadn't felt like I had.

She occupied my thoughts all the way to Brooklyn. She stayed there as I made it to my apartment, as I changed into my gym clothes and got in a five-mile run through the park, even managed to make it as far as the Old Stone House, knowing she wouldn't be there, not on a Thursday, not during the week. Still, Willow invaded my thoughts until I couldn't see the sidewalk in front of me. Until I stopped running altogether and shuffled back to my building like a punk, too winded, too worn out by the day to do more than remember the taste of her skin and just how sweet her laugh had sounded.

Midnight, three hours later, and a shower, a decent hoagie, and two Blue Moons still didn't manage to make me sleepy or wear me down. I thought about Sookie and what she felt as she died. That had been lodged in my chest like a spear-sized splinter. Funny thing about those dreams; they didn't seem like dreams at all. Not the ones about Sookie. Not the ones about the library and the big son of a bitch in love with that redhead. I felt it all—that fear, that love, that powerful lust. It came at me like a wave, sticking me in the chest, constricting my breathing until my eyes burned. Then Willow took over, wrestled away the dreams and filled me up like a spirit, taking away the voice that tried in vain to remind me I didn't need anything or anyone. I'd walked away from one person today. God knew I had no problem doing that. But Duncan and his slick ways were nothing like Willow. He didn't haunt me. His smile, his laugh, the gleam in his eye did nothing for me; not like Willow. She overpowered me like no one ever had.

"Shit," I said to myself, sitting up in bed because that faint jasmine scent still hung onto the sheet and pillow. Something came over me then. It was the urgency to be rid of her, to exorcise her from that room. I stripped off the sheets, pulled the pillows from their cases and grabbed the comforter. Willow had been wrapped up in it, her naked body against the thick fabric, and I wanted her gone, right then. I wanted her out completely.

I ran down to the laundry room and stuffed everything into the washer, and poured in bleach and detergent, determined to eradicate her. I promised myself I wouldn't think about how much that jasmine had comforted me, how the smell of it got me sleepy, kept me there. I wouldn't think of how the night before I'd missed her so much the pillow got tucked under my chin, how I'd fallen asleep smiling from the smell on the fabric.

Didn't matter now. Now there would be nothing for me—no business, no Willow, and I'd have myself back. There wouldn't even be dreams, not with Sookie being gone. Not with her story at an end.

The machine rumbled to life, rocking me as I leaned against it, closing my eyes at the rhythm, and I scrubbed my face, wondering why I couldn't get the sick feeling, the regret, from my stomach.

Returning to my apartment, I found the living room dark and quiet when I walked into it. I grabbed the tennis ball on the console and the remote to let Coltrane speak to me. That should work. It had before, though not that first night. Not when Willow interrupted my entire world and tugged me into her apartment.

"*Shit.*" Another recall and I was back where I'd been in my bedroom, thinking about that first night, and the others afterward, thinking about that kiss on the roof and the sting of her leaving my place.

She was a witch. I'd known that for months. She worked

some kind of wonderful spell on me, and no matter how I fought it, I loved being under her power. Outside, the night was inky black and perfectly still. No wind, no rain, nothing that would keep her from the roof. Nothing in that apartment would keep me from it either.

My chest ached a little as I climbed the stairs, and I didn't think it was because of the exertion. Some part of me knew when I took my last step and opened that roof deck door, that I'd find her out there, so when she wasn't there, that ache in my chest tightened even more.

The cityscape was boring; Brooklyn always had been. The only thing remarkable about it was the bridge in the far distance, but that was more New York than Brooklyn, no matter the name or how close it was to us. Out there in the city, everything moved and bustled. In Brooklyn, on my roof, everything went in slow motion. Especially when I turned and, with a jolt, spotted Willow hunkered down, her head hidden behind the long back of the lawn chair as she rested in it.

That wild hair was up in a bun and little flyaways framed her sweet face. She held a box in her lap but didn't touch it, didn't do much of anything but stare forward. Then she seemed to notice me, and sat up straighter, which is when I caught a glimpse of the bottle of bourbon under her arm. Her face was drawn, her features tight with tension, but she didn't speak when I moved close and sat, sharing a seat with her.

I nodded at the bottle, but kept my voice calm. "You feeling a little southern tonight?" She'd told me the first night about her granddaddy and his love of cigars and whisky. I'd almost half-expected to see her puffing on a stogie.

"A lot southern," she said, drinking from the bottle without watching me.

"You're not from the south, Will." There was a small twitch on the left side of her mouth when I called her that. She'd smiled wide and happy the first night I'd used her pet name, like the sound of the endearment had made her all fuzzy headed.

She set the bottle down next to her hip, steadying it with the crook of her elbow before she pushed the box on her lap toward me. "My folks stopped by yesterday. It's been exactly two months since my great-grandfather died, and they wanted me to have this box. Dad thought it had been lost, all this…stuff…"

"What is it?"

She waited, licking her lips like she had cotton mouth before she answered. I wasn't sure what to make of that expression. It was serious, a little worried. "Pictures, letters, rings he bent and twisted from silver dollars and pennies during the war when he was on watch." She pulled one out of the box and slipped it on her pinky. It was old, dingy copper, splotched green, but Willow stared at it like it was a Tiffany diamond. I liked the look on her face, how, for a second it made me forget that I wanted her gone, that she'd walked away so easily.

"I remember you mentioning him dying."

"Yeah, well, my folks thought I'd want this stuff. It's all the things that meant the most to him, except maybe us."

Her fingers were small, the nails short but trim, and when she handed over a small black and white picture, my fingers grazed hers, lingering as I held the old photo with a little reverence. Not long ago, I'd kissed each finger, and let them run over my body, across my naked chest. There were no calluses, nothing that would take away her softness, nothing that made her seem hard around the edges.

"It's him and…I suppose one of his friends, when they were kids back in New Orleans."

I stopped then, frowning when I glanced down at the picture. "My great-granddaddy was from New Orleans. They were all Creole. Or so my Dad claimed." The two boys in the picture, a light-skinned black kid and a white boy with light hair, were smiling, laughing at something behind the camera, maybe the person who took the picture. Something felt odd, something that twisted my stomach, and I caught a flash of déjà vu. It filled up my chest and made it hard to breath.

"Who is this?" I asked Willow, turning it over to see only two things written on the back. "Summer, 1927" and "D and S".

"My great-grandfather and his friend. He's in this one too," she said, digging around in the box before withdrawing another image.

The edges of the picture were frayed and the corner on the bottom left side was torn off. But they were clearly the same two boys, both standing on either side of a pretty girl. Her hair was curled, hit just below her ears, and she had dark eyes with the smallest slant to them. That twist in my stomach got worse as I concentrated on the girl, trying like hell to remember why that face looked so familiar, why I knew what the sound of her voice was like or how she looked when she laughed.

"That's...I don't..." And then, it hit me, like a slap across the face. It hit me hard and dramatic and I stood, the photo dropping from my fingers. "That's impossible."

Around me the night got cold, like a twister had somehow swept through the city, not disturbing anything on the streets—no trash cans or post signs along the sidewalks, no tourists taking long shots of the Brooklyn Bridge. Everything was still and quiet, except for the ripping rhythm of my heart and the sweat that formed on my forehead.

Willow looked scared when I stepped back, her wide eyes. "What is?" Willow asked, picking up the picture from where it had fallen on her chair. "Nash?"

It occurred to me then that maybe this was all tied in to Willow after all. All this...this weird connection, the memories that rose up inside me since I met her. I was a man of logic and science. I didn't believe in things like angels or second chances or different lives. I believed in life and death and that both only came around once. But Willow didn't. At least she swore she didn't. That's why she'd left me the night we slept together. That's why she swore she couldn't be with me. Having no faith meant I couldn't have Willow. But this…this connection, it was too much. It was just too damn much. It literally shook the foundation of what I thought I believed.

"What is this?" I pointed at the picture, at the face I'd seen so many nights. The smile was the same, the smooth, dark skin, the flash of laughter in her eyes. It was her, I knew it. But good God, how? "What the hell is this? My God, Will, how is this even possible?"

"What…"

"Your granddaddy?"

"Great-granddaddy," she said, moving her head into a tilt. "What about him?"

"This…" I took the picture from her, head shaking, unable to keep a tight grip on the picture. "That's…that's Sookie."

Willow stared at me, mouth dropping open. "How do you know about Sookie?"

I blinked, eyes narrowing before I answered her. "She's…she was my great-grandpaw's sister. But she died, Will. She died in…"

"A fire."

The noise I'd heard fogging up my head, clogging

sense and reason, turned into disbelief and fear, all went away with Willow's words. Something burned me up from the inside when I looked at her. Something that made my head swim and my chest flood with dread and worry as she stepped closer. For the first time since I'd met her, I worried Willow was someone I wouldn't be safe around. A harbinger of something unexplainable. The touchstone of something that simply could not be.

"They chased her," she said, her voice strained, waiting for confirmation. I gave it, my head moving in the slightest nod.

"Those white men. Dempsey's father and his friends," I said, speaking so low that I had to strain to hear her.

I fell against the brick wall behind me, my fingers shaking, my palm sweating. She knew. She'd seen Sookie same as me. Willow had dreamed the same dream.

"How is this possible?" I could hear the alarm in her voice, the disbelief.

"Willow…"

She shook her head, fingers trembling as she covered her mouth. "Nash…I saw it." She watched me, pleading, like she needed me to understand. The tremble in her fingers worsened, and a small shudder worked over her shoulders. "I watched the whole thing happen. I…I watched Sookie die."

Willow

There were flashes I did not recognize. Swirls of memory, the feeling of loss and want and anger—it all swam around me, filled my head so that when I dreamed, there was no rest.

My bedroom was silent and cold. It felt like a tomb, a dread that even a touch of light and the slip of laughter could not splinter. It was my cave away from the possibility of what I'd seen, what I'd always believed, and how, with one conversation, Nash had dismantled that belief.

"Maybe you should take a vacation." Effie's voice was calm, soothing over the phone, but even with the cool she covered herself with, I caught the hint of worry in her inflection. "Head out somewhere peaceful…the coast, or…*oh,* I know. Virginia."

Virginia reminded me of the places Riley recalled with such clarity. I couldn't go there. I couldn't go anywhere and not remember the life she'd led and the man she'd loved. She was everywhere.

Riley had loved Isaac. I knew that. She'd loved him like Dempsey had loved Sookie. Those dreams were fainter, the memory not as strong, but running like a current through all those lives was the pulse of something strong. Something that wouldn't be denied. Something, I knew without knowing how or why, that demanded to be felt.

"Or…"

"I think I'll just hide in my bedroom," I told Effie, settling my cell phone on the pillow next to me. The earbud wires got lost somewhere in the tangle of my hair and the pillowcase. "I just want to…I don't know…rest a little bit. Hide from the world." I exhaled, not liking how quiet Effie had become, as if she was gearing up for an argument and needed to decide how to begin it. "You ever feel that way, Effie? You ever just want to forget the world for a little while?"

"Of course I have, sweetie. Everyone has, but you know…"

"Then that's what I'll do." I'd already decided to hang up before she finished speaking. "I'll call you tomorrow. For now, though, I just need to sleep."

Washington D.C.

Senator Mansfield had given a great speech before the formal dinner. There was talk of honor, justice and liberty. The room was crowded with the elite of D.C. insiders—men and women who'd worked with the late President Kennedy championing Civil Rights. Others came in later, when Lyndon Johnson promised to finish that work, and now it was time for toasting the people who had chipped away at another chain of injustice, my parents among them.

"That man, he would make a good president," my mother said, leaning close to my father.

"Maybe so, my love." Dad shot a wink across the table, and then turned to his two law clerks. "Work isn't done, not by a long shot, though." he added. The clerks were a pair of young, idealistic Harvard grads eager to take on D.C. single-handedly. But first, Dad emphasized, they'd need to learn the difference between pleadings and briefs.

Ryan sat next to me, smiling like he wanted desperately to ask me how my weekend at the cottage with Isaac had been, but I kicked him under the table when he started to drop cryptic hints, flashing a wince as Dad watched over the rim of his glass.

"What's happening with the two of you?" He leaned close, elbow nearly toppling over his half-empty water glass. The room was noisy with people moving around and socializing, and I could barely make out his question.

"What do you mean?" Ryan asked innocently, clearly not disadvantaged by the crowd and the rolling noise of clinking dinnerware and emptying glasses.

"The pair of you, all night, you've been snickering and talking behind your hands. You want to share your secrets?"

"Nothing worth sharing, Dad," I quickly cut in. He didn't buy it, that much I gathered by the way his eyes met mine and held them for a beat longer than strictly necessary. My father was a busy man and he took his work seriously, but that didn't mean he'd ever give up being a parent, regardless of how old his kids had grown.

"Come now, Eric, leave them." my mom said teasingly, leaning in so he could hear her over the dinner buzz. "They are both here, yes? Both under one roof. You will scare them away with your meddling." My

mother's Polish accent had grown slightly more pronounced, due to her being on her second glass of chardonnay, but it only made her sound more charming.

Our parents were like two kids, still besotted and smitten after some twenty-five years. Dad kissed her forehead, and she momentarily laid her cheek on his shoulder.

It was true that I had been conspicuously absent from the family home over the past few months, taking the odd call from each of them or dashing off a quick note after my mother had dropped off another box of cookies or homemade pierogi at my dorm room, but that was about it. My mother was not one to pry, but my dad was understandable suspicious—after all, I was his only daughter. And, as much as I hated to admit it, I had been drawn into the D.C. social scene that, like it or not, impacted the way things got done.

"Does this low talking have anything to do with why Trent is sitting over there with his parents and not at our table, Riley?"

"Dad…"

"I know you two had a fight, but I think everyone expected you to have patched things up by now…"

I smiled at him even as something shifted in my chest. His tone was mildly teasing, and had we been somewhere else, I might have taken the opportunity to admit to him right there and then what had gone on between Trent and myself. But now certainly wasn't the time or the place, not with our table full of colleagues my parents had worked so hard with over the past year. I wasn't going to let his bringing up my love life ruin the evening.

"Daddy, please." I downed what remained of my red, dissatisfied when it did little to boost my resolve, and decided deflection was my best course of action.

"You know that a girl doesn't kiss and tell."

He shrugged, patting my mother's hand when she whispered in his ear. "Whatever it is, Trent seems to have no problem with broadcasting it. It's pretty obvious he's fixated on you. He's either been mooning over you all night, or shooting daggers in your direction. Damn, Riley, what on earth did you do to him?"

"Me?" I said in mock shock, but next to me Ryan straightened in his chair, holding my hand still when I balled my linen napkin in my fist. But try as I might, I couldn't keep up the façade. "It wasn't…" Thank heavens Ryan was there, giving me a wide, teasing smile but whispered, "Now's not the time, Riley" under his breath.

"Well, it looks as if we're going to find out, anyway." Dad said, standing and smiling at someone behind me.

I turned, and saw Trent and his father heading towards our table. I shot Ryan a panicked glance as Dad moved forward to shake hands with Mr. Dexter, and then motion at two empty chairs that sat at our table. Ryan, however, looked just as stricken as I did.

Mr. Dexter had been working the room, typical for the consummate social climber he was, always worming his way into the good graces of whatever cabinet member or high-ranking staff member could push his personal agenda. While I was not exactly enamored with his behavior, it was not uncommon nor even remotely surprising in this city. Everyone in D.C. wanted power, except maybe my parents, and that came hand in hand with double dealing and promise breaking. Trent's despicable behavior hadn't been learned in a vacuum—men like Trent and his father were used to getting whatever caught their eye, be it women or influence or power. Once they got them, they moved on to something else. My rejection of him was a challenge that Trent just couldn't let pass.

"You look beautiful, Riley," Trent said, leaning toward me with that watery-eye glint that I supposed he thought made him look charming, flashing me his million-dollar smile. It was all I could do to keep from snapping at him to leave me alone, but I opted instead to ignore him.

My father spoke to Mr. Dexter in animated tones, high spirited, but every so often he would glance at me, mildly curious as to why I dutifully ignored Trent even as he continued to speak to me.

"You can't be civil?" Ryan asked sotto voce, and I cut him a cool look, silently telling him to mind his own business. My brother leaned back, pretending to look to his left while scooting closer to me so as not to be overheard by Trent, still hovering at my shoulder, wine glass in hand, but waving to someone across the room. "You being with Isaac is one thing. But you know if you ignore Trent, questions are going to be asked. Is that a conversation you're ready to have? Is that something you want to share with these nosy people?"

I closed my eyes, wishing for once that I could escape my life, shoot far away from my family and the lives we lived in Washington D.C. In that moment I only wanted to be on some imaginary island with Isaac, forgetting the world and everything in it but the two of us. No one mattered, no one existed in that place, but me and the man I loved.

"Riley, are you all set for classes this upcoming semester?" I started, hitting my elbow on the table as Mr. Dexter's booming question cut through my private reverie and struggled to gain my composure as I noticed everyone around the table looking at me, politely waiting for my answer.

I crossed my leg, keeping my ankle out of reach of my brother's nudging foot. "Yes," I answered Mr. Dexter, falling back on my most practiced, sugary sweet expression. "I've enrolled in a course on the fall of Constantinople, one on statistical methodology, and Dr. Matthis is doing a seminar on the Protestant Reformation. Should be a good semester."

Trent's father smiled at me patronizingly. "Indeed, indeed," he crooned, but I don't think my answer even registered with him as he turned his attention to my father. "It's good you let her continue on with studying, Eric." His hand fell on my father's shoulder, in an attempt at a shared camaraderie. "Mind, it's best not to let young women become too invested in their studies."

"And why's that?" My father asked, his good-natured smile never lowering, but I could see the muscles in his jaw suddenly clench. Mom must have sensed something in his demeanor, in the way she sat up straighter, as if preparing to intervene if need be. "A good education is such an important part of any young person's development, women as well as men. Why on earth should my daughter, anyone's daughter, not be invested in their education?"

Trent's father didn't know my dad that well. Their paths crossed, yes, especially with Trent and me dating for a few months, but I don't believe they'd ever spoken about anything personal, certainly not outside of work. From the look of the effort my dad was having to put forth to maintain his composure, I guessed that was likely a good thing.

"Ah, so," Mr. Dexter said, dismissing my father's question and turning to his son. "Trent, you must bring Riley back around next week. Uncle Ray will be in town; we'll have to take the boat out to show *him the lake. You'd like that, wouldn't you, Riley?" He smiled at me as if he had just bestowed on me a great honor, nodding once as his own confirmation, fully expecting me to agree. When I only glared back at him, Mr. Dexter cleared his throat, obviously not used to his gestures being met with anything other than delight and gratitude.*

"Riley would love…" Trent jumped in, answering for me when I opened my mouth to speak. But his thoughtless assumption of control shattered the resolve I had made to at all costs remain civil at what should have been just another Washington dinner. In one fleeting moment, my father's clenched jaw and red face, and my mother' look of glittering concern, made me realize that they would stand behind me regardless of the consequences.

"I'm sorry, Mr. Dexter," I said, standing to face him, my voice solid and clear, "but Trent will not be 'bringing me around' next week, nor will I be accompanying you and your family to the lake." I was aware that other conversations around us were quieting, and while I had no intention of making a scene, I also had no intention of letting any kind of charade Trent was maintaining continue at my expense. "In fact, I will never again allow a man who thinks hitting a woman in the face is acceptable behavior to date me, or have anything to do with me, even if his last name is Dexter."

There was a brief pause as the admission sunk in, and then a number of things happened at once. The buzz in the room started up again, gossip no doubt spreading like wildfire. Mr. Dexter looked at me askance, broadcasting disbelief as his eyes darted surreptitiously around the room as if tallying up 'aye' or 'nay' votes in his head. Both Mom and Ryan had stood up to join Dad, who had drawn himself up with his eyes glaring, but knowing me well enough to wait and see what would play out before stepping in. Mom laid a hand on Dad's arm, her gesture at once both restraining and supportive. And Ryan stood between them all and me, despite the shock on his face—I'd told him about Isaac but not about Trent hitting me. But he was still my big brother, giving me the chance to pull Trent aside and hiss my now unbridled accusations at him.

"You had Isaac fired because you knew he cared about me," I said, my voice pitched for Trent's ears alone, even though he looked ready to spontaneously combust. "He's a good man, but you just couldn't stand it, could you? Him in the company of something you wanted? You saw him walking me home that night after you hit me. You saw him kiss my hand, didn't you? It must have made you livid, knowing that he was more of a gentleman than you'll ever be."

But with that I had pushed him too far. A man who hit a woman may be using bad judgment, but he was still a man, might even get a few sympathy votes from the other mover and shakers in power. But a man who not only loses his woman, especially to someone like Isaac, and then has to listen to her taunt him about it? That could not be borne, and Trent lashed out with all the fury of his trampled privilege and scorned pride, careless of how his words rang out around us.

"You think that makes you special, running off with someone like that? I'm a fucking Yale graduate, Riley. My father is on the president's staff, and you chase after some colored idiot who mops the floors in a library? You choose him *over* me *when you know I'm the better man?"*

You could have heard a pin drop.

"No," I said, throwing the napkin that had been bunched in my hand all this time down on my plate. "You're not the better man, Trent. You're not even a tenth of the man Isaac is. You can't touch him." And before anyone could say anything else, before the hum of voices started back up again, before my brother could catch me or my parents catch my eye, I walked out of that room, straight-backed, head held high, feeling like my chest was going to explode. And feeling free.

"Stop fidgeting."

"I ain't."

"You are. Just...oh, my God, he's broken out the bourbon."

"Riley tells me you're working on your entrance essay to Lincoln." My father handed Isaac the glass, and he took it, standing when my mother entered the room to sit next to Dad on the sofa.

Isaac lowered himself into the chair next to me with his back straight and his grip on the sweating glass vice tight. "Yes, sir. Riley's helped me sound like I might not be so thick-headed." He smiled when Dad laughed, and I felt something warm heat my chest.

But that calm didn't last long. It was an awkward mess, this whole meeting. But Isaac had insisted as soon as he'd heard about the confrontation at the Matheson dinner; it just was a question of when and under what circumstances. We had spent weeks arguing over how to handle that first meeting, and my father had been frustrated with constantly asking to meet Isaac. But now, after a single conversation, we had decided that the 'where' and the 'how' were not nearly as important as the 'now'.

So here we were, facing my parents as they sipped on their drinks, with Ryan smirking behind his glass as he watched the whole ridiculous event unfold while I questioned the wisdom in the entire thing, and Isaac tried his best not to fidget.

We should have disappeared to New York, sending a "See you" postcard to my folks on the way out of D.C. But Isaac wouldn't hear of it. Despite how nervous he'd been to meet them, how worried he was that my parents wouldn't approve, he still was insistent on showing up— on time.

"Well," Dad said, nodding as he moved the ice around in his glass. "There are programs available at Columbia and Georgetown too, in case you were interested in other universities aside from Lincoln. It's not the only good school in D.C."

"Eric, dear, there is time, yes? Don't force him into a thing he may not wish, not so quickly." Mom was being a diplomat, smooth and calm as she spoke, but I knew behind her polite words, she was worried. She was a Polish Jew whose family had seen the worst in the war, including how quickly the boys from gentile families had dropped their Jewish girlfriends once the pogroms started. D.C. wasn't Poland, and the war was long over, but the tension would never fully leave her. No doubt my mother fretted over what Isaac and I would have to face for staying together.

Dad relented, nodding to Isaac in way of an apology for making assumptions about his plans, and I absently pulled my bottom lip between my teeth as yet another when a wave of nerves hit me. They didn't know. None of them, not even Ryan. Any plans they might think

Isaac might aspire to wouldn't matter to my folks much, not by the end of the evening.

For his part, Isaac could not stay still. He'd already gone through his panicked and pacing phase when I told him. Even then he'd insisted, and insisted yet again, despite my protests, that no matter how hard it might be, we needed to face this openly. So here we were, staring at my family, wondering when the tension in the room would break.

It wasn't that my parents were unfriendly. They were always generous, always kind, but since my admission that Trent had slapped me, I'd noticed their worry for me had grown. I'd kept something monumental from them, and that was hard for them to take. This dinner tonight wouldn't make it any easier.

The conversation lulled, and Isaac looked down at the drink in his hand. In one graceful movement he downed it, then turned to me, and my breath caught with the look I saw in his eyes—his worry, his excitement, his deep and unassailable love. He raised his eyebrows the tiniest bit, and I responded with an infinitesimal nod.

He set down his empty glass and stood, his fists balled nervously at his side. "Mr. O'Bryant, ma'am?" My parents looked up at him, calm, expectant, while Ryan continued to lean on the windowsill, a willing observer. "I'll ask your pardon for the way all this…" he waved a hand between us, at a loss for more of an explanation. "This…what's happened, as I say, I'm sorry for it all to come out like it did, surprising you all in front of your people in public like that."

Mom relaxed her face, laying a hand on my father's leg. "No, dear. Is not necessary…" Dad took her fingers, linking them with his own, stoically watching his melting ice cubes as Isaac continued.

"We wanted to tell you in our own way, in our own time, but sometimes life just doesn't play out like you expect."

I could see my family out of the corner of my eye, but all my focus was on Isaac, willing him strength and encouragement as he stood up there, making what was surely the hardest speech of his life.

Still my father watched the ice in his glass, my mother smiled, my brother slouched offhandedly. They waited, as Isaac stood with his eyes downcast. As time seemed to stretch on, my mother, always the one in charge with making everyone else feel comfortable, broke the silence.

"Riley?" she said, pulling my attention to her.

"Ma'am, please." Isaac wanted this. He'd wanted to be held accountable. "Please," he said again, "I feel it's…it's my place."

He waited for my father's slow, reluctant nod before he spoke again. "I want you to know that I would never disrespect you all, and not Riley. Not ever. But I feel…" when I grabbed Isaac's hand, he moved his head, a small gesture that told me he knew I was there, at his side. "We feel for each other…deeply, things that are…I believe are real. And it wouldn't be right, me coming here, saying what I have to say and not asking your pardon first."

Ryan moved to lean on the back of the sofa, his gaze flashing to me before he cleared his throat. "Tell us."

"As I say, Riley and me, we care…we love each other. So, I reckon it's a good thing, just not the best of timing…" He glanced at me, then looked my father straight in the eyes. "Sir, I've gotten your daughter pregnant. And I want to marry her. Not because of the baby but…well, because I love her. I love her a lot. She's…she's the only

family I've got."

That hadn't been a lie. Isaac had taken me to Charlotte the week before, where his sister, Clara, had been visiting for the weekend, but when we knocked on the door, smiles bright, hands shaking with nerves, she'd refused to let me in. She'd made him choose. Me and the baby, or her.

He hadn't even taken a breath before he answered her.

"No contest." And then he led me off the front stoop and back to the Bel Aire.

Now, in my parent's living room, I caught my father's gaze, something flashing behind them as he watched Isaac. I couldn't read it, but it seemed to keep him from being able to react to our news.

My mother, however, instantly started to cry. "Is not you," she told Isaac, wiping her eyes. "She's my baby."

"I've got some money saved up," Isaac told her, his words came out in a rush. "I'm not very religious myself, but whatever Riley wants the baby to be is fine with me."

"Riley…what of your studies?" Mom said, as my father walked over to the window, staring out across the yard and into the street beyond, the muscle along his jaw tight and working.

"She can always finish later, Mom." Ryan's smile was wide as he walked toward us, unworried as he shook Isaac's hand and kissed my forehead. "I think it's great news. Really. Congrats, sis."

But my mom was still struggling with the notion. "How will she study with a baby?"

"Mom, this is Riley we're talking about. She'll figure it out."

Ryan held her hand, his grin ridiculous, and she dabbed at her eyes and nodded in agreement, which warmed me to the bottom of my heart. It was then that she seemed to realize how quiet my father had become. Mom looked over her shoulder to where he stood looking out of the window. "You have nothing you want to say to your daughter?"

Dad nodded, his focus still on the view outside that window. The fall weather had turned the cherry trees to green masses and the large oak trees that lined our street had the most beautiful stretch of red and gold leaves. I wondered then what my father was thinking; was he disappointed in me? Did he worry what would be become of us? Of his first grandchild?

"Dad?" Still he made no answer. My stomach started to churn, and I was of half a mind to grab Isaac's hand and hightail it out of there. I stood up and touched his fingers, pulled him into the adjoining dining room, away from my mother's cries and my father's stoic reflection.

"Isaac, I'm scared. Do you think we should go?"

I looked up at him, into those odd amber eyes and that beautiful smile. The damned fool that I loved was smiling. Then he reached down to touch my face.

"Riley..." he said, and he wasn't faltering, but searching for the right words. "These are the bones I live in. They take me through this life good or bad. I can't tell you what that's like." He dropped his hand from my face, and I held my breath, not sure what he was trying to say. "You can't know what it's like, neither, just the same as me not knowing what it is to be you. We all have our burdens to carry, and I don't pretend like mine is any heavier than anyone else's. I only know

that from the first day I met you, you asked me to add weight to my burden. You wanted me to pretend that the world won't do its damnedest to break us. You and me and now this baby, it's gonna tear us to pieces."

"Isaac…I don't care what anyone else in the world thinks."

He nodded, his fingers soft on my face, his smile still glowing. "That's just it, Riley. It's gonna tear us to pieces, but damn if I ain't eager to catch each one of 'em while they fall. I love you, Riley, something fierce. God help me, I do."

Isaac leaned forward then, lifting my chin and kissed me, soft, sweet, just long enough for any noise in the other room to go quiet. We looked into the den, realizing by how my mother's sniffles had eased, how Ryan's grin had gone all wide and stupid, that my family had heard everything Isaac said. He pulled me back into the den, and I looked over at my father and noticed his nod, his hands now in his pockets. Through the window behind him I could see the cherry blossom buds as they were blown from their branches, to swirl and scatter in the wind.

Finally, Dad cleared his throat, releasing a long exhale through his nose.

"The ACLU assigned Bernie Cohen a case about a mixed-race married couple in Virginia. Whispers are that it'll end up in the Supreme Court. They're hoping to make the ban on interracial marriages unconstitutional." Dad scratched his chin, pressing his lips together as he kept his returned his attention outside of that window. "Cohen has a fine case, and I have a feeling they'll win." He turned toward us, his expression still solemn. "But that won't be for a while, well after my grandchild is born."

"And now?" Isaac asked, his voice low, not sure of what Dad was driving at. To be honest, neither was I.

"Technically they're called miscegenation laws," Dad said, "aimed at criminalizing marriage between races. A felony offense, pretty serious. They are common all through the South." Dad turned then, and looked right at us, the ghost of a smile on his face. "But not in D.C."

There was a cloud over my vision. My family came to my attention hazy, like they weren't quite made of anything solid. It felt odd, this sensation of my body being so weak, so wrung out, my limbs like lead and all around me, in this strange place there were voices that I couldn't quite make out buzzing. Not really. I knew that in the corner, my parents were huddled together, my mother crying, sniffling, as the doctor said things I couldn't understand. Blood loss? Weak constitution? He couldn't be talking about me. Ryan was there too. His face was drawn and his skin pale, but he was at my side, forcing a smile, as he looked down at me.

"Sis?" His voice was so soft, and I thought it was funny somehow—my loud, obnoxious brother sounding small, awed.

Then, there came the smallest squeak of a sound and that cloudy haze drifted, left my breasts aching as that cry grew louder. A baby. My baby. I wanted to reach out for it, but I was too tired, my arms too heavy.

"Shh, hush now." That deep, rich voice felt like warm water over my cold skin, and I leaned toward it, loving the sweet cadence of Isaac's voice. "Hush now, Winston."

I remembered that name. It was a like a song in the back of my mind, something that was sweet and gentle, something I wanted to keep inside me, right next to my heart. And just like that, it came back to me like a wave, rushing forward, that I had a husband I loved and a baby, a son that was the most perfect creature I'd ever seen.

"Riley?" Isaac's voice was deep, but soft, not a whisper but a brush against my subconscious. "See our son? You see what a beautiful baby we made?"

His voice cracked just then, and behind me, in that fog, I heard my mother's cries and the low call of my father soothing her. But my gaze was hungry for the baby, for the perfect shape of his round face and the smooth contours of his skin. Winston. Winston. My son.

"Riley?"

"I see," I told Isaac, leaning toward his voice and the smell of baby powder and clean, sweet soap. "I see." Even though I didn't. Even though I'd never wanted anything more. That fog grew thicker then, so thick I couldn't breathe. So thick there was nothing I could do but let it swallow me whole.

Nash

Breath and fire all mingled, shuttered and sparked like electricity in my chest. I couldn't get air into my lungs, I couldn't fight hard enough, grip tight enough to make her stay. No, she had to stay. There was a baby. *Our baby.* There was a life to lead. *Our life.* We were together and then… apart.

"No. No!"

The scent of baby powder clogged in my sinuses, and I still felt the soft, heavy weight of a baby in my arms. I came awake, cradling nothing to my chest, my face wet, my breath uneven, a gasp that rent through with a sob. Tears I cried for my woman. Tears that came for someone I didn't know. Had I ever known her?

Eyes tight, I saw all those faces. They looked familiar, like an echo of memory, something I knew was mine, but couldn't get a grip on. My room was dark, but the light outside was bright, cracked through the blackout curtains around my windows. It was morning, and I was alone. The sheets draped around my hips were wet, and my chest felt damp. It had been a dream and like the others, it had felt so real. It had felt like it belonged to me.

Isaac loved Riley. I knew that. Felt it deep inside me.

He'd loved her when she cried in the library with her lips busted and bloody. He loved each tear as they came, and it was only her mouth, her touch, that had kept him from finding that Trent asshole and ripping him to pieces. It was only Riley's sweet words and sweeter taste that kept him from risking his own neck to be with her. No matter that Lenny warned him. No matter that the world was set against them. Isaac had loved Riley with a fierceness that made it impossible to do more but keep on loving her. That scared him; that made him brave.

But she had given him a son. He'd had a link to the world, a name and place and moment that would keep her with him always. Riley had given him a reason to get out of bed each morning. She'd given him a family.

I sat up straighter, elbows on my legs, hands on the back of my head, trying to steady my heartbeat. It raged quick and desperate. The dream was dimming, but the emotions, the feelings Isaac felt, swam inside me like she had been *mine*, like *I* had lost her.

And when I remembered what Isaac felt, how it seemed to him that his heart had come right out of his chest, like someone had taken a light that lit his entire world and snuffed it out, I did something I hadn't done since my mother's funeral. I sat in the middle of my bed and cried.

Riley had not been mine. That boy, the baby Winston, had not been mine, but I wept like they were. I cried for the loss. For the memory. For the man I'd never known and the life that had been stolen from him.

"Damn."

I fell onto my mattress, dragging the back of my hand over my face, pushing back the ache in my chest until it became duller. Until it was only a small thud that smarted like a bruise and not the gash that pulsed and bled Isaac dry.

Outside I heard voices, many of them, workers likely, a few crews had been tackling potholes down on the street below. It was the noise—their voices, the thump from their radios and the squeak from their tires that I tried to focus on; anything to move the ache of my dream from feeling so real.

I wondered, idly, as I lay there, if I'd called out in my dreams. Had I spoken Riley's name? Had I begged her not to die? Had Willow heard me? Despite myself, despite the argument we'd had two nights ago, I still couldn't shake her from my thoughts. I couldn't ignore the connection she seemed to hold between all the strange things that had been happening in my life. Had I had been wrong about everything? No one could make me dream impossible dreams. Not unless their juju was real, and by the sweat drying on my forehead and the slowing pace of my heart, I began to believe that Willow's was.

"You're doing this," I'd told her, face tight as I'd yelled at her. "You planned all of this, didn't you?"

"How the hell could I do that?" She'd waved the picture at me, and I caught a glimpse of Sookie's smile. "I'm not supernatural, Nash. I can't make up pictures from ninety damn years ago, and I can't make it that you have the same dreams as I do!"

But it wasn't logical, not any of it. It wasn't possible. And I knew it, even before I'd accused her, I knew she hadn't done anything. It was deep down, in the center of my brain, that reality. It told me Willow had only reacted. It told me she was feeling everything I had, reliving the same lives I had.

But how?

The sheets rustled as I turned, arms stretched out over my head, and I stared off at nothing, reliving the dream of that day at the hospital. Most likely the worst day of Isaac's life. He'd watched her blink twice, her gaze on him, then shifting to their son. There was softness in her expression, the peace that comes when you know you don't have to fight anymore. It relaxed the tension in her facial muscles and made the whites of her eyes seem brighter. Isaac had watched Riley do all that while she kept her attention on their boy. He'd placed the baby next to her and she closed her eyes, her lips moving like a twitch, her face leaning toward the soft, sweet scent of newborn skin, like she knew, even as she faded, that her baby was there, sleeping next to her.

"My sweet," he'd whispered, so low that only she'd hear him. "My sweet girl. I love you, Riley. Always will." Then Isaac kissed her. Her skin was warm, but pale, and one final rattle of breath went out of her. "What do I do now?" he asked, but she was gone, soft like a first kiss, bitter like a rainstorm. She left him, and he could not keep hold of her. He could not stop her from going.

My eyelids felt heavy as the flood of pain came on me again. It was worse, this feeling, than anything. Worse than watching Willow walk out of my room. Worse than hearing the click of my front door when she left. Worse that seeing her standing too close to another man in the lobby, no matter that she swore he'd only hired her to make two dozen cupcakes for his niece's birthday. Worse than the jasmine of her scent fading more and more each day I kept away from her. Worse than the look on her face when I took off, leaving her on the roof deck, a catch in her voice as she called after me.

I banged my knee against the bedside table when I sat up, but I didn't feel it. Couldn't. My mind was full of Isaac and Riley, of that baby. Of Sookie and Dempsey and the horror of it all. Of Willow. Of how heavy and thick it all felt as every one of those faces crowded inside my head.

Willow had tears on her cheeks when I walked away from her two nights ago.

I hadn't believed her when she swore she'd done nothing to me. No, I didn't know if I believed her or not, but accepting what she said would have meant everything I have believed before had been a lie.

I left her alone out there. Because I was afraid and confused, I'd just left her...

Isaac would have given anything to keep Riley with

him. Sookie would have done anything not to let the smoke and fire take her, to have her chance with Dempsey.

But I wasn't willing to stop and even consider that I might have been wrong, to keep Willow with me? To be with her and never want her to go away from me? What in hell was wrong with me?

The sheets fell to the floor when I left the bed, and I started then to rehearse what I'd say to her. "I'm sorry" didn't seem good enough, neither did "I can explain…" because nothing would make up for the way I'd left her.

"Please forgive me" sounded a little better, but even as I spoke it aloud, tugging on my shirt and slipping my feet into my Chucks, it still seemed off, not nearly good enough. I'd crawl on my knees if that's what she needed. I might not understand what was happening, and despite everything, I still couldn't wrap my head around past lives or anything like that. But, I wanted her. No, it was more than that—I needed her. Apologies might not be enough, I thought, jogging out of my apartment and into the stairwell, taking steps two at a time as I went, but they were all I had. I'd thrown away everything else.

How long had I spent acting like she was an irritation? Months? Like I was too fucking important to waste my precious time on her, and then, when I'd finally gotten my head out of my ass, I ended up walking away.

I was a fuck-up, something solidified and certain, I decided, as I got to her floor, skirting around two guys in gray overalls as they carried boxes toward the elevator. An epic fuck-up who would die alone, apparently.

The door to Willow's apartment was open, and I slipped inside, bypassing another coverall-wearing guy with no neck as he held a lamp in each hand. A knot formed in my chest and the further I came into that apartment, the larger that knot got.

The crowded space that normally looked like a Technicolor wet dream was sparse. I only just noticed with all the furniture missing and windows, free of curtains or tapestries, that the walls were a soft gray and the floor, usually covered by blankets and rugs, was dark oak. Without Willow to decorate this small chunk of the world, it seemed lifeless and boring. I could relate.

"Hey!" I called, stopping the mover before he could punch the down button. He paused, moving his chin toward me in answer to my call. Standing in front of him, I'd guess he might have been 5'6 but no taller than that and had small, glassy blue eyes. "The woman who booked this gig, where is she?"

He shrugged, ignoring me as he elbowed the button on the wall. "I just move the boxes and furniture, man." The bell chimed and he walked inside the elevator, adjusting the lamps. "There was a car outside next to our van, but it's full. Pretty sure she's gone already."

Willow

My great-grandfather liked to talk about the old days, especially when he'd smoked too many stogies and had too much bourbon.

"It's not the same, Buttercup. It's not how it used to be." Normally "it" had something to do with the government and the mess politicians made of it. But my grandfather wasn't a typical grumpy old man. He didn't bemoan the world because he missed the way things were in the past. He complained because we still, in his view, hadn't gotten our shit together.

"Two hundred years and only one black president and still, after all this time, no women. If I had my way…"

He'd go on and on, hours sometimes, and then, when he had gone quiet, when the fire had gone out of him, he'd sometimes talk about the things that normally were shut up inside of him. My great-grandfather was the last. After him there'd be no grandparents on my father's side of the family. He knew it. Often, he'd apologize about it.

"No man should have to bury his children or his bride, Buttercup, and I've done that more than once."

Some nights he'd gotten quiet, and the anger and loneliness inside him had rushed through him like a windstorm. Those were the nights he'd played Coltrane loud and told me about his childhood. "No one should live the way they made me. I wouldn't wish that on my worst enemy and, *cher*, I've had plenty." That also came out when he drank a lot—the hidden French words he never used when sober. The childhood back in New Orleans had done something to him, and it had never left him completely. That's the way of things, I guessed. We never really lose who we are.

"Who would be your enemy, Gramps?" I'd asked him, not understanding how this gentle old man could ever piss anyone off. "You're the best of them all."

"No, Buttercup. Not by a long shot. That was your granny, God rest her. Your granny and our sweet girl."

He never talked much about either of them. Only when the bourbon came out and Coltrane came on and even then, it was the same stories—the time his daughter had learned to ride a bike; the day his wife came down the isle of a tiny Berlin church wearing a borrowed dress and her hair up in pin curls. "Perfection," he'd called them, and he'd meant it. I'd always wondered if anyone would ever think that of me.

I almost thought Nash had.

The boxes were pushed one on top of another, as tight in my car as I could get them, with quilts and throws tucked between them and the seats as I stuffed my things inside. The decision to leave had come after my mother promised to clear out the old cottage on Lake Winfred. It would be warmer there, warmer than the city had been. I had never liked the winters in New York. Something set in my bones made me long for a lake and the peace inside a cottage no one knew about.

"You can have it for as long as you want, sweetie." There was a pause in my mother's voice, something that told me she was worried. "But why do you want to give up that apartment in the city? I thought you liked Brooklyn. I thought you were doing well with your booth at the Farmer's Market, and you'll never find a rent control like that again, you know."

If I'd told her the truth, I'd spend an hour on the phone promising my mother my heart wasn't as broken as it felt. I'd have to lie to her and say that Nash hadn't hurt me, that what I felt between us was one-sided and stupid.

"Just want a change of pace," I'd told her, knowing that she'd pick up my tone, that she'd hear the small lie behind the elevated, forced inflection.

"Willow…"

"Mom, I promise." Another pitch higher this time and I threw in a laugh. "So tell me about the trip to Costa Rica this spring."

She had. My mother had gone on for twenty minutes about the group of teenagers she and dad were bringing with them to help build wells in the thick of the jungle, while I pushed my clothes, my dishes and books into boxes. Already I planned to walk away from Brooklyn because staying hurt too badly. It wasn't enough that the dreams consumed me. They kept me up. They blocked my sleep patterns and diluted my aura. I felt it heavy on my skin, like a bruise that covered my entire body.

Those memories soaked into my mind like oil—clinging until there was only the sight of Sookie holding that rope and the horror I felt, the terror on her beautiful face as she stared down at me. I could still smell the thick smoke that choked me, I still heard Sylv's prayers as he said them over and over. Then, she fell, and part of me, of Dempsey, died. I felt it slip away like a second skin. I felt it leave and knew it wouldn't return.

And Riley…my God. The slip of her world as it went away, the soft weight of her baby on her chest. The warm press of Isaac's sweet kiss against her…against my mouth.

"God…"

This was not the time to think of it. Not when there were taxis zipping through the streets and a construction crew coming closer to our building; tar from their truck puffed great swells of thick liquid into the air, and the smell made me a little queasy. I had a lot to do, anyway—miles and miles to go tomorrow before I made it to Lake Winfred.

I ran the back of my wrist against my eyes to dry my face and picked up another box, stuffing it between three frames and my father's old turntable. It was an ancient thing, something Grandpa Ryan, my father's father, had given to him, something I was sure *he'd* gotten from *his* dad, my great-granddaddy O'Bryant. It had been broken for years when I found it after Grandpa Ryan's death, and my father wanted me to have it. "A family heirloom," my father had joked, handing it over to me along with old Fats Domino and Muddy Waters vinyls. "Use them well," he'd told me.

Now that turntable was snug on the floorboard of my car, ready to go with me to the cottage. There would be no neighbors to disturb with my music and, God willing, no memories to haunt me when I got there.

"Where do you want these?" a mover asked, motioning with the two lamps in his hands.

"Those can go in the van. They're headed to storage."

No need to bring those along to the cottage, when my mother had likely already seen to it that the place was outfitted with food, dishes, and toiletries, not to mention lamps. The rest of my things would go to a storage facility in the city. My rugs and tapestries, many of my books, most of my cooking supplies all would be there, forgotten until I'd licked my wounds for an appropriate amount of time and decided where I'd start over again.

I shut the trunk of my car and opened the passenger side door, pushing the seat back to feel around for my cell when my elbow shoved against something I thought was my jewelry box, but instead turned out to be the small wooden box my parents dropped off just a week ago.

The clasp was gold, and there was a heavy inlay of filigree along the sides and at the corners. Fleur de lis from the look of them, all faint with age. Opening it, I felt the soft fabric that lined the box, the silk pattern and heavy threads, and wondered where my granddad had found it and what had made him keep it.

There were dozens of pictures, some I'd flipped through the first night I got it, smiling at all those images of great-grandpa and great-grandma Nicola when they were young. He was so handsome, his eyes bright even in the dull black and white photo. She'd never smiled as widely as him or laughed as much, but then her childhood and what her family had endured during the war was something not easily forgotten.

Among those pictures were others I hadn't had a chance to go through, and letters, mostly from my great-grandmother's cousins in Poland after the war. There were pieces of jewelry, some that Gramps had made, others that looked store bought. At the bottom of the box was a small journal. Flipping through the pages, I caught sight of the dates, some going back as early as the late thirties, all in my great-grandfather's tight, precise handwriting.

I debated looking through it, despite all the noise around me and the activity of moving. The movers were nearly done, and another small voice in my head told me to toss the box in the van, send it and the memories away to storage while I tried to run from them, from the dreams and from Nash. I stood up and a rush of emotion came over me, as I caught a glimpse of another picture, this one clear, the faces in it laughing. I knew one face. Had seen it before, months before, when I moved to Brooklyn. He'd given me the key to the apartment. He'd swore I looked just like my mother...

"What are you doing?"

Nash's voice pulled me out of my shock, and I blinked, squeezed my eyes tight to refocus as he moved closer. A swift breeze picked up and the smell of Nash's cologne whipped around me like a snake, firing up sensation and heat and all the things I was trying to avoid with this move.

"What do you want?" I asked him, closing Gramp's box and shoving it under the passenger seat of my car. I would shoot for aloof, impassive, I told myself. I would pretend that I wasn't affected by the heat from his body as he came up next to me or how the low, deep lull of his voice when he whispered my name didn't make my heart skip a beat or my palms sweaty.

"Willow." It was a low, sweet sound, like music. It remind me of the piercing moment in a chord change, when the saxophone player took a breath, the way your body goes still, how anticipation keys up your senses until you aren't sure how wise it would be to wait for the next note.

"Nash, I need you to..."

"What do you need? Tell me. I'm...I'm sorry for leaving."

"Leaving?" I asked, stepping out from the car to slam the door shut. I fished my keys from my pocket and turned on him, not caring that the sidewalk was thick with people moving by us, that the movers had slowed to watch the exchange. There was a construction crew a few feet behind my car and the heavy scent of tar grew thicker. "That's why you're sorry? Because you got freaked out and left me out on the roof?"

"No. I don't mean…"

I hadn't realized just how much anger I was holding inside, but now that I let some of it loose, the rest couldn't be held back. "Not that you made me feel like I was insane for—" One of the movers took out a cigarette and lit it, his attention on us and not his co-workers who awkwardly moved a large chest of drawers toward the van. "You made me think I was insane for…thinking what I think. For believing what I believe in. You called me insane, you called me a witch, you pretty much told me I was fucked any way you look at it."

"I'm sorry," he said, holding up his hands. For a second I thought he might reach out, try to touch me, and I prepared myself for it, ready to push him back. "I don't think you're insane. I don't. I just think there is a lot of…" Nash looked around the sidewalk, nodding me away from the car to get us out of earshot of the nosy mover. "There's a lot of things that can't be explained."

"They can," I said, a little louder, my temper returning with the frown he gave me and the stubborn way he looked away. "You just happen to call the explanations crap." A few small, indiscernible words came out of his mouth, but Nash didn't repeat them loud enough for me to hear.

"Can we go upstairs?" He nodded toward the building, even took a step toward it before I shook my head. "Why not?"

"I don't live here anymore." It was true. I'd sent Mom's university friend, Mr. Lewis, my key that morning. The super would find another tenant, and I'd be gone soon, gone for good.

"Willow. Please. I don't like this…" he waved between us, finally scrubbing his face when I folded my arms over my chest. "Where are you going? How long…"

"That's not important. It's not…don't worry about it."

This time when Nash looked at me, his large hands moved to the back of his neck, rubbing hard, as though he needed to release the tension that had grown there. "It's damn well important to me, Will."

I wanted to smile at him then. I wanted Nash to open his arms and tell me he loved me. I wanted him to admit he believed me…that he simply believed in things he couldn't see, things that didn't make sense to the logical mind at all. But he had let me just walk away. He didn't try to fight, he didn't try to think outside the box he'd put himself in. He'd turned his back when coincidences couldn't be explained. Worse yet, he'd accused me of trying to trick him, even though he had felt the very same things I had. Those dreams were memories—we shared them. Even if we didn't understand how, they meant something, and rather than being amazed, he'd run from them. From the truth. He'd run from me.

I tried one last time.

"Why, Nash? Why is it important to you?"

Say it, I thought. Please. *Tell me you love me. Say, 'Because of everything' and mean it.*

"I'd...*damn*..." Nash shrugged, looking uncomfortable, looking a lot like a kid standing in front of a grown-up, being asked to explain why he'd misbehaved. But Nash wasn't a kid. No matter if he'd acted like one often enough. He took to rubbing his neck again before he dropped his hand, smiling, but with no conviction. "I'd hate to see you go. The place would be too quiet without the noise you make and then there's the cupcakes..."

He stopped joking when I lowered my shoulders, gripping my keys in my hand as I stepped back into the street, meaning to yank the door of my car open to show just how angry I was. I heard the first syllables of my name come from his mouth, then screams to my left, the screech of tires and the blast of a horn. The stench of street tar was all around me, thick and metallic, heavy and cloying. The smell, it was awful, and still it enveloped me, poured up into my sinuses and wound its way inside my head, and for a second, I let the smell take me...

Sookie gripped the chain tight and I wanted to stop her. I wanted to kill my father, kill them all, all the damn fools that had started this. They screamed about the rain, the flood that came out in the river. They cursed Sookie, they cursed her mama like it had been their fault for running from the threat when it came. Fools, fucking fools, all of them.

She looked down at me from so high above, and I read my name on her lips. I wanted to catch her. I wanted to go with her into the smoke. I wanted...

She dropped fast. I ran. Sylv did. We tried to catch her. But she was too far away.

We tried to stop the world from spinning.

It went on and on, and part of me died with her.

I loved her. My first love. That love had lived; it always would. Inside my veins, inside my blood. For one brilliant moment in time, that love lived.

She went pale before the baby came. Like she knew. My darlin' Riley had known it could happen. Her body was a thin thing, not like her heart. Not like her spirit. Sometimes a body isn't built for a spirit that is bigger than the world itself. Sometimes it fails and sometimes that failing destroys the world. It wrecked mine.

She was weak, they told me. There had been too much blood loss.

The baby had come, and he was a soldier, a strong champion that grew and lived with the same fire his mama had.

But Riley was pale when I saw her. She hadn't the strength to lift her head from the pillow. Couldn't even hold the baby when they brought him in.

"You do it. Please."

I took my boy, stronger than his mama, stronger, if I'm honest, than I was just then, and I held him because my darlin' asked me to. I held him close and let him lie beside her, wondering if she knew him. Praying she did. Believing she would.

"Riley?"

She'd been too pale. Too damn pale and those eyes slid closed. Dear Lord, how I loved her. How I loved her so. That love had lived, it always would. Inside my veins. Inside my blood. For one brilliant moment in time, that love lived.

I loved her. It came to me along with Sookie's fear and Isaac's bottomless sorrow. It came to me when Willow fell, when her keys hit the street and got crushed beneath the metal wheel of the tar truck. It came to me as I shot forward, as I grabbed her and held her, away from the noise and chaos behind us.

With everything inside my veins, inside my blood, I loved her.

Nash

"I'm sorry. Oh, sweet God, Will. I'm so sorry."

It didn't matter: the crowd, the worried onlookers who huddled around us, the construction crew all sweaty from work and fear, the movers, unused to such drama in their normally mundane lives. All I saw was the color coming back to her face. All I felt was the death grip of her fingers on my collar. "Willow, I'm so sorry." I could say it a million times and it wouldn't be enough. None of it. "Please, forgive me."

"Nash…" her voice was weak, but loud enough that it made me look down, a wild rush of relief running through me as I touched her face, her shoulders, as I kissed her over and over until the small sound of my name came again. "Please…just let me breathe."

"Are you hurt? You fell." I held her back, fingers everywhere, running over her arms, holding her hands, moving them out of the way to get a clearer look at her. Her sweater was torn and she'd lost a tennis shoe in the tumble to the tar-slick ground, but she wasn't hurt. Thank the powers that be, she wasn't hurt.

"I'm fine." She pushed on my shoulder, and I helped her up. "Can we…let's go inside, okay?"

"But you need a hospital or…there could be internal injuries or, hell…"

"Will you stop?" She waved off the construction foreman when he got closer. "Really, he's overreacting. I'm fine. Just tripped on my own damn feet and nearly bought it under that truck."

"Ma'am..." the guy protested, coming closer.

"Seriously, the track was a good five feet from where I fell. It's fine, honestly. No worries at all."

Willow moved to her car, grabbing the door, before I stopped her. "Where are you going?" I couldn't believe she was still thinking of leaving, now. She opened her mouth, and I thought there was something biting she was going to say, something that would have me doling out more apologies, so I didn't give her a chance.

"I'm sorry. I'll say it a thousand times, I swear. I'm sorry I was an asshole to you. I'm sorry I let you walk away." I stood so close to her now Will had to rest against the car door to look at me. For once, she was uncharacteristically quiet. "You asked me why it mattered, you leaving? It matters, Willow. It matters because I love you. It matters because I don't want to go to bed at night wondering where you are, wondering if you're safe or sad or tired or happy or a billion other things." I took her face, lowering my voice so only she could hear me. "It matters because God or fate or the universe or whoever clearly wants us together. Because Sookie and Dempsey didn't get a happy ending, and Isaac and Riley got theirs taken from them. I don't know who they are,

Will. I don't know if it's you or me or people who share our blood. I don't care about any of that, about the why, about the how. I only know that I want you—that you twist me up, that I'm sprung, so stupid sprung over you. It matters, you leaving. It matters because I don't want you leave without me."

I didn't wait for her to answer. I didn't need to hear she loved me. I knew it. It was in every look she'd ever given me. It was in the sweet swirl of her mouth on mine. It was in each touch, each laugh. The words didn't matter to me at all.

"Nash," she said when I leaned down to kiss her.

"Yeah?"

"I need to get something out of my car. Then, let's go upstairs. I…" she looked around, grinning at two movers when they passed us by. "There's something I need to show you."

Nash

The building was quiet. No lights lit up the hallways and no answer came when we knocked on the door. "We should check the roof."

Will nodded, holding my hand when I offered it to her as we headed toward the stairs. "You said his cell was disconnected?"

"Yeah." I held open the door, letting her in front of me as we climbed the stairs. "Been at least a week since I've heard from him. But then sometimes he goes AWOL. He always shows up again." She moved through the door, holding it open for me when I came behind her, and we walked toward the cages where Roan kept his pigeons.

"Think he'll show up again?"

But I didn't answer Willow. There was a little too much worry crowding my head, coupled with all the other confusing things that had happened that day. The cages were empty.

"There were pigeons. Hundreds of them." I waved at the empty cages, two sets of six rows, all vacant, even the water from the dispensers and the feed in the bowls were gone. In fact, the only thing that remained of the birds were some random feathers and a single spattering of droppings. Everything else had been cleaned away.

She moved around the cages, closing the open doors, her head shaking as she looked first at me, then around the roof. "I don't understand why…"

"What is that?" I asked, pointing at a red envelope stuck between two of the cages. Will was closer and grabbed it, but once she looked at it, she smiled. "I'm guessing this is for you."

Will handed it over, and I copied her smile, spotting Roan's messy scrawl on the front: "My man…"

When I opened the envelope there were numerous sheets of neatly folded paper and a silver key which fell from between them. *Read this inside* was jotted on the outside of the pages. "What does he…"

"Here," Willow said, picking up the key to hand it over. "There's more to discover, it seems."

The old bastard had slipped his apartment key in the envelope, something that struck me as monumental since I'd never gotten even the smallest glimpse inside his place before now. But the key had a number, 1313, and I knew exactly which door it would open, though none had numbers.

"Come on."

We headed to the last door on the third floor, a place Roan had told me he had taken over when he moved into the building because he liked to watch the sunrise from that spot. It gave him a clear view of the park.

A slip of the key and we were inside, exploring the nearly empty apartment. There was no furniture anywhere in the large loft space, which I guess hadn't always been a loft. Heavy wood beams stretched from one end of the room to the other, and in the center, near to where a small kitchenette sat in a corner, two more beams ran vertical on either side. It looked like Roan had used a small air mattress to sleep on, but it was deflated, and a thick blanket sat in the center, folded neatly with a pillow on top of it.

"Didn't leave much, did he?" Will asked stepping away from me to nose through the row of upturned boxes and the books that lay scattered across the brick floor. She squatted down, picking up one by the corner, a smile tugging on her mouth when she read the cover.

"What is it?" I asked, coming toward her.

"*The Ancestor's Tale,* by Richard Dawkins. My mom has this one. In fact," she said, standing up to hand over the book. "I'm pretty sure Roan…or Mr. Lewis…whoever he was, gave it to her."

"Sneaky asshole."

There was a makeshift wall dividing the main living area and when I walked to the far side of it, I came face to face with an expanse cluttered with photographs, printed images, sketches and graphs. Multi-colored strings of yarn linked one image to another, mapping out relationships, drawing one generation to another. I decided whatever I thought I knew about my old mentor was going to get thrown right out the window—along with so much that I once thought I believed.

"Son of a bitch," Willow said, voicing my thoughts as she came to stand next to me. Almost all of the pictures were old, some going back a hundred years, maybe even earlier than that. "Nash, the letter."

Until she mentioned it, I'd almost forgotten. "You read it," I said, stepping closer to the wall. There was a clear division, with a length of black string separating one section of pictures from the other. At the top of the right side was the messy scrawl of "Simoneaux." To the left, came "Lanoix." Those names were familiar and, by looking at the pictures, I started to get an idea why.

Some were in color—those I only glanced at. Some, like the one Willow had shown me earlier that night, were of Roan, or the man who I thought was Roan. Near the top, taped to a brick, was a picture that Will's great-granddaddy had also had in his little box of keepsakes. There were four people in this one—Sylv and Sookie, standing next to Dempsey, all smiling, all glancing to their right, looking at a tall man with dark skin who wore a jaunty fedora. The picture in the old man's box had listed four names: three we knew, and one we didn't. Sookie, Sylv and Dempsey were familiar, but not the man who went by "Uncle Aron." Yet even though the name wasn't familiar, the face certainly was. He hadn't been Aron when Willow met him as Mr. Lewis, her mother's university colleague who'd given her the key to his rent-controlled apartment. He hadn't been Aron, but Roan, when I got to know him as one of my college professors, then my mentor; he was the one who, four years ago, clued me in about an apartment building in Brooklyn that I might want to check out. Now his face was in a decades old photograph, while the letter he had written only a day ago was in my hands.

"Read it, please," I said to Will, my gaze never leaving the images. Hundreds of faces reminded me of my kin; many looked like Will and what I guessed her own people had looked like.

Willow unfolded the papers and began to read. "Nash, you're reading this letter because things have aligned. Finally, I hope. For the duration of your life, at least, I pray."

As I listened to her voice, I studied picture of Sookie and Dempsey. Something about the boy's face in this one seemed vaguely familiar.

Behind me, Will continued. "There are things that should not be explained. Things I wish I could tell you, but fear you'd never believe, about me, about the life I have led. You told me of the dreams you had and the memories you shared with your Willow. First, let me say that you have not lost your young mind. You aren't being set up for some prank, and Willow isn't a witch, no matter how hard you try to convince yourself she is." She lowered the page, telling me with the quick arch of her eyebrow that she wasn't amused.

"You told him I was a witch?"

"Willow, you yanked me into your apartment inside of a minute of laying eyes on me, and then you announced you wanted to cleanse my aura." I turned, facing her, hoping my smile would disarm her look of skepticism. "Wasn't long after that I started having the dreams. What else was I supposed to think?"

She smacked my arm with the paper, but smiled while she did it, holding back a laugh. "A witch? Really? Do you see me wearing a pointy hat?" I opened my mouth, gearing up for another apology, but Willow looked down at the letter again and started to read. "And you aren't experiencing these memories because you've lived them before. Reincarnation is a dream made up by folk who can't believe there is only one go around in life. They cling to it, to the hope that they will get a second chance. This isn't yours. Well, not completely."

I turned back to the board, focusing on the same boy, tilting my head to stare at his smile and the shape of his chin.

"There is a connection you feel with Willow because it has existed for a very long time and most probably will continue to exist for many generations into the future. It will not end with your life or with hers. It will go on, you see, as long as the world does."

Will came to stand next to me as I continued to examine the picture on the wall. When she caught sight of what I was looking at, she lowered the page she had been reading, and lifted up a hand her mouth, which was suddenly hanging open. "What?" I asked, frowning. "What's wrong?"

She shook her head, as though she wasn't sure what she was looking at. "I didn't realize it with the other pictures." She pointed at the board, right at the picture I'd been staring at. "Dempsey. He's so young in this picture. I've never seen him so damn young."

"What do you mean?"

She looked at me, pressing her lips together like she wasn't sure how to make the word unfurrow from her throat. "Dempsey is my great-grandfather, Nash."

I looked between her and the board, seeing the similarities, the shape of her cheeks, just like Dempsey's and the sharp point of her chin. They were identical, but that didn't make sense.

"How?"

"I... I don't know." She immediately went back to the letter, skimming through the words, her eyes moving down the page until she came to a line that widened her eyes. "…after Sookie and Babette died, Dempsey's father blamed Joe Andres, telling the police, those not in Simoneaux's pocket, that it was the fat man that had started the fire. Dempsey did something stupid, I'd say, though it did free us all up to worry less over that rotten family. He told the sheriff that he'd seen his father start the fire, told him he'd testify if he needed to. Knowing his own son was willing to testify against him, the old man didn't put up a fight, and Simoneaux got hauled off to parish prison. Dempsey's word, it seemed, was enough to put his daddy in jail for murder and destruction of property—but it wasn't enough to keep himself safe.

"We took him to Alabama after the trial, then on to the Army recruitment station where he signed his name as Eric O'Bryant, and O'Bryant is what he remained until the day he died."

Will lowered the letter again, stretching a hand out to rest it on my arm, like she needed me to keep her from falling. Her face was open, her features expressive as she blinked and seemed to look inward, as though there were too many thoughts clouding up her mind and she need to sort them out.

"That means..." she looked at the board, searching for a name, maybe a face, and after a few moments she covered her mouth again, pointing at the string of yarn that ran from her great-grandfather's picture to a smaller one further down. "Nash, look. It's Riley. Riley and Isaac."

I had to look closely at it, and there was Riley, standing on the steps of a synagogue with an older version of Dempsey at her side, next to an older woman—Riley's mother I guessed— and a man that looked even more like Will than her great-granddaddy. I nodded to the man and Will smile. "That's Ryan. That's my daddy's daddy, Nash. Riley's brother Ryan. I'd never put the name together. *Riley.* They never talked about her. Not ever. I only knew her name because it was in my grandfather's prayer book. I saw it when I was ten and asked him who she was." She stared at the image again, stretching a finger toward it. "He said Riley was his sister who'd gone off to heaven a long time ago. Then he made me promise never to mention her to Gramps. He said it would hurt him too bad to talk about her."

Next to Riley was a tall, broad black man. There was a small grin on his face, and he held Riley close to his side, but he stood ramrod straight, like a soldier, and I wondered how long Isaac went on that way, being on guard, once Riley was gone. I wondered if when he was alone with Riley he smiled the way I did when Willow looked at me.

"Isaac," I said, pointing to the picture, then frowning when I fingered the string that ran from his wedding picture, then across the board to the second family tree. "Holy shit."

"Nash…"

I pointed at another picture, this one with Isaac too, but Riley was missing. He looked younger in that picture and there was nothing resembling a grin on his face as he stood next to a face I knew. I'd seen it in a handful of pictures in the family album my mother kept in the front room of our small apartment. It had been next to her family Bible, and the envelopes she said were for important papers. Nat and my birth certificates, my parents' wedding license, the number to the detective who always called to check on my father if he'd gone too long falling asleep on the front porch.

Next to the Bible she'd stacked a thick photo album. There were baby pictures of me and Natalie, things that only a first-time parent would keep—locks from our first haircuts, pictures we'd drawn in preschool and dozens of photos from her family in California. In the back of that album were a handful of images, not as well kept as my mother's, all of our father's people. His parents, who had died one night, just like my mother had, exactly for the same reason. My grandfather Lenny had gotten drunk. We'd heard rumors from the family, things that got passed along like how many husbands a certain cousin had or how many times someone had been in jail. Lenny had been a drunk, and had passed that habit down to my father. There had been whispers told behind our backs, when the gossips thought Nat and I slept: Lenny and his wife Clara had never gotten over the loss of her brother. They'd been close at some point but had fallen out when her brother married a woman Clara didn't like.

I'd only heard the story once, but knew it well enough that seeing my grandfather and Isaac wasn't as much of a surprise as it should have been.

"It's Lenny," I told Willow, nodding toward the picture.

"Isaac's friend?"

"And my father's father, Will."

"What?"

We traced the string, how it moved up, linking Clara to Sylv, Sookie's brother. I glanced over at the O'Bryant tree, moving my fingertips along it and saw the timelines were nearly even. For every Lanoix family member that married and had children, so went an O'Bryant. Nearly every year since Sookie's death, there had been a birth, a marriage on Willow's side of the family.

"It's the same," I said, glancing at Will, noticing that her eyes had gone wide again as she quickly scanned Roan's letter.

She moved her fingernail over the pages, stopping when she came to Isaac's name. She looked up at me. "He almost..." Will shook her head and I caught the glint of tears between her lashes. "Isaac might have had a good life," she read, "with his son Winston, and maybe that would have been enough. But for Winston's birthday, he wanted the boy to meet his family, to bring him to his sister and hope that his son would be the one to bring them back together." Will's throat worked, as though she had to swallow the large knot that blocked her voice. "The plane they were on crashed somewhere off the South Carolina coast and Isaac and Winston went on to be with Riley before the boy had turned five."

"That was why..." I closed my eyes, wondering for a second if things would have been different. If my life would have changed if Isaac hadn't crashed with his son, if his sister and Lenny had never been forced into the sorrow that took over their lives. "My father said once his folks were sad people. There had been so much loss. Too much, it seemed. He said they never laughed. They never..."

Willow came to my side, curling an arm around me, and I hugged her close, looking at the pictures, the endless strings that weaved in and out, that touched and moved and connected all these lives.

"What else does it say?" I asked her, and she lifted her hand, passing over the letter for me to read.

"There is a force at work that cannot be explained," Roan had written. "Something that moves through the ages. The same thing that made it possible for me to be an uncle in New Orleans, that brought me to Riley and Isaac in a D.C. library, and also to a young woman who wanted to learn, so she could show her young daughter, Willow, that a woman was a force to be reckoned with. It led me to you to me as well, Nash, when you were scared, when you needed a father because yours had not been one at all.

"This force—this power— directs, guides us, plants within us the memory of generations, things that should have been and weren't, things that could have been, yet failed. And sometimes, as you probably are realizing by now, those should-have things will try again and again, searching for a fitting end, searching for a finality that will lead not to sorrow, not to loss, not to failure, but to joy. I cannot name it, this ancient, sacred thing. I can only follow it, obey it, and hope that one day it ends with love. In my bones, my friend, I believe that it will, and that you will be one of those happy endings. For you, Nash, have found everything you need in the woman at your side."

Later, Willow lay on my chest, our bodies sweaty and slick, our heartbeats slowing as we lay naked, sated in my bed. There were boxes and bags all over my floors. Her toothbrush had been unpacked, and we shared a pillow. I thought the jasmine scent would never leave my sheets, and in the same thought I realized I didn't want it to.

"A hundred lifetimes, I bet," Willow said, staring up at the ceiling with her fingers moving over my arm.

"What?"

"A hundred. All those people, moving together. All the lifetimes spent searching, wanting to come together. We can't be the first, Nash." She lifted on her elbow, resting her palm against my chest as she watched me. "How sad would it be if after all those lifetimes it's you and me who get our happy ending and no one else." She laid back down, turning to rest her chin on my chest. "Doesn't seem fair."

"No," I said, pulling her closer. "I don't think it's fair at all."

"Why us, do you think? After all this time…why is it us?"

I'd thought of nothing else on the taxi ride home. We'd splurged, celebrating Roan's departure with a cab ride back to Brooklyn and a pizza delivered ten minutes after we'd lugged Willow's suitcases back into the building.

"Maybe it's because no one learned." I felt her move her head, her hair rustling against my shoulder. "It's like this country and all the people who are still clueless. We kill each other, we fight and fuss, and we forget that there was a time, not that long ago, where we were even more divided. It's two hundred years, and we're still divided. Maybe all those people in our families, maybe they were divided too. Maybe because the world was, they couldn't get past that to someplace where they could be happy."

"And we can?"

I nodded, a non-answer that gave her pause. She was warm against me, a solid weight that was soft, and sweet, and so new and exciting. Her life and mine were moving together, real and honestly, closing the gap on the distance that seemed to have always divided our families.

"Sometime, next year, I need to go to California."

"To see your sister?" She was curious, and I tugged her further up my chest. I'd been thinking about Nat since we read Roan's letter. How family and blood cross tides of time. How there had been so much anger, so much loss, and nothing ever got settled from holding onto it. I didn't want that for me. I didn't want it for Natalie, either.

"Yes," I told her, swallowing as the words came. "To see Nat and...to see my father. It's been a long time." I exhaled when Willow relaxed against me. "I've hated him for a long time, Will. But...I don't want to anymore. It's time to start healing." She nodded; I felt the movement of her chin. "Will you go with me?"

"Of course," she said, kissing my chest. "I'll go anywhere with you."

She hummed when I kissed her, holding her face between my hands, feeling our bodies twining together. "We can have our happy, Will," I whispered to her, "the two of us. I know we can. I know it with everything I am."

Roan

The Nation farm was a sprawling place, well-appointed, with a small cottage off to the side of the main property and a larger, woodframed home in the center. I watched it all, leaning on a tree that years before, lifetimes before, Sookie and Dempsey had hid beneath, holed up in the tree house that had long since fallen to shreds and ruin.

They could not see me, watching, the children running around, their laughter loud and sweet against the slow wind that blew the scent of honeysuckle and the tease of sugarcane into the air.

"Riley, you want to bring the baby inside?" Willow called, and I watched her, the slim waist only marginally rounder than it had been when she was young. There were small strands of gray coloring her chestnut hair, but she wore hardly any wrinkles at all, despite her years. Those years, it seemed, had been very kind to her.

Around the end of the porch, Nash manned the grill, a beer in one hand and his grandson at his hip, nodding toward the surface that sizzled and burned with steaks and burgers. "No," he told the boy, "not yet. You have to wait til just before they're ready to add the sauce."

Nash, too, had grown a little rounded about his middle, his hair still full, but duller, his eyes now covered with glasses that he rarely took off.

The farmhouse had once been a tiny, two-room shack built by hands who'd seen too much work and not much care. The years came fast and with them the broken walls that were mended and the structure that grew wide, larger to accomodate children and grandchildren and then cousins when they came, when old granny **Bastien** had seen her children scatter to the wind, to death and travel, and her granddaughter fall to her reward, taken much too soon by smoke and fire.

The home was now a large place with a wraparound porch and double wooden entry doors, finely crafted with inlays, the craftsmanship something to boast and crow about. But that was not the way of Mr. Nation or his wife of twenty-five years.

They had seen fit to return to Manchac when their four young children became too wild for the confines of their Brooklyn brownstone. And so it was that Nash brought his family back to the swamp, to the place where it had all began. There the children grew up, the boys— Winston, Roan and Isaac—and a girl with wild auburn hair and tawny, dark skin. Her they called Riley.

They had been here for fifteen years now. Fifteen years since Bastie's place had been extended, since the Simoneaux kin were all too happy to take Nash up on his offer to buy their land. It was nothing at all to a man of his means, a man who had become succesful, and content with the things he had built, more so by the life he was leading. And so Bastie's old farm reached out, extended beyond the hidden trails that led to the old fishing shack, right to the sugar cane fields that Nash had torn down. It was a project of immense effort, as was the deconstruction of the Simoneaux mansion that had not been touched in some forty years, falling in to unreclaimable disrepair. The shelters and rehab stores got the woodwork from the foyer and the fine trim and millwork that had not rotted in the years of neglect. The rest of the mansion went to ground, became ash and dirt—a difficult but very satisfying project. Nash and Willow set tracks and built cottages that could one day house their children and their families, if they so desired.

Those two great lines, divided for so long, had been settled, at least for now. But joy had come at a great price. There is always a price to pay. It had come in smoke and fire. It had come with fret and worry, with blood and tears, with loss, with anger, with pain. Yet joy endured—it came and went, then came again, until the girl with the wild, chaotic hair and the boy who could not be bothered with love or joy at all, had paid the toll, settled the debt so many had left waiting.

And like before, like lifetimes before, the memory remained, passing into one life, into the next, through bone and blood and cells that made up one life and then another.

There it stayed.

THE END

AUTHOR'S NOTE

There are no political debates in this novel. There are no demands that you support one person over another or that the minutia of media fodder and the overwhelming worries so many of us face on a daily basis be dissected and explored. No resolutions will be offered.

This book, these characters, do something I think we all should—it explores love. It's just that simple, just that complex. There are no boundaries for these couples, not ultimately, and what I hope you'll understand about the nature of these kinds of stories is that they are vital. All of them. They are real and honest and sometimes very cruel. But they are very, very necessary.

You cannot call yourself a tolerant, compassionate person and see the differences in others as a threat to your own wellbeing. You cannot profess to love everyone as your faith or beliefs demand, and still think you are better, you are more deserving or that your privilege makes you right. It doesn't.

These couples understand that love—honest, real love—transcends. It does not judge, it doesn't set limitations or see differences. Love stretches, it strengthens, and it is absolutely essential. It gives you hope for a better day, the one we pray is coming.

"Love is patient, love is kind. It is not jealous, is not

pompous […] it does not brood over injury, it does not rejoice over wrongdoing but rejoices with the truth. It bears all things, believes all things, hopes all things, endures all things," (1 Corinthians, Chapter 13).

Without love, we are pointless.

With it, we are infinite.

FAMILY TREE

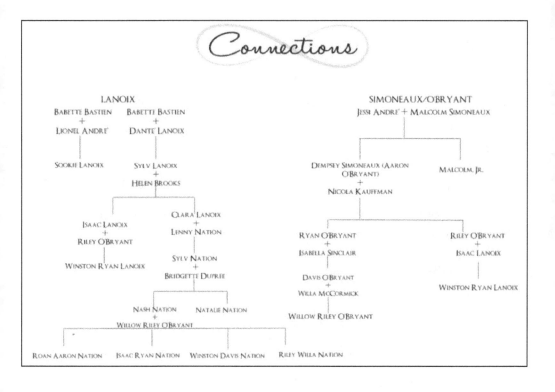

Connections

LANOIX

BABETTE BASTIEN
+
LIONEL ANDRE'

BABETTE BASTIEN
+
DANTE' LANOIX

SOOKIE LANOIX

SYLV LANOIX
+
HELEN BROOKS

ISAAC LANOIX
+
RILEY O'BRYANT

WINSTON RYAN LANOIX

CLARA LANOIX
+
LENNY NATION

SYLV NATION
+
BRIDGETTE DUPREE

NASH NATION   NATALIE NATION
+
WILLOW RILEY O'BRYANT

ROAN AARON NATION   ISAAC RYAN NATION   WINSTON DAVIS NATION   RILEY WILLA NATION

SIMONEAUX/O'BRYANT

JESSI ANDRE' + MALCOLM SIMONEAUX

DEMPSEY SIMONEAUX (AARON O'BRYANT)
+
NICOLA KAUFFMAN

MALCOLM, JR.

RYAN O'BRYANT
+
ISABELLA SINCLAIR

DAVIS O'BRYANT
+
WELLA McCORMICK

WILLOW RILEY O'BRYANT

RILEY O'BRYANT
+
ISAAC LANOIX

WINSTON RYAN LANOIX

DISCUSSION QUESTIONS

- Because of his upbringing, Nash has never held much of a sense of familial connection, with the exception of his twin sister, Natalie. How different do you think he would have been if he'd grown up with a stable family environment?

- There is a divergence in Willow's worldview and Nash's. Would these differences impact how Nash and Willow raised their children? Do you think it impacted their decision to return to the swamp farm?

- The issue of race is central to the motivations of various characters in INFINITE US. In your opinion, is the world much changed from Sookie's time to Nash's? How are these two time periods alike?

- What character impacted you the most?

- With what character could you most closely identify?

- How did you feel about the slip between time periods and how they are accessed?

- What did you dislike about the story? What did you like?

- INFINITE US follows characters that are at odds with the world around them (Sookie and Dempsey vs. their families, Isaac and Riley vs. Trent and the Civil Rights-era world they lived in and Nash and Willow and their own personal demons). Do you experience similar issues in your daily life? How do you cope with them?

- The past and present are woven throughout the story. What do you think Nash and Willow learned from their family? Do you think they would have had the same connection had it not been for the dreams?

- What's your guess about Roan and his role in each of these couples' lives? Would there have been a different outcome for Nash and Willow if he had not intervened?

ACKNOWLEDGMENTS

This was a beautiful journey to take with Nash and Willow, Isaac and Riley, and Sookie and Dempsey. I can't remember having this much fun or feeling things so deeply when I wrote as I did during the INFINITE US writing process. I hope you feel a small bit of that when you read it.

Sharon Browning, my editor, thank you for your insight, your patience and the wonderful way you make me sound like I have any idea what I'm doing. (I so do not). She is always the final touch, the master craftswoman who makes sure what you read is logical and well executed. She's my Yoda, guys. Always.

Thank you to my fantastic Sweet Team: Trinity Tate, Veronica Varela Rigby, Lisa Bennett, Jessica D. Hollyfield, Amy Bernstein-Feldman, Kayla Jagneaux, Heather McCorkle, Joy Jagneaux, Jennifer Jagneaux, Tina Jaworski, Naarah Scheiffler, Laura Agra, Betsy Gehring, Allyson Lavigne Wilson, Allison Coburn, Chanpreet Singh, Emily Lamphear, Sammy Jo Lle, Michelle Horstman, Jazmine Ayala, Melanie Brunsch and Joanna Holland for their amazing support and especially to Christopher Ledbetter, Lori Westhaver, Judy Lovely, Carla Castro, Heather Weston-Confer, Jennifer Holt, Trish Finely Leger, Karin Enders, Barbara Blakes and Marie Anderson-Simmons for the impeccable beta read. Thank you, particularly, Marie for schooling me on the important of the Omegas. I'm sure Mark would agree they'd definitely spank those Alpha Phi Alphas every time.

As always thank you to Chelle Bliss and Penelope Douglas for your constant friendship and support. Thank you, sincerely to Christine Case-lo for the research and explanations of epigenetic memory.

Thank you to all the reviewers, blogs and readers who have supported me throughout my publishing journey and to Ena with Enticing Journey, Nicole with IndieSage, Jo with Give Me Books, Love Between the Sheets, Natasha with Natasha is a Book Junkie and Maryse Black for all the help spreading the word about INFINITE US. Thanks to Murphy Rae for her patience in the cover design process and to my Manuscript Mixens and the lovely ladies of the Relentless Reviewers who cheer so, so loudly for me.

To my Corporate Hell sisters—Barbara Blakes, Marie Anderson-Simmons, Kalpana Singh, Sarah Cooper, Sherry Jackson and Karen Chapman, thank you for the lunch breaks, the laughs and your unfailing support. I love you all!

Thank you to my girls, Trinity, Faith and Grace and to my Himself, Chris, who never once believe that I will fail. You make my life a true blessing.

ABOUT THE AUTHOR

Eden Butler is an editor and writer of Romance, SciFi and Fantasy novels and the nine-time great-granddaughter of an honest-to-God English pirate. This could explain her affinity for rule breaking and rum.

When she's not writing, or wondering about her *possibly* Jack Sparrowesque ancestor, Eden impatiently awaits her Hogwarts letter, writes, reads and spends too much time watching rugby, "Doctor Who" and New Orleans Saints football. Currently, she is imprisoned under teenage rule alongside her husband in Southeastern Louisiana.

Please send help.

WEBSITE – edenbutler.com
TWIITER – twitter.com/EdenButler_
FACEBOOK – www.facebook.com/eden.butler.10

Subscribe to Eden's newsletter http://eepurl.com/VXQXD for giveaways, sneak peeks and various goodies that might just give you a chuckle.

CPSIA information can be obtained
at www.ICGtesting.com
Printed in the USA
LVHW03s0052020818
585615LV00003B/553/P